Before We Began

TANIA UNSWORTH

PENGUIN

FIG TREE

FIG TREE

Published by the Penguin Group
Penguin Books Ltd, 80 Strand, London WC2R 0RL, England
Penguin Group (USA) Inc., 375 Hudson Street, New York, New York 10014, USA
Penguin Group (Canada), 90 Eglinton Avenue East, Suite 700, Toronto, Ontario, Canada M4P 2Y3
(a division of Pearson Penguin Canada Inc.)
Penguin Ireland, 25 St Stephen's Green, Dublin 2, Ireland (a division of Penguin Books Ltd)
Penguin Group (Australia), 250 Camberwell Road,
Camberwell, Victoria 3124, Australia (a division of Pearson Australia Group Pty Ltd)
Penguin Books India Pvt Ltd, 11 Community Centre,
Panchsheel Park, New Delhi – 110 017, India
Penguin Group (NZ), cnr Airborne and Rosedale Roads, Albany,
Auckland 1310, New Zealand (a division of Pearson New Zealand Ltd)
Penguin Books (South Africa) (Pty) Ltd, 24 Sturdee Avenue,
Rosebank, Johannesburg 2196, South Africa

Penguin Books Ltd, Registered Offices: 80 Strand, London WC2R 0RL, England

www.penguin.com

First published 2006
1

Copyright © Tania Unsworth, 2006

The moral right of the author has been asserted

'I Passed for Sane' by Adrian Mitchell, from *Heart on the Left; Poems 1953–1984* (copyright © Adrian Mitchell
1997) is reproduced by permission of PFD (www.pfd.co.uk) on behalf of Adrian Mitchell.
Adrian Mitchell Educational Health warning! Adrian Mitchell asks that none of his poems be used in
connection with any examinations whatsoever!

Set in Monotype Dante
Typeset by Palimpsest Book Production Limited, Polmont, Stirlingshire
Printed in Great Britain by Clays Ltd, St Ives plc

A CIP catalogue record for this book is available from the British Library

ISBN-13 978-0-670-91280-3
ISBN-10 0-670-91280-8

In loving memory of Frances Adkins

Prologue

There was nowhere to go and nothing to do. Absolutely, entirely nothing to do. Even the matter of our boredom – held up and studied from all sides – had long since been exhausted as a topic of conversation. We sat around the shed in a vacant silence, broken only by the rustling of Julia's fingers as she picked at the insides of the sofa.

'You'll ruin it doing that,' Nancy said at last.

'So what? It's already completely fucked.' She fitted a scrap of foam to the elastic band stretched between her fingers, aimed carefully and flicked it at the bare light bulb overhead. 'It's mine, anyway. The whole shed is. I could set fire to it if I wanted.'

'You'll never hit it with that stuff,' I said. 'It's too light. You need something heavier.'

She positioned another piece of foam between her fingers. I watched the shadow of her hand – huge in the yellow light – stretch out against the half painted wooden planks of the shed, darkening Nancy's head and shoulders where she sat, with her back to the wall, knees drawn up tight against her chest.

'We could tidy this place up a bit,' I suggested. 'That would be something to do. We haven't even got rid of all the cardboard boxes yet.'

'Storage,' Julia said.

'For what?'

'I don't know. All the imaginary homework Nancy tells her mum she's doing whenever she comes over.'

'That's not funny,' Nancy said. 'I have to tell her *something*.'

'I still think we could make it nicer in here,' I said. 'I thought that was the idea. We haven't even finished the painting . . .'

'It wouldn't matter what we did, it's a dump,' Julia said. 'I mean, take a look outside. It's not even dark yet but we've got to have a light on in here.' I glanced out at the grey summer dusk still holding to the sky, though the trees and dense shrubs of the garden had already given way to night. 'We could try cleaning the window, couldn't we?'

Julia made a snorting sound. 'It's the same way in the *morning* isn't it? Black hole of Calcutta . . . without the heat of course.' She paused. 'Black hole of Oakville Street.'

'If there's a black hole around here,' I said, 'it's old bag Ivy's sitting room.'

'Or maybe her bog. I don't think you could get a blacker hole than Ivy's bog.'

'I like it,' Nancy said, her eyes fixed on the ceiling of the shed. 'I like that about it.'

Julia snickered. 'Why? Spent a lot of time there, have you?'

'The shed,' Nancy said. 'I like that you always need to put the light on. That way, you never really know what time it is.'

Julia gave me a look. 'Sometimes I hate talking to Nancy,' she said. 'She's always off on her own little track. It meets up with the general conversation every so often and then it sort of trundles away again . . .'

'What's so great about not knowing the time?' I asked.

'I don't know. Because then it wouldn't matter, would it?' She hunched forward intently, her eyes narrowed in thought. 'It could be any time or any day. It could be last week for all you know.'

'It might as well be last week,' Julia said. 'Seeing as how we're in exactly the same place we were then. Same positions even. You wouldn't have known we'd ever moved.'

2

'All we ever do is sit around,' I complained. 'We're no differ-ent from the dossers down the street.'

Julia selected another piece of foam, eyeing the light. 'Not true. We're sitting around because we're waiting. For things to happen, you know?' She took aim and fired. The pellet made a slow arc and hit the centre of the bulb, sending great shadows swinging abruptly from side to side across the empty walls and shabby furniture.

'All the dossers are waiting for,' Julia said, 'is for things to end.'

1   *The Whistle*

I

He was still wearing the whistle. Odd, how I fixed on that detail. Perhaps it was a refusal of sorts; the mind fastening itself to the particular in an effort to avoid the general. As I stood in the doorway, frozen, disconnected, all I could think of was that he had left it on for a reason; a kind of message.

He'd made a pile of books to stand on, kicking away the top few copies when the time came. *Ten Steps to an Organic Garden*. A particularly unsuccessful title. I'd ordered too many. I sometimes make mistakes when it comes to judging the market. Not often, but sometimes. And again, I had the sense that this was somehow significant. That if I'd ordered fewer, or sent them back earlier . . . I took three or four steps forward and grasped him around his legs and lifted him, trying to get some slack into the rope so that he could breathe, my face against the cloth of his trousers. He smelled of soap, of bodily fastidiousness. He was very heavy and the moment I touched him I knew I'd made another mistake. I should have gone to the phone and called for help.

As I shifted him, his right hand swung at me as though he would bat me away and for a second, I felt the tips of his fingers, cold as glass against my forehead. I didn't look up at his face. I stood there for what seemed like a long time. My muscles aching, my cheek pressed against his thigh. I held him for too long perhaps. But it would have made no difference. I couldn't do anything to help him. I don't know why I kept holding him except to say that letting go felt like an abandonment. A second death for him.

I lowered him finally, bending my knees carefully to avoid jolting the body, and called for an ambulance. His shoes were highly polished, but there was nothing unusual in that. Simon was always very groomed and I imagine he would have taken special care over his last appearance.

Two policemen arrived almost immediately after the ambulance and suddenly the small basement was full of people. They appeared very large, these officials; all bulky clothes and pounding feet. Even their breathing seemed deafening. I was there when they finally took him down and for the first time I looked at his face. His skin was pale, the features puffy and surprisingly placid and I marvelled how I could have imagined before that he was still alive. I must have been deceived by his very stillness, my eyes instinctively supplying movement for a second or two. It sounds like such a small thing, an ordinary error, but I found myself dwelling on it.

I told the police he'd worked for me for the last two years and gave them what personal details I could, although what I knew didn't appear to be the kind of information they were looking for. They looked very similar, the two policemen. Broad faced, rather expressionless. They spoke slowly, not unkindly, with a seeming lack of curiosity that made me a little uncomfortable. Neither of them wrote anything down although one had a notepad which he kept glancing at as though waiting for me to say something worth recording.

'I touched him,' I said, 'I tried to lift him. I thought he was . . .'

'These things are best left to the professionals,' the policeman said.

'Yes. I'll try to remember that.'

5

He gave me a rather sharp look. 'I should have called straightaway,' I said hastily. 'I do see that.'

'Is there anything else?' the policeman asked.

I thought about what I knew of Simon. He seemed to have no one. At least no one that he spoke about. It used to puzzle me a little. He was thirty-three, quite nice-looking in a quiet sort of way. But there was something locked-in about him that must have discouraged others. He carried himself like a person under siege. As if being alone and being gay put him into an entirely different category from everybody else. I have to admit it frustrated me a little, this air of martyrdom. It seemed . . . self indulgent. But then when he was attacked, six months before, I saw that the line drawn between himself and the rest of the world had been a real one after all.

It was one of the things I told the police about. I thought it might be important although they didn't dwell on it, not asking any further questions. I explained that Simon was attacked outside a bar after closing time. I remember that it surprised me a little to think of him in bars, but even he must have needed company from time to time. There were three men, one with a knife, waiting a little way down the street. They took him all together, the men, smashing his face against the pavement, breaking a rib. I don't think they had any intention of stopping before they killed him. Simon, at least, felt quite certain this was the case. That in that moment, there was nothing in the world those men wanted but his utter annihilation. And that, I think, was the worst of it for him.

He returned to work after three weeks, seemingly recovered. But he was changed. I didn't know then how deep the alteration went, only that he seemed to move differently from before, with a kind of resignation, like someone who had lost one certainty and found another. That was the time he began wearing the whistle. The whistles were meant to make people feel more safe. More in control of things I suppose. I think that you were meant to wear them when you might be in danger; after dark perhaps. But Simon wore his all the time.

He wore it as if it was more than merely a practical necessity; as if it were a badge. I used to think he wore it with a certain pride; a drawing of attention to his own vulnerability that was not without defiance. But after his death I saw that he had not worn it like this at all. Instead it had been a kind of brand, the sign of someone marked. He must have known it would be me who found him. Leaving no suicide note, only the whistle, self-mocking, reproachful. I needed help, the whistle said, more clearly than any written word. I carried my need for you to see, against my heart, day after day.

I used to think I was fond of him, but after discovering him down there in the basement I began to feel differently. A confused kind of resentment – the sort reserved exclusively for those we feel we have wronged – took hold of me. I thought of myself clutching his dangling legs and wondered, if I had to do it again, whether I could bring myself to touch him.

A cold word, fond. Used for those we find it easy not to think about from one week to the next.

I've read that hanging doesn't hurt too much. Those who have survived it report a feeling of great heat in the head, lights flashing before the eyes, a rushing, roaring sound in the ears. Most lose consciousness very quickly. Simon used a rope for the job. It left a long, deep herringbone mark on the other side of his neck from the knot.

I wish I hadn't noticed that. I wish I hadn't even looked.

We stayed closed for the rest of the week. I was the manager there and thought of it as my shop, although it was actually owned by my ex-boyfriend Lucien's mother Andrea – pronounced 'An*dray*a' – as she was always so careful to point out.

I had a lot of ideas for the place. Oxford, after all, was an ideal location for a shop like mine. But Andrea wasn't big on risk taking. 'Do you think we're quite . . . ready for all that?' she'd say in that soft way of hers when I suggested we start a newsletter for regular customers or organize evenings for writers to read their work. 'It's such a lovely idea. Perhaps in a little while . . . yes, later.' I could have tried harder to persuade her, or failing that, looked for a better job. But I kept putting it off. I didn't have the energy and besides, it never felt urgent enough. Very little did.

I went into the shop every day that week but I did nothing. Instead I moved here and there, impelled by a sense of purpose that always deserted me before I was halfway across the floor. I kept thinking about the moment I first saw Simon hanging; how quickly, how easily, the world had been shifted by the simple, familiar action of going down a flight of stairs and opening a door. It seemed preposterous that something so trivial could cause such change. And a sense crept over me that something equally trivial might have the power to turn the world back again. To the moment just before I found him. Or further back, before he decided on his own death, to some ordinary, harmless afternoon in the shop; myself behind the till, Simon dusting the postcard spinner and keeping an eye on the closed circuit television for shoplifters downstairs.

He had his own way of dealing with thieves, designed to minimize the kind of confrontation that would have been a horror for him. He would knock three times on the staircase – neatly, almost politely – to let them know they had been spotted, always giving them the same brief look, half reproachful, half sympathetic, when they emerged, moments later, bags empty. It meant they came back of course, hoping to escape notice another day. In time we got to know them by sight. Simon even became quite attached to several especially persistent individuals, greeting them with a small, ironic wave of his hand when they entered the shop . . .

I used to tell him he should be more firm, that next time it happened, he should call the police. He'd nod, in that careful way of his. He knew I would never force him to make the call and knew that I was incapable of making it myself. It was a weakness we shared, although we never spoke about it.

II

In the days and weeks following Simon's death, I became aware of something within myself to which I could give no name. A sensation, that although newly recognized, carried with it an uneasy familiarity. It was like a building whose construction takes place right before your eyes, the site bull-dozed, the scaffolding erected, without you registering any change in your surroundings. And then, one day, some finishing touch – the installation of the window frames, the painting of a sign – brings the whole to your attention.

I was on my way home from the bus stop, walking with my head down, retracing the shadow of my own steps, laid down a thousand times on the empty ground. Suddenly, something caught my eye, a movement in the bushes on my right-hand side. I looked up and saw a bird perched there, barely a foot away. It was plain brown, slightly larger than a sparrow, and it appeared quite unafraid of me. It turned its head slowly to one side, with an odd, almost jerky movement and sang two or three notes.

I stopped and stared at the creature. It turned its head and sang again, an alien sound, too sharp for a living throat. It did not look at me, seemed not to know I was there. And there crept into my mind the thought that it was not a real thing at all, but a clockwork bird. An old-fashioned toy, wound up to amaze a child. I turned away and walked on, disturbed in a way that seemed beyond understanding.

I didn't tell anybody about this incident. Nor that there were other times when it seemed to me that I walked through a world mysteriously altered. As if some small, but unmistakable slippage in the normal running of things had taken place. At these times it was as if I moved, not in the present at all, but in the small fraction of time immediately following it. The way a woman turned from me in the street, the unexpected changing of a traffic light, suggestive of events already over and done. As if I walked in my own shadow, in the brief aftermath of my own passing.

A sense of invisibility possessed me then, a helplessness. Small decisions seemed of utter significance. I stood by the vegetable section in Safeway's, unable to decide between one grapefruit and another, turning the fruit over in my hands, paralyzed, foolish. I felt I was already halfway into that other country where the people live that we see but never look at. The mutterers, the twitchers, the ones who always stand a little too close. I put the fruit down and forced myself to move forward, my feet sounding too loud against the floor, the light in the shop giving everything a green, underwater look.

The feeling always passed, in a moment or an hour. What would I have told anybody anyway? That I had a problem choosing groceries? The whole thing seemed both too monumental and too petty to attempt to explain.

At night, I lay for hours without sleeping, listening to the sound of my own breathing, the hiss of wet tyres on distant streets. It was at these times that I thought most of Simon, my mind searching through the details of his face, his smallest gesture before turning, slowly at first, with many sideways steps and half retreats towards that other time. That other death.

I went unwillingly, although it wasn't far away. You can give something no particular thought and still be thinking of it all the time. And the connection, after all, seemed an obvious one.

They go somewhere different, Nancy said, the people who die young.

No contradictions for those dead, I thought. No changes of heart. Their lives unfold complete before us, with all the deceptive simplicity of parable. And we are left, grasping for meaning, making shapes with our hands in the dark.

There's a sensation that follows disaster. It feels like movement, but it's only your feet beating far below you in the water, keeping you in sight – in reach – of the unbroken surface just above your head. It feels like breathing, but it's someone else drawing the air in and out of your lungs. Someone who knows what you don't; that weeks turn into months and then to years. For the first time, I wondered how long a person could spend in that manner, forgetting, with the passage of time, that there was any other way to be; seeing everything that happened – Simon's death, his silence, all the things said and left unsaid – not as independent events, but merely repetitions of the same endless, dull refrain.

Perhaps, I thought, it was Oakville Street that I needed to get back to and the summer we were fourteen. To Julia and Nancy and the postcard of Wilfred Owen taped to Nancy's bedroom wall. His army uniform buttoned up to the neck, his hair parted clean down the centre and cut so short at the sides you could still see the razor marks. Those dark, dark eyes. Full of a look not ever seen before. A kind of knowing. His own and yours too. Of all that had been and all that was still to come.

III

For a long time I kept a photograph of Julia, Nancy and I tucked into a small pocket in my purse. It disappeared after a while, but I can still picture it. It was black and white, taken in a photo booth, our three heads crowding together in the small frame. Nancy at the rear, pressed against the background curtain, her eyes caught shut in a blink. Julia in the foreground, face distorted by proximity to the camera and, behind her right shoulder, my own disembodied head, craning forward like someone trying to see over a hedge. All three of us were laughing, our mouths agape with overwhelming merriment.

I remember the day of the photograph too. Woolworths in the town centre. We laughed so hard that Nancy wet herself. There was a puddle on the seat of the photo booth and we had to run out of the shop for fear we would be caught and made to clean it up. Nancy lifted her skirt and showed us her legs, striped orange from pee and stolen fake tan.

It has been a long time since I laughed like that. I have lost the knack of it and besides, the world no longer seems as funny as it did then.

What did I remember of that year we were fourteen? Nothing but fragments. The significance of them came only later, stitched with the thread of assumption, with the need to make order. Was it the truth I remembered, or only the stitching? Each act of recall becoming a memory of itself, layer upon shifting layer. It suddenly seemed impossible to separate my recollections of what had happened from what I thought had happened, or what I had imagined happening; my past a series of hooks on which to hang a fiction. And myself, too, a character in the story. When I looked back, it seemed I saw myself no longer as observer, but one observed. A figure quite whole and separate, as distant from me now as those remembered friends.

IV

I told almost everyone I knew about my experience of finding Simon and each telling was the same. At first – in the few moments before actually relaying the information – a kind of excitement would grip me. I suppose it was simply the drama of the situation – the fleeting sense of self-importance that goes along with being the bearer of such news – but there seemed more to it than that. There was an urgency, a sense of expectation behind my impulse to tell and retell. And then, the moment after I had made the announcement, after the expressions of dismay and sympathy and shock from my various friends – sometimes even in the midst of them – this feeling of urgency would vanish and a sensation of hollowncss would take its place. I would stop talking or try to change the subject, suddenly beset by a vague, inexplicable disappointment that lingered for a while until I thought of another person to call, someone else who may not have heard the news.

A day or so after I came back from Simon's funeral, I found one of those ancient typewriters – black, with keys that make a loud thumping click against the page – in a junk shop. I brought it into the shop and set it up on a small table near the poetry section with a chair and a sign inviting customers to sit down and write their own impromptu verse. Something for those small moments of inspiration I thought. Even though Simon never expressed much interest in the poetry section, it felt like a kind of memorial.

For what seemed like a long time, I kept finding small traces of him around the shop. A ball of Blu-tack with his thumb-print still fixed on the surface, a coffee cup with Nescafé dregs around the brim where his lips had met the china. I took the cup to the sink to wash it, hesitating before running the tap. For a moment or two, I imagined that he could see me, was watching as I obliterated even this small evidence of his existence.

'I'm sorry, Simon,' I said, slowly wiping the rim of the cup with my hands. 'I'm sorry, but what else can I do?'

He used to eat his lunch on the table next to the sink. Sandwiches from home in a small ziploc bag. When he finished eating he shook out the crumbs from the bag, folded it up and put it away for the next day. You might have described his gestures as fussy, but I think they were more the actions of a person who, having learned to have no expectations that others would take care of him, makes every movement, however trivial, an exercise in self-solicitude.

I could tell that he felt uncomfortable around people. He always used to say that he could do his job much better if it wasn't for the customers. What he really liked doing was organizing the books, placing them where they belonged. He would move around the shop, scanning the shelves, and when-ever he found a volume out of place, something seemed to shoot through him – a tiny tremor of outrage – expressed in the way his hand darted out, forefinger prodding the top of the spine in an almost accusing fashion. Then the replacing. Using the flat of his palm to slide the book home with a brisk, almost theatrical gesture as though reproving a recalcitrant.

We didn't always agree on a particular book's categoriza-tion, but he usually got his own way in the end. I thought of him with a copy of *A Passage to India* in one hand, trying to slip it into the gay section without me noticing.

'It doesn't go there, Simon.'

'But E. M. Forster . . .' His face had a stubborn, helpless look.

'The section's for writers who deal with gay themes. There aren't any gay themes in *A Passage to India*.'

'Well,' he said, as though he was about to dispute this, although I suspected he hadn't read the book. Despite his job, Simon wasn't much of a reader. I think the circumstances of his own life were story enough for him.

'It just doesn't belong there,' I said. He hovered patiently, sensing weakness, the book still in his hand. 'Okay,' I said. 'If we've got two copies, you can put one there. I don't suppose it matters.' He watched me silently. 'But only if we've got two,' I added. 'And that really is the last concession I'm going to make in the gay section.'

I think he raised his eyebrows at that. A tiny gesture that you'd have missed if you hadn't been looking carefully. I always thought Simon could express more in a single twitch than most people could in a lengthy speech.

Ten days or so after he died, I found a business card that must have belonged to him. It was tucked between the invoices, in the sort of place you might choose to put something you hadn't any use for, but were unwilling to throw away.

Dr Peter Byrne, Senior Registrar in Medicine, John Radcliffe Hospital.

The name was familiar, although it was a while before I could place it. And then it came to me. Peter Byrne was the man who'd come to Simon's rescue when he was attacked. He'd been passing on the other side of the street at the time. I remember thinking how unlikely it was that somebody would do this – put themselves in danger for the sake of a stranger. It was appropriate, I thought, that he should turn out to be a doctor. Saving lives must be a habit with him. He'd been hurt himself in the fight; stabbed in the arm or the leg.

I'd forgotten the precise details. But I did remember that he'd been taken to the same hospital as Simon. They must have spoken at some point.

The card was slightly frayed at the edges as though it had been kept in Byrne's pocket for some time. Or, more likely, as if Simon himself had carried it around with him for a while – pulling it out perhaps to read and re-read the name. Had he called the number, or simply thought about doing so?

I held the card in my hand, looking at the name, thinking of this stranger, Peter Byrne. It was unlikely that he knew of Simon's suicide and it crossed my mind that I should tell him. It was perhaps unnecessary, but I did feel as though I might want to know, if I were him. Wouldn't I always have a special interest in the life I had saved, no matter how distant? There was something else too. It occurred to me that Simon might have told Peter Byrne something or revealed it unwittingly perhaps, that I had not been privy to. Something concrete – quite beyond dispute – that might explain his suicide.

I sat there for a while, considering the pros and cons before deciding that perhaps it wasn't a good idea after all. The news would be upsetting. And Byrne might think it odd, rather misplaced. I had no evidence that the man had had any further contact with Simon in the months following the attack.

I put the card back among the papers on the desk and went upstairs.

V

It had been a while since Lucien had visited the shop, so I was slightly surprised to see him striding through the door. He looked around for a moment or two and then caught sight of the typewriter.

'What have we here?' he said.

Lucien and I had gone out together for more than three years, before recently deciding to go our separate ways. It was either that or move in together. The logic of this choice had made perfect sense to me when he first explained it, but then Lucien always made sense when you were with him. It was only afterwards that you felt confused. It was all to do with his theories about monogamy – or pair bonding as he called it. How some people were less well designed for it – biologically speaking – than others.

'Nice touch. Very ... whimsical,' he said, fingering the typewriter keys.

'It's just an experiment.'

'No, I like it. I do. Something for all those closet bards out there. You know, the ones who don't have pen and paper of their own.'

'What do you want, Lucien?' I said, wondering exactly when it was that I had stopped finding him funny. His humour had always been one of his greatest attractions. Nobody would have described him as good looking, with his over-large nose and thinning hair, but he had a certain irresistible confidence that drew you in, made even the smallest amount of attention from him seem flattering. I'd once met one of his former girlfriends and seen photos of a couple of others. They were all what I would describe as very attractive – even beautiful. And there was something about this fact and the way Lucien acted in general that made you feel as if you were the lucky one in the relationship. It wasn't anything he said or did. Perhaps more what he didn't say. Lucien wasn't prone to making compliments, although he was possibly the most flirtatious person I had ever met

'I was just passing,' he said, giving me a look. 'Wondered what you were wearing today.'

'Well . . . the usual glamorous outfit . . .' I stopped, aware that I was simpering slightly. No matter how annoyed I was with Lucien, he always seemed able to inspire this reaction in me, this grinning foolishness. It was because he was so good in bed. It was simply – shamefully – nothing but that. I had not known what that phrase really meant until I met him. I had always thought it a rather loathsome description, conjuring up images of bedpost shackles, Olympic thrusting and the kind of stamina that expects – demands – a correspondingly superhuman response. But sex with Lucien was not at all like this. Perhaps it was the relative lack of direction elsewhere in his life that made him so focused in bed. His whole energy, his entire thought seemingly gathered there, in the touch of his hands. His face changing too; that sense he normally conveyed of being before some imagined, applauding audience, replaced by a look of complete, utterly gratifying absorption. That was his gift. To make you feel, for as long as the encounter lasted – and frequently with Lucien, it could be all afternoon – that he was totally, and quite help-lessly in love with everything about you . . .

He pulled the paper out of the roller with an abrupt jerk of his hand. 'Let's see what immortal words we have here.'

'Oh Lucien, *don't* . . .'

'*Lollipop, lollipop*,' he read, '*oh lolly, lolly pop*.' He paused. 'Then there's a whole bunch of letters . . . jawaalp i frum-mmpok . . . very profound.'

'They're not all like that.'

'You see, that's your problem,' he said. 'You take everything far too seriously.'

I had never known how to respond to this particular accu-sation of his – one of his favourite utterances – since denying it merely strengthened his case. 'So what's new?' I asked, trying to change the subject.

He shrugged. 'Had a meeting with Channel Four that went pretty well.'

'Sounds promising,' I said. Lucien produced television documentaries. Or rather, he had produced one, two years ago. It was a half-hour show about a blind plastic surgeon in Los Angeles who got his standard of female beauty from groping classical sculpture. It was a perfect subject for him. Nobody could ever accuse Lucien of taking things too seriously. Since then he had produced nothing, although he was always on the verge of developing new projects.

'Have you talked to Andrea recently?' he asked. He always called his mother by her first name. It suited his bond with her which had never seemed to me particularly filial, but instead had the fond, slightly exasperated intimacy one associates with old friends or former lovers.

'I'm seeing her tomorrow. We really have to talk about getting a replacement for Simon. I can't run this place by myself.'

'Ah, yes . . . Simon.' He grimaced briefly. 'That must have been quite an experience, finding him like that.'

'Yes, Lucien. You could say that.'

'You should have taken pictures.'

I stared at him.

'Don't look so outraged. That's what I would have done.'

I thought of Simon's feet dangling pigeon-toed, the neat bows of his laces. 'No, you wouldn't,' I said, 'believe me.'

'Okay, so maybe not. But I'd have *thought* about it.'

'You're sick, Lucien. You know that, don't you?'

He grinned, leaned towards me as though he was about to kiss me, then pulled away at the last moment. 'I'll call you,' he said, seeming not to remember – or rather not caring – that our relationship was meant to be over.

*

About an hour later, a couple came in and stood in the doorway for a moment or two as though uncertain they were in the right place, hovering with the air of people not used to asserting themselves. I could imagine that finding their way here had been something of an enterprise; the man studying his map on the train, unwilling to ask directions; the woman in cheap court shoes and dark suit. The same suit, I noticed, that she'd worn to the funeral.

'Mr Peterson,' I said, with a sinking feeling. 'I wasn't expecting . . .'

The man nodded a couple of times as though taking charge. 'You know my wife,' he interrupted, pushing her forward slightly. He was short, rather stocky, with that air of aggression some men assume when they are uncomfortable socially.

'Yes, yes of course,' I said, although I'd met her only very briefly, outside the church, when the service for Simon was over.

'We just thought we'd come in,' she said apologetically, 'as we were in town . . .' She had a podgy, unremarkable face, her eyes spoiled by heavily drooping pouches, but her voice was light, rather beautiful. She stepped forward hesitantly and held out her hand.

'It's nice to see you again, Sophie. Simon talked a lot about you.'

'It's good to see you too,' I said, hoping I sounded as though I meant it. There was a short, awkward pause.

'We just thought we'd come in . . .' she said again.

'I'm so sorry about everything,' I said. 'I thought Simon's funeral was beautiful.'

'Yes, it was, wasn't it?' she said valiantly. 'We had very good weather.'

During this exchange, Mr Peterson had remained quite silent. Now he seemed to gather himself slightly, his lips tightening into a small grimace.

'So this is where Simon worked,' he said, with false heartiness. 'The bookshop . . .' He looked about him, seemingly
unable to proceed.

'It's very nice,' Simon's mother said. 'Really lovely.'

'Thank you,' I said. 'I can show you around if you like.'

The moment the words were out of my mouth, I cringed.
What could have possessed me to suggest a tour of the shop?
I could imagine how it would sound. *Here, on your left, we have
new hardbacks; on your right, a tasteful selection of postcards and
downstairs, the very spot where I found your son dangling by his
neck . . .*

'It's really just what you see,' I said quickly. 'We're hoping
to expand one of these days . . .'

'It's very nice,' Simon's mother said again. She raised her
hand to the counter and patted it a couple of times. 'Simon
enjoyed working here,' she said softly. 'I know he did.'

'I liked him very much,' I said.

I wanted to tell her about how Simon used to deal with
the shoplifters, how carefully he avoided humiliating them.
But I couldn't find the right words.

'He was a very kind person,' I said.

She nodded sadly. 'Yes, yes, he was.'

There was another long pause.

'Did he seem ill to you?' Mr Peterson said suddenly, in a
loud voice.

Mrs Peterson made a gesture of protest. 'Frank,' she said,
'please . . . you said you wouldn't . . .'

'I'm only asking aren't I?'

'Ill?' I repeated.

He had a tight, almost angry look. His hands deep in the
pockets of his overcoat, his head thrust forward slightly. 'You
know,' he said. 'That disease they get.'

Beside him, Mrs Peterson wrung her hands. I used to think

nobody actually did this – that it was just a figure of speech – until I saw her. She had the palm of her left hand in a tight grip and was rubbing her right thumb over the skin with a hard, compulsive motion that seemed quite involuntary.

'Please,' she said again, very urgently. 'We've talked about this.'

I looked Simon's father in the eye as steadily as I could. 'I don't think he was . . . sick,' I said. 'At least he never told me he was. And I don't think Simon ever took a day off work that I can remember. Apart from – well – that time when he was in hospital.'

He sniffed slightly and glanced away without replying. The tight look had not left his face, but it was clear he had nothing more to say.

'We should be going,' Simon's mother said, twitching the sleeve of his coat.

I came around the counter and held the door open for them. When they had gone, I flipped the OPEN sign and fastened the top bolt. I went downstairs and sat at the desk for a while without moving. Then I picked up the phone and after locating Peter Byrne's card in my in-tray, dialled the number.

It didn't seem like it at the time, but now I see that there was something spiteful in my desire to call him; to tell this stranger who thought he had saved Simon, that no, he had not saved him at all. His effort pointless, his heroism misplaced.

I got a woman on the line; an operator at the hospital. She told me to wait while she paged him. After a long pause, he came on, his voice loud, almost brusque.

'Doctor Byrne? You don't know me. My name's Sophie Barrett. I worked with Simon Peterson, the man you . . . helped. I'm afraid I have some very bad news.' Now that I was actually talking to him, all my earlier misgivings came flooding back. I shouldn't be doing this, I thought belatedly, ploughing on.

'I'm afraid Simon killed himself. I thought you would want to know.'

'Simon Peterson?' he said, even more brusquely. 'Have you called emergency services?'

'No, no,' I said, 'no, it's not an emergency. It happened a week or so ago. I thought . . . since you knew him . . . because of what happened . . .'

'Simon,' he said. 'Yes, I see.' There was the muffled sound of voices on the other end of the line.

'I'm just calling everyone who knew him,' I lied.

'Yes,' he said. 'I appreciate the call. Thank you.'

'You're welcome,' I said as he clicked off.

I put the phone back on the receiver, picked up Byrne's card and tore it into four pieces. Then I went back upstairs and opened up the shop again.

VI

I used to get a lot of students in the bookshop and sometimes, when I was in a certain sort of mood, I'd start thinking about who they saw when they glanced at me. Someone not very much older than they were, but already in a place that they, in their confidence, would never expect to find themselves: sitting behind the till in a shop without any clear plan for the future.

In retrospect, perhaps I stayed too long in Cambridge, moving out of my parents' house to a room barely a mile away while I studied English at the Tech. My mother certainly thought so. 'What's wrong with you?' she demanded to know. 'Why on earth are you hanging around here?' At the time I put it down to her prejudices. It was no secret that she hated the city and was only waiting for the earliest opportunity to leave it herself. But I can't deny that I never found a good answer to either of her questions, nor why I spent so much time on my PhD, or stayed with Lucien for as long as I did, or even stuck with the bookshop although I was paid so little I had to borrow the money to get to Bristol for Simon's funeral.

I admire people who know what they are doing. They have substance. Sometimes it seems to me that even the outlines of their bodies look clearer, as if they have been drawn with a bolder, thicker line . . .

Julia was like that. I hadn't spoken to her in over a dozen years, but I'd seen her name many times in the *Guardian* and elsewhere, read her reports of turmoils in the Middle East, the former Yugoslavia. Her writing wasn't as elegant as some, but it had momentum; a controlled version of that tearing impatience, that eagerness that I remembered so well about her.

Julia was something of a mystery when you looked at the rest of her family. They were loud, rather jovial in an unsubtle way; keen on camping holidays and practical jokes. Her mother was a large woman who had stayed at home to look after the children, her father a chemistry professor at one of the colleges. He collected old laboratory equipment as a hobby. Their sitting room was filled with glass vials and antique Bunsen burners and photographs of them in anoraks on the Isle of Wight. I never paid much attention to her younger brother who seemed destined to be just like his father, with his boy scout badges and Meccano sets.

Now I think of it, Julia was perhaps more like them than I thought at the time. But in her, their qualities were transformed. Their heartiness translated into vitality, their outdoorsy enthusiasms becoming, through some genetic alchemy, something finer and more rare; a boldness of spirit, an appetite for adventure. She was tall like her mother, but with none of her burliness. Slender, long-legged, wearing her clothes – even at fourteen – with a kind of casual glamour that I never achieved either then or now.

I'd thought of trying to contact her from time to time over the years, but never had. I suspected that if Julia and I had met at any other time in our lives, at college say, or later, we wouldn't have become friends. Even at fourteen I felt different from her. I was the one who held back; content to drift in the slipstream of her energy and Nancy's strange, involuntary passions. We were friends of circumstance and time; our friendship the camaraderie of prisoners for whom the outside world is only a distant, future dream. This being so, our separation was hardly surprising. We were already on the brink of it that summer. With increased independence, Julia would soon find other friends, girls from her school who lived far beyond our little street. And when, in her sixteenth year, her family moved to London, I lost her completely.

But after Simon's death and with the year already turning towards autumn, the impulse to call her came again, stronger than before. There was the agreement that we'd made, although I thought it was impossible that she would have remembered it. Most people – and Julia in particular – would have put it out of their minds years ago.

At the time, of course, we attached great seriousness to the thing. I don't remember who first suggested it. Perhaps it was Nancy, in her dark berth under my bed. There wasn't enough space in my small room for the three of us when we spent the night together there. I had the bed and Julia the narrow strip of floor to my left and Nancy made do as best she could beneath me. We never altered these positions, despite Nancy's complaints that the bedsprings caught in her hair whenever she tried to turn over.

'We should make a pact. To meet up. After ages and ages.' Now that I thought of it, it must have been Nancy. It was just the kind of suggestion she would make.

'Why?' Julia asked, without much interest. It was very late and we had been talking for hours. We were all at that precise moment when conversation seemed utterly exhausted, but sleep was still something that needed to be held off for a while yet.

'I don't know. Just because.'

'Stop moving so much,' I said, 'you're making the whole bed shake.'

'It stinks of pee down here,' Nancy complained, for perhaps the tenth time. 'I hate your cat.'

'I think it's a good idea,' I said. 'Meeting up. We should do it so . . .'

'So we can see if Nancy ever changes her hairstyle,' Julia cackled. 'Or if my boobs ever grow larger than raisins.'

'So we can . . . remind ourselves,' I said, struggling to find the right words. 'You know, of what we're like now. Right this very minute. Like a time capsule or something. Because we might not remember otherwise. Not what it's like *exactly* . . .' I trailed off, unable to explain myself properly. It seemed ridiculous to think we could ever forget even the smallest detail of our life. But if, by some far-fetched possibility we did need a reminder, I sensed that it would be impossible to find alone. It was only with the three of us together that we would know what it meant to be fourteen again, here in this place. As if we all carried separate pieces of a map that only made sense when they were joined . . .

We were silent for a while as the idea took hold. 'When we're all thirty,' Julia said suddenly. 'We should do it then.'

She paused to do the arithmetic. '1994. We'll all be thirty by the end of 1994.'

We would meet on November 20th, we decided. At midnight, by the lions in Trafalgar Square. It was the only landmark we could all agree on, our knowledge of the city being sketchy in the extreme. Nancy held out for Madame Tussauds for a while, until Julia pointed out that it would, without doubt, be closed at midnight. We told each other we would write down the date and keep it safe, but I didn't have to. I had no trouble remembering it.

But Julia would have forgotten. I felt sure of that. And I would feel embarrassed reminding her. She would think me childish, or worse, pathetic. No, contacting her at this late stage was out of the question. I told myself the impulse was irrational, nothing more than a futile effort to find comfort where none could exist. Of the three of us, she had always been the one best able to make sense of things. But that was long ago and we were different people then.

2 Mr Watson

I

Ivy was the one to blame. Nancy always said it was Ivy's fault. But really, it was Julia's cigarette and the only reason she was smoking it in the first place was because of the séance.

The séance was Nancy's idea, of course. She had arranged a circle of Scrabble letters on her bedside table and was staring at the tiles – grubby from years of handling – with fierce anticipation. Her eyes seemed even larger than normal; her small body hunched forward; the ragged fringe of her hair giving her a neglected, vaguely delinquent look.

'It's ready,' she announced.

I lay on her bed and stared at the ceiling. I hated Sunday afternoons. I hated their empty feeling, as if everything was already over and done with, even though it was still hours before the bells of St Luke's would start their dismal clamour, tolling for the liberation of Friday, the promise of Saturday, the death of the whole weekend. Even the June sun, striping in between the drawn curtains of Nancy's bedroom, had a drained appearance, like something left over, pointless.

'Come on,' Nancy said. 'I thought you wanted to do this.'

'You wanted to do it, you mean,' Julia said, from her seat on the floor. 'It's not going to work anyway. It's stupid.'

'No it's not,' Nancy said. 'I know a lot of people this has worked for.'

'Like who?'

She ignored the question. 'The glass has to be upside

down. In the middle, the exact, perfect middle.' In the dim light of the room, her face looked paler than usual, almost chalky.

'You have to put your finger on top. Lightly. Like this . . .'

We did as she said, Julia with an exaggerated flourish, her silver rings clinking slightly against the glass.

'I think Sophie's scared,' she said.

'I am *not*.'

'What are we supposed to say?' Julia asked.

Nancy hesitated. 'Is anybody there?' Julia and I looked at each other.

'Is anybody there?' Nancy repeated in a louder voice. She lifted her chin and closed her eyes. 'Is anybody there?'

'Perhaps we should ask for someone in particular,' I suggested.

'No, no.'

'Perhaps Wilfred . . .' Julia said.

Nancy's eyes flew open. 'It's not like that. You're meant to let them *come*.'

'Okay, okay. No need to wet your knickers over it.' It was the sort of expression that Julia was always coming out with. 'That girl is crude,' my mother used to say. 'I don't know where she picks up the things she says.' I didn't think Julia picked them up from anywhere. They just seemed to emerge spontaneously.

'It's just that if we don't ask for anyone in particular, we'll end up with some boring git or other,' Julia said.

'They won't be *boring*, Julia,' I said. 'I mean, they're dead, aren't they?'

'I don't see what that has to do with it,' she said. 'If you're boring when you're alive, you're going to be doubly boring when you're dead. Like most of the teachers at my school. Like all the newsreaders off *Look East* . . .'

'I hate those newsreaders,' I said. 'The minute they start talking, my brain sort of shrivels up.'

'Come *on*,' Nancy cried. 'We've got to really, really concentrate.'

'Is anybody there?'

Beneath our fingers, the glass seemed to shift very slightly before sliding a few centimetres to the left. My heart lurched.

'It's going to the "y",' I said.

The glass picked up speed. It was gliding now, moving from letter to letter. '*Yes*,' I said, 'it's saying yes.' Excitement gripped me. Before we started, I hadn't expected the glass to move like this. But now, feeling it slip so readily beneath my fingers, I found I wasn't very surprised at all.

'What – is – Your – Name?' Nancy intoned, as though addressing a foreigner. 'Are – You – Male – Or – Female?'

'Ask one question at a time. You'll give it a heart attack,' Julia said.

I wondered how she could joke. Under my finger, the glass felt hot. It was because we were all touching it, I told myself. It was no more than that.

'Are you dead?' Julia asked with relish. The glass quivered and began to move again.

Yes.

I sucked in my breath, glancing quickly around the room. Nancy frowned. 'Can't you say anything apart from yes or no?'

'I don't think it can,' Julia said. There was a pause. 'I've got an idea!' Julia said suddenly. She leaned forward, repositioning her finger. 'Is there anyone here,' she began, 'is there anyone here, in this room, who is going to be famous?'

'Don't ask it stuff like that!' Nancy cried. 'What kind of a . . .' She was interrupted by the sound of the glass moving at great speed across the table. The three of us watched as it circled once, twice and then stopped, with great finality, in front of Julia.

'Well, there you have it,' she said with satisfaction.

'You cheat,' Nancy said. 'You bloody cheat. You were moving it, weren't you?'

'Only a little . . .'

'Typical,' I said. 'I knew you were moving it.'

'You did not. You should've seen your face.'

'You weren't moving it all the time,' Nancy said. She reached for the glass, placing it in the centre of the table again, her hands trembling slightly. 'I know you weren't. I felt it . . .' She had that look on her face again. The one that made you feel sorry for her, and want to hurt her too. Just a little. Because it was so easy.

'I felt it,' she insisted, putting her finger back on the glass. 'We've got to keep doing it.'

Julia and I looked at each other. 'Waste of time,' she said.

'Maybe it would work if we did ask for a particular person,' I suggested. 'I don't know anybody dead. Do you, Julia?'

She thought for a moment then shook her head. 'No,' she said, sounding regretful. 'Just my granddad. But he's too old . . .'

'I know!' I said. 'There's this friend of my mum. Or a friend of one of her friends. Their son died recently. About two months ago. I heard her talking about it. A climbing accident in Scotland. He was only about seventeen. He broke his back, I think.' I was hazy on the precise details. 'There were these other two people with him and they fell too, only they didn't die. They had to stay there all night with him dead because the helicopters couldn't get out to rescue them until the next morning.

'It was in the papers,' I added, noticing Julia's look of doubt. 'The other two people had to use the dead boy's clothes to keep warm or they'd have died too.'

'What was his name?' Julia wanted to know.

'I don't know. Kevin. Kevin something. It was in the papers.'

'Kevin something!' Julia snorted. 'Told you it was a waste of time.'

'How did they know?' Nancy said, breaking her silence.

'Know what?'

'That he was dead. The other two. How did they know?'

'Probably because he'd stopped breathing, Nancy,' Julia said. 'You know, that thing you do with your lungs . . .'

'Yes, but it was dark wasn't it? And they must have been hurt too and it might have been hard to tell. I'd have thought it would be hard to tell for *sure*.'

'What are you on about?' I said. 'I mean, he's dead *now* isn't he?'

'I don't think you die straightaway when you break your back,' Nancy continued. 'I think you kind of lie there for a bit.'

'Sort of twitching,' Julia added. 'Yeah, probably . . .'

'I still don't get what the point is.'

'They took his clothes didn't they?' Nancy said. 'But if they didn't know for sure he was dead, they might have taken them too early. By mistake. Then he'd have died of the cold, wouldn't he? Even if he was going to die anyway, they'd have made it faster. But perhaps they did know. Perhaps they took them, knowing he was still alive. Thinking he would die soon and needing the extra clothes to save themselves. I don't think that's the sort of thing they'd tell anyone about. They'd keep it a secret. I think we should ask him. I think we should ask Kevin Something exactly how he died.'

There was a moment of silence.

'Oh come on then,' Julia said. 'There's sod all else to do.'

Nancy's movements became more hurried. I knew it was because her mother would be home soon. Back from her afternoon collecting cancer envelopes door to door. Her mother collected for everything; cancer patients, famine victims, guide dogs for the blind. She never managed more than a dozen envelopes or so, despite the way she stood there on the step, with that urgent, apologetic look on her face, as though it was she who needed help with a brain tumour rather than all those children in Addenbrooke's Hospital. The minute she got back, Julia and I would have to leave because she'd want Nancy to help her with the counting.

Nancy had told me about the counting. The envelopes scattered thinly on the kitchen table, her mother making her check and re-check the figures. 'How come there isn't twenty-five pounds there?' her mother would say in a bewildered voice. 'I felt sure I'd get twenty-five. At least. Count again.' And then the rummaging in her own purse to make up the imagined amount, pretending that she'd collected the whole sum. As if ten or fifteen pounds was somehow wrong, and only the magical sum of twenty-five would do.

Nancy's mother was a small woman. Fine boned. She moved and talked very fast. Her little hands darting in front of her face with panicky gestures as though she was forever warding off something. She couldn't have been much more than thirty-five or -six although I considered her old at the time. I didn't know which was worse; the fact that she still made an effort with her appearance, or the way she almost always got it so wrong, with her unfashionably short skirts, faded from being washed too many times and her collection of jangling charm bracelets. I knew that Nancy was ashamed of her. Not in the way that many of us were embarrassed by our parents, but with something far deeper, unmoving and relentless. Perhaps, I thought, it was something to do with the fact that there was only the two of them to keep each other company.

'We're calling for Kevin,' Nancy said. 'Kevin who died very

recently. In a climbing accident. Are you there, Kevin?' Her eyes were wide. I was sitting so close to her, I could see a tiny image of the bedroom window – quivering slightly but perfectly clear – reflected in each dark pupil. Julia's knee bumped against my leg.

'Stop shoving.'

'I'm *not*.'

'Shut up!'

'Kevin,' Nancy repeated, in the same hollow-sounding voice. 'Are you there?'

The glass began to shift and she leaned into the movement, her body taut.

Yes.

'What is your last name?' The glass spun, found a letter, moved on again. 'M-O-F' I spelled. 'Another F . . . it's stopped.' I gave Julia a suspicious look, but she was staring at the glass as though its movement came as a surprise. 'Is that right?' she mouthed.

'I don't know. Maybe. Something like that.' I searched my mind. 'Yes, it started with M. I do know that. It definitely started with M . . .'

Our fingers rose a fraction as we hesitated.

'Don't break it!' Nancy said.

We were all whispering now. No noise came from the street outside. It was always quiet, this street, but even on a Sunday you could usually hear sounds from the world beyond its edges: traffic, thin cries of children, the low hum of the city that enclosed it. Now, even this distant clamour was silenced. As though the world had shrunk back, I thought, and our street had somehow grown; stretching itself out to fill the emptiness beyond.

'Kevin,' Nancy said. 'Tell us how you died.'

Our three fingers were touching each other now. Almost

as if they were joined together. The glass made a small, scraping insect sound as it circled the table.

'C.A.N.T . . . F.E.E.L . . . A.N.Y.T . . .'

We pulled away at the same time, before the third word had been completed. Julia had a stupefied expression on her face, but it was Nancy I looked to. She had brought both hands up to her mouth, fingers pinching her lips. Her eyes were blank.

'I think that's enough,' Julia said in a loud voice.

There was a moment in which none of us moved and then Nancy took her hands away from her face and without saying anything, replaced her finger on the glass.

'Don't!' Julia said.

'Are you still there?'

The glass was motionless. I stared at it, half expecting to see it take flight. But now that I wasn't touching it any longer, it seemed whatever had possessed it a minute before had quite gone. It was simply a beaker, a perfectly ordinary item, something I had drunk from perhaps a dozen times, leaving it wet on the draining board in Nancy's untidy kitchen without another thought.

'Do you see us?' Nancy pleaded. 'Kevin, do you see us?'

And the moment she spoke, I had the sense that it wasn't the three of us, sitting there, that she was referring to, but something far greater, unclear and borderless. Her mother was part of it perhaps. And this house too, with the back gate that never fastened properly and the weed-infested garden and the Sally Army sofa in the living room. The church bells ringing from underwater towers. Her own dark thoughts.

'This is just too creepy,' Julia said. 'I'm going to have a cigarette.'

She fished for a ragged packet of ten Benson & Hedges in her jeans pocket.

'Got a light?'

'How many of those are you smoking a day?' I asked, distracted.

'A couple,' she said, discovering a box of matches in another pocket. She had perfected the technique of striking a match using only one hand, performing this trick with a casual bravado that never failed to impress me. At the sound of the small flare, Nancy seemed to come to.

'You can't smoke in here! Mum will kill me . . .'

'I'll do it out of the window.'

'She'll smell it.'

But we always did what Julia wanted. She drew the curtains aside and lifted the sash without further argument.

Nancy's bedroom window looked out onto the street which was so narrow that traffic often had to drive up onto the kerb even though parking was only permitted down one side. The pavement was even more cramped. You had to duck your head to avoid untrimmed hedges and a single bicycle left by someone's gate was enough to block the entire path. We all lived so close together, that sometimes at night, if I lay very still, I thought I might almost hear the sound of neighbours breathing all around; the tiny creak of bedsprings as they shifted in their sleep.

With a few exceptions, all the houses were semi-detached, and if you leaned out far enough, you could see the gate of my house two doors down, separated by the forbidding aspect of Ivy's front yard, a grey, concrete expanse, empty of plant life, with a large stone urn in the very centre. If geraniums or pansies had ever grown there, they were now only a distant memory. I thought it looked like something that belonged on top of a grave.

I joined Julia at the window.

'Give us a drag.' We leaned out as far as we could in an

effort to prevent the smoke from curling back into the room behind.

'That man's outside again,' I said. 'The one who's always crying.'

I was looking at the house directly opposite, where three men – one in a chair, the others leaning against the wall – lounged with stoical inertia, the expressions on their faces too distant to be read. On a fine afternoon like this one, there was usually a similar group sunning themselves or venturing further down the road, with unsteady, concentrated gait. They were the reason, as my mother was endlessly pointing out, that the house prices in the street stayed so low. It was the person who owned the building who was to blame; the Spanish landlady who kept junk in the back garden and offered rooms to drunks and derelicts. 'That Woman', my mother called her, convinced it was all some scam with the local council. There were no curtains on the windows of the house and at night you could look right in. Not that there was much to see, apart from a mattress leaning up against one of the walls.

'You mean Weeping Tom?' Julia asked, sounding quite pleased at her own pun. 'That's what I call him,' she added.

'He's always wiping his eyes with a hankie,' I said. 'That's all he ever does. He just sits there and cries and wipes himself . . .'

'He's not crying,' she said scornfully. 'His eyes are just watering.'

'How come?'

'How should I know? He's sick I suppose. He's out of it.'

We watched the man curiously, taking turns to puff on the cigarette. Behind us, Nancy had seated herself on the bed and was quite still, lost in some dream.

'That was weird,' I said in a low voice. 'I mean, how did the glass move? It was like something was inside it or something. And it knew the last name. How did it know that?'

'I don't think we should tell anybody else about it,' I added.

Julia took a drag and narrowed her eyes. 'Want to know something?'

'What?'

She leaned in close, whispering. 'Nancy was pushing it.'

'No. No, that can't be right.'

'It's obvious. I could tell.'

'But did you see her face? How could she fake that?'

Julia didn't answer. Instead she started humming the music from *Doctor Who*.

'Shut up, she'll hear you. She's not . . .'

I was interrupted suddenly by a movement below. The net curtains hanging in Ivy's front room had twitched; minutely but unmistakably.

'God, she's looking at us!' I ducked abruptly back into the room.

'Who?' Julia craned her neck.

'Ivy. She's spying on us. Get in. Don't let her see . . .'

'That old bag next door?'

'*Julia*,' I half shrieked. 'She's going to see the cigarette.' I could imagine the old woman pressed up against the window, her face all jowly, her eyes vengeful.

Julia peered with renewed interest.

'She'll tell my parents,' I said.

But Julia didn't seem to hear. She levered herself so that the whole of her upper body was clear of the window, with only the tops of her thighs against the ledge to give her balance and took a last, long drag on her cigarette. And then, with an impudent movement of her wrist, she waggled the butt in Ivy's direction.

'That's given her something to gawk at,' she said with satisfaction.

II

'Have you been smoking?' my mother asked sharply.

It was a couple of days after the séance and she had been talking to Ivy. The warmth of the day had drawn the old woman out to the front of her house where she stood, one hand resting on the gate, the other buried deep in the pocket of her tent-shaped dress, a disgruntled expression on her face, as though the pleasant weather, by obliging her to leave the comfort of her chair, was one more mark on the long list of wrongs that fate had dealt her. I knew that if there had been a way – some back route into the house – that my mother could have taken to avoid the encounter, she would have done so. But there was no getting away from the woman.

'Sometimes, I swear to God, I think that woman was put on earth to drive me crazy.'

'It wasn't me,' I said. 'It was Julia. She's always smoking.'

'Well Ivy says she saw you. On Sunday.'

'If you're going to believe *her* . . .'

'Is that my sweater you're wearing?' my mother said, abruptly. 'I can't believe you're wearing that sweater again without asking. Just because I let you borrow it once . . .'

'I'll take it off, *okay*?'

I went upstairs, pulling it over my head angrily. At the top, I sat down. Below, in the kitchen, I could hear my parents talking about Julia and I wanted to listen. I often eavesdropped on them in this way, unseen, silenced by frustration and baffled rage. My parents never seemed to speak clearly, but in a kind of code that muffled everything they said and gave it an obscure, disturbing significance.

'Her parents spend all that money sending her to the Perse,' my mother was saying. 'It just goes to show. I don't know what they think they're getting for it. It's sheer snobbery, sending a child to private school in this city. The girl seems to do as she pleases.'

'She's not a bad kid,' my father said, after a small pause. He sounded tired. 'You should see some of the . . .'

'Well, that's the problem isn't it? Just because she's not being brought up by drug addicts who molest her, you think everything's fine. You're not living in the real world anymore.'

'Not the real world . . .' my father said. 'My God . . .'

'Don't start. I don't need it. God, I hate this street. When I think, we could have bought in Victoria Park.' She stopped. 'Could you at least turn off the radio when we're having a conversation?'

'We couldn't afford Victoria Park even then,' my father said, without moving.

'I would have thought they could have done something about the state of the pavement. It's been months . . .'

'Perhaps we should get Miss Pemble on to it.'

'I'm not joking, Tony. I mean it.'

And then my father's voice, low with a kind of resignation that sounded like disdain.

'I'm a social worker, Margaret. That's what I do.'

I got up and went into my bedroom and put *Station to Station* in my cassette player. I had most of Bowie's albums on tape. My recordings weren't perfect. There were long, crackling pauses between songs, or else no pause at all, but they were better than nothing. I pressed the fast forward button, stopped and then rewound.

Golden years . . . golden years . . . nothing's gonna touch you in these golden years.

I sat down on the bed, staring at my brown school skirt with its hem coming undone and my end-of-term shoes, which had never been right, even when they were new. A sense of enormity possessed me. Vague, profound, tethered to nothing but a few slim ropes, a great white sail of a feeling, bellied out with mysterious longing and sadness and hope.

I wondered if I was the only one who ever felt like this. As though I'd come up against a kind of wall around the world. Invisible, made of nothing but movement, most of the time I didn't even know it was there. But sometimes, cycling across the Common, with the long shadows of the trees striping the bright grass, or listening to certain songs, or simply sitting there in my bedroom, surrounded by everything that was familiar and would never change, I felt it in my mind. A great wave of a thing, very close, rushing by so fast it fooled you into thinking it was still.

Julia didn't like David Bowie. Nor did Nancy. Nancy never listened to music of any kind. She had Wilfred Owen instead.

She hadn't talked about him for a while, but I knew she had an exercise book with all his poems copied out and every November 4th – the day he died – she lit a candle in her room. She said it was in memory of him, although I wasn't sure how you could remember someone who'd been dead for sixty years. But Nancy talked as though she'd known the man. She had a picture of him stuck up on her bedroom wall which she called a 'photograph', although anyone could see it was just a postcard she'd bought from a museum gift shop.

Nancy had no friends at her school. She never brought anyone home, or talked about anyone there. It puzzled me a little. Apart from her frumpy clothes, she didn't look very different from everyone else. She wasn't like Mandy Pratt in my class, with her wide hips and purplish hands who spent every lunch hour covering books with sticky-back plastic for the school librarian. You weren't supposed to speak to Mandy, or even look at her, accepting these rules without challenge, because if it wasn't Mandy, it might be you, sitting there in the library, day after day.

Julia, effortlessly, triumphantly popular herself, had her own theory about Nancy's lack of friends. 'It's obvious isn't it? She's a complete Woho.'

'Woho?'

'World Of Her Own. Not even on the same planet.'

'I never heard of that.'

'That's because I just made it up,' Julia said rather smugly.

'I still don't see . . .'

'It puts people off,' Julia pronounced. 'She could have tons of friends if she really wanted. It's not that hard.'

I thought of Mandy Pratt on the last day of term. We didn't have to wear uniform on the last day. We could wear anything we wanted. Mandy wore dark blue men's jeans, one size too large. She walked down the corridor with her arms dangling like someone out of a joke Western.

'I don't know, Julia,' I said. 'I don't know about that.'

I never questioned the conditions of being fourteen. I thought perhaps they had always been there, and it was I who was to blame for not noticing them before. Like someone walking in a field, lost in a dream, who lifts their head for the first time and sees that there are fences all around . . .

'What are you doing?' my mother said from the doorway.

'Nothing.'

She looked at me with exasperation. 'Why are you sitting like that? Slumped over. You look like the letter C.'

'I've taken off your sweater, if that's what you want.'

'You know very well that's not what I want.' She glanced at the garment lying balled up on the bed beside me. 'It's not your colour anyway,' she said.

My mother was prone to statements like this. She had a great many rules for the way things should look. She could form an opinion of a person's character it seemed, based solely on the fact that their curtains matched the sofa. Apparently this was not a good thing, although I could never fathom out quite why.

My mother had been to art school and earned a living teaching photography at the Tech. As a sideline, she ran a small portrait studio off Mill Road – an arty neighbourhood, the closest Cambridge ever came to bohemia. She specialized in portraits of babies and children, developing the pictures in a dark room set up in the basement of our house. I was very intrigued by this job of hers, although she never showed much enthusiasm for the work. Instead it often seemed to make her angry. 'You should have seen the cellulite on that baby's bottom,' she'd say in a disgusted voice. 'Thank God for the infinite mercy of soft focus.'

I'd learned that she wasn't making conversation with such announcements. Responding only added to her general irritation. Perhaps my father had learned this too. For all that they lived and slept and ate together, it seemed to me that my parents were nevertheless both quite solitary. Like people pressed together on a crowded train, who through some quality of stillness, some rigidity of glance, maintain their sense of personal space.

'You suit cooler colours,' my mother continued, 'lilac, pale green . . . We should go shopping for you. Get you some new things.'

I hunched forward, visualizing the outing; my mother and I, walking into town. Down Castle Hill and over the river, noisy with punters. The wet hiss of the poles, drawn up hand over hand, the hapless cries of novices floundering beneath Magdalene Bridge. Town was always crowded at this time of the year; swarms of students from the foreign language schools teetering along on rented bicycles; tourists milling about the college walls, peering reverently through ancient, wrought-iron gates, shading their upward gaze against the crenulated sky. I barely noticed such sights myself, my eyes moving with indifference over the vast, elaborate entrance to John's, the soaring façade of King's College Chapel. Only sometimes, in passing, I might catch an accidental sight, through a deeply shadowed archway or half-closed door, of what lay behind the walls. Green, ordered courtyards; briefly glimpsed, where the light looked different from elsewhere. As though it drew on some other, richer source.

But it was to the far more familiar and dismal halls of Eaden Lilley's or Marks & Spencer's, that my mother and I would be headed. It was always one of these two, even though there were other shops in town that sold clothes specifically for my age group. I knew that Tammy Girl, wedged in a shabby corner next to the Wimpy, was out of the question. Tammy Girl was cheap. Tammy Girl was mysteriously, unforgivably common. But there was also Miss Selfridges. Julia bought her clothes there. *Her* mother never made her stand in the dressing rooms at Eaden Lilley's trying on flared trousers and hopelessly small polo-necks.

I could tell I disappointed my mother on these shopping trips. I was beginning to be aware that I was a different shape from her. Shorter, far more rounded. 'No, no,' she would say, in a voice that reverberated around the store. 'That doesn't do anything for you . . .' The knowledge of my inability to make her happy hung over me, weighted with guilt and frustrated love.

'It's been a long time since I bought you some new clothes,' she insisted.

I could always get some trousers, I thought. I could take them to Julia's house to straighten on the sewing machine there. All I had to do was make another seam on the inside of each leg and then cut away the extra fabric. Julia had done it to a pair of jeans, making them so tight her legs went numb while she was waiting in line for the cinema . . .

'All right. I don't mind,' I said.

She patted my leg awkwardly. 'Saturday then. Just the two of us.'

I went outside to see if Nancy was back from school yet and found her walking up and down on the gravel path by the side of her house. It had been a long time since anyone had tended to the area and the gravel was thin in places, with tiny weeds beginning to show between the stones. Nancy's feet were bare and she was swearing softly to herself.

'What are you doing?'

She looked up. 'Don't make me lose count. If I lose count I have to start again.'

I stood by the gate and watched her.

'You look like a spastic,' I said.

'Three hundred and forty-four,' Nancy muttered. 'Three hundred and forty-five. I have to get to a thousand.'

'Why?'

'I'm toughening up my soles.'

'Why?'

She ignored the question. 'Julia's been banned from the house,' she said. 'I told you my mum would smell the smoke didn't I? She's not allowed to come round any more.'

'Your mum can't do that,' I said, outraged.

'You're still allowed.'

'How long is she banned for?'

'I don't know. Until my mum stops going on and on about it.'

'You're going to really hurt your feet if you go on doing that.'

'They're already bleeding a bit,' Nancy said with satisfaction.

'That's the whole point. When they heal up I'll be able to walk with bare feet anywhere.' She reached the end of the path, tottering slightly, turned and walked back towards me again. 'They'll be completely hard. Like leather.'

'It's so unfair about Julia,' I said.

'Do you want to go to Watson's?'

'Now? I thought you were meant to stay in when your Mum's working late.'

'I'm already out aren't I?'

'Do we have to?'

'Julia's going,' Nancy said, settling the debate. 'But I have to get to a thousand first. I can't go until I get to a thousand.'

We walked together down the street, on our way to Watson's. It was late, the light uncertain under a blank, grey sky. Behind us, Miss Pemble came pedalling along, back straight, eyes fixed. She swerved a little as she went by, and I glanced automatically at her slightly worn brown lace-ups.

There was a rumour that despite Miss Pemble's respectable appearance and general air of self-righteousness, she had not, in fact, removed her shoes for over five years. Julia swore that this was the case, claiming that Miss Pemble slept and even bathed with her laces firmly tied. There was fungus, she said – tiny mushrooms – growing between her toes. If this was true, Miss Pemble seemed unaware that her secret was out. She pinged her bell officiously as she passed and soon disappeared from view.

At the end of the road, we stopped for a moment. 'Do we have to go to Watson's again?' I begged. 'One of these days we're going to get caught. I mean it. It's only a matter of time.'

'*You're* not going to get caught,' Nancy said. 'You never do anything.'

'I stand there don't I?'

'You can't get sent to jail for standing,' Julia said. 'Come on. Whose turn is it anyway?'

Watson's was a chemists; a long, low shop on the corner of Victoria Road, with windows looking out on the street. It stayed open until ten at night, seven days a week. I had always suspected the shop's late closing hours resulted less from industriousness on Mr Watson's part, than from the sheer difficulty of shifting his hugely fat body out of the small space behind the till; a feat worthy of Houdini, to be delayed for as long as possible. Mr Watson was so large that it was easy to overlook his other qualities. It was only on closer inspection that one registered his pale, unfriendly features set in perpetual lines of dislike or noticed that from time to time another, quite different expression would cross his face. It was a strange look, both comic and disturbing, which I found hard to properly describe.

'I went last time,' Nancy said, regretfully. 'It's your turn, Julia.'

I could never decide which of my friends it was worse to watch shoplifting. Julia had a bold approach to thievery; filching items from right under the nose of the man with a recklessness that sickened me with anxiety. Nancy, by contrast, was far more furtive, using a sleight of hand that made it difficult to see what she was doing, even when I was staring right at her. But she made up for this by sheer ambition, risking everything for some of the most expensive items in the shop.

They differed in their choices too, each selecting things according to long-established but opposite principles. It was a matter of pride to Julia that she only took things she had absolutely no desire to own; thus transforming the act of theft into a kind of sport. Nancy on the other hand was entirely practical. She took what she liked and wanted, often spending long – and to me, agonizing – minutes in the shop before making her selection.

Only once had I ever taken anything myself. A stick of cherry lip-gloss. I remembered the episode well. The long, terrifying walk up the centre aisle, guts sinking into my knickers, and then my hand darting out to seize the small item, not checking to see whether I was being observed, suddenly quite desperate for it to be done, whether I was caught or not. Looking, as Julia later described it, like a myxomatosis-infected rabbit. The lip-gloss remained in my pocket for a while, unused, emitting a small, unpleasant charge each time my fingers came into contact with it. Julia was right. I was nothing but a coward.

Nancy and I stood outside the shop and watched her saunter casually inside. She smiled at Mr Watson briefly, fingered a packet of tissues near the counter and drifted towards the feminine hygiene section. Mr Watson's eyes followed her. I saw that he had that expression on his face again; a slightly fixed look, but not openly so. As if he was hiding something, I thought. Pretending everything was normal, just as Julia was, but all the time with something secret and wary and intent behind his eyes. As he watched her, he lifted his fat hand away from his body and began rubbing the edge of the counter, palm against the wood, with a tiny, persistent motion, almost mechanical in its repetition. As if he was unaware that he was doing it at all. I turned to Nancy. 'Do you see that? What he's doing?'

'What?'

'He's staring at her. Right at her. She's going to get caught. I mean it. This is the time she finally gets caught.'

'No it isn't,' Nancy said, staring down absently at her sandals; a pair of Jesus Creepers; the sort of shoes that only children wore and secondhand by the look of them. Her mother never bought her anything new, I thought, with a fresh surge of outrage.

'I can't believe your mum's banned Julia,' I repeated for about the tenth time.

'She thinks she's a bad influence.'

'But it wasn't even you doing the smoking. Can't she understand that?'

Nancy made a face. 'She's always going on about trust and then she doesn't . . . I don't care, I don't care what she says. I was trying to read my book and she kept on and on.'

'It was just one cigarette. You can't get cancer from one cigarette.'

'I was trying to read,' Nancy repeated, 'and she gave me the Talk anyway. I had the book up to my face – I was even turning the pages, but it didn't make any difference.'

I had heard Nancy mention the Talk several times before, but she was always vague on the details of what it was actually about. Perhaps, knowing it word for word herself, she assumed everyone else did as well. What I did know was that the Talk involved what had happened to Nancy's mother. The story – heavy with warning – of how she had dropped out of college to bring Nancy up all by herself, and how much better everything would have been if she had done things completely differently.

'I don't see what all that has to do with one cigarette,' I said. 'That you didn't even smoke in the first place.' She shrugged absently, her mind on other things.

'Julia's being ages,' I complained. 'I'm honestly going to have a nervous breakdown if she doesn't get out of there soon.'

'It was a really good book,' Nancy said. 'Wilfred Owen's biography. They've got drafts in it. Some of the poems, all the drafts he did of "Anthem for Doomed Youth". Five of them.' She gestured with her hands. 'Black ink. A fountain pen, I think. You can see . . . you can see all the changes he made.'

Her hand movements became more agitated. 'You can see his *mind* changing.'

I looked at her silently, not sure what to say.

'There's a bit where he crosses out one word. It's right at the end. He crosses out "patient" and puts "silent" instead. The ink there, it's faint in the first letter and then comes out darker. Like he wasn't sure and then he suddenly was. Like it suddenly came to him.'

I liked it when Nancy talked like this, although I didn't know exactly why. It seemed to put me – for a moment or two – into a different time. A time when humiliation was still unforeseen and the only rules were the kind you could break.

'What difference does it make between that word and the other one?' I asked.

She stared at me, with a baffled, shut-off look. 'I just keep reading that poem,' she said finally.

I knew she had the thing by heart already, because she'd recited it to me once, months ago. I couldn't recall what it was really about, only that it was sad; something about soldiers dying. But I remembered the sound of her voice; almost singsong, the words expressionless as muttered prayer. And I wondered how many more times she would go over it, transfixed by some ecstatic sorrow that I had never known and perhaps never would.

'I wish Julia would hurry up,' I said. 'I really, really do.'

Julia had stolen a small bottle of bubble bath and a box of tampons. She emerged triumphantly, hands in pockets, and we all walked quickly away, down towards the river, past the sweetshop on the corner and the small, shady rec.

'Sorry it took so long,' she said, 'that creepy bastard never took his eyes off me.'

'I don't know how you got away without being caught,' I said.

She gave me a look of mock incomprehension. 'Jesus, Sophie, I *wonder* . . .'

'What?'

It was quite dark by now. Below the footbridge leading to Jesus Green the weir roared, sounding deafening in the surrounding silence. We stopped on the far side and sat down in the shadow of the bridge, on the sloping river bank. During the day there were often people fishing from this spot and small children feeding the ducks. On summer weekends there was usually an ice-cream van parked on the other side of the path and people playing tennis on the courts beyond. But now the place was deserted and almost completely silent, apart from the distant noise of traffic.

It felt a little daring to be out at night – just the three of us. But our sense of liberation was tinged with aimlessness. We had nowhere to be and nothing in particular to do. Julia unscrewed the top of the bubble bath and sniffed the contents.

'Smell this. It's disgusting. Why would anyone buy this crap?'

'It's quite nice,' Nancy said. 'I quite like that.'

'No, it's not. It smells like cat's pee. It smells like under Sophie's bed.'

'It's not my fault the cat goes there,' I said, aggrieved. 'He's only done it a couple of times anyway.'

Behind us, the park seemed very wide and dark. In the daylight, the tree-lined avenue that crossed it in a long diagonal was clear and broad. But in the darkness, it appeared to have narrowed, forming a dense tunnel; the single, far-off lamp-post at its very centre casting a weak, shallow light that was soon lost amidst the trees. In the last few months, there had been assaults made on women in Cambridge and the Fens. Nobody knew whether one man or several were involved, only that there was a consistency to the attacks, a pattern forming. I thought of this briefly as I sat there, but my unease was an abstract thing, easily put aside.

Julia slithered on her bottom down to the water's edge and began to pour the bubble bath into the river.

'Things happen after a Badedas Bath,' she said.

'That's a complete waste,' Nancy said.

'Why? Do you want it? So you can stand at the window like in the adverts? Wearing nothing but a towel with a cheesy man holding the reins of a horse looking up at you from the street.'

'I just like it,' Nancy said.

'I bet you think that man has come to give her the horse. You do, don't you? You think that's what happens after a Badedas Bath; a man appears and presents you with a pony.'

'I used to think that,' I said, 'when I was about *ten*.'

'What really happens after a Badedas Bath,' Julia continued, still pouring, 'is that you end up smelling like shit.'

'Talking of smells,' I said, 'you're banned from Nancy's house. Her mum smelled the smoke. Plus Ivy said she saw you.'

Julia shrugged. 'That's pathetic.'

'My mum says Ivy's budgie is the reincarnation of Hitler or someone,' I said. 'She says that's the worst punishment you could have, to come back as Ivy's budgie.'

'No it isn't,' Julia said. 'I think Hitler came back as one of those socks you put on in shoe shops when you're trying on shoes. You know, the ones like tights, all shrivelled up, with loads of ladders in them.'

'I hate Ivy,' Nancy said suddenly. 'My mum says I have to

go round and apologize to her. Even though I didn't do anything. It's all her fault anyway.'

'You can't be reincarnated as a sock,' she added. 'You have to come back as something alive.'

'Your mum must have a really good sense of smell,' Julia said. 'I mean, most of the smoke went out of the window, didn't it, Sophie?'

'We'd have probably got away with it if you hadn't stuck that cigarette practically up Ivy's nose,' I pointed out.

'There's this teacher at my school,' Julia continued. 'He can smell anything. I mean it. He can walk into the library and if you've been eating crisps there within the last five hours, he can tell. Not only that, he knows the *flavour*.' Her voice changed to an accusing growl. 'It's Smoky Bacon! Smo-ky Ba-con!'

'Can't we just get rid of the tampons and go?' I said. 'My parents are going to kill me if they find out I'm here.'

The box of tampons was one of Julia's more inspired thefts, since she had yet to have her first period. I had started the year before and was deeply ashamed of the fact that I still used sanitary towels. I stood in the loos at my school, peeling off the sticky strip on the back of each towel with infinite slowness. If you did it too fast, it made a loud, tell-tale ripping sound. 'We know what you're *do-ing!*' Monica Freely had once shrieked through the cubicle door after I had pulled the strip too hastily. Monica had red hair, big white front teeth and unerring radar for the weaknesses of others. She banged her fist hard against the cubicle door. 'Still using those great big jam rolls?' she yelled.

Julia unwrapped each tampon slowly, dangling them by their string over the water before letting go. 'I wonder if they float or sink,' she said with interest.

'They sink,' Nancy said. 'But only when they're completely soaked through.'

We didn't question her authority on the matter. Nancy had started her periods when she was ten. She was the only girl in the whole of junior school who had to wear shorts like the boys during P. E. Everyone else still ran around in their vests and knickers.

Julia dropped the last of the tampons into the water, followed by the empty box.

'Disgusting,' she said with relish.

III

My mother was not in the habit of throwing dinner parties and always made elaborate preparations on the rare occasions when guests came to the house. She stood at the sink washing squid tentacles under the running tap, her long, pale fingers almost the same colour as the fish. It was another grey day, the sky low, the wind rattling the leaves of the apple tree outside the kitchen window and making the square-shaped garments hanging out on Ivy's washing line flap heavily against each other.

In recent weeks, the old woman had taken to knocking against the shared wall of our two houses, a signal that she needed help. There was never anything wrong; just the usual list of small ailments and complaints and from time to time my mother would try to ignore the summons, but the knocking – beginning fast, then slowing to an intermittent tap as though delivered by a rapidly weakening arm – was so tormenting that she always gave in. I used to wonder why she simply didn't tell Ivy to stop, seeing as she disliked her so much. Perhaps it was as simple as the fact that my mother thought that if anything happened to the old woman, it would make her feel bad.

My father had another theory. 'You know that landlady is going to snap up her house the minute she dies, don't you?' he'd said once, after a couple of glasses of wine. 'Then we'll have a whole crowd of new neighbours who'll do a lot more than just knock on the wall.'

'That thought has never occurred to me,' my mother said tightly. 'If you're suggesting that I'm only . . .'

'I'm just stating the facts,' my father said.

While my mother prepared food and arranged bowls of peanuts on the coffee table in readiness for the party, my father sat with *The Cambridge Evening News* in the living room. Nobody he knew had been invited, they were all people my mother worked with. I wasn't sure my father had any friends beyond casual acquaintances.

For quite a while I had stopped having any real conversations with my father. We had always been close before, but now this seemed a distant thing, separated by something other than simply the passage of time. We still had our Sunday morning ritual of course. My father at the stove, cooking pancakes for me as he had done for as long as I could remember. The same careful laying out of ingredients on the kitchen counter, the same silent examination of the bubbles on the surface of each golden puddle as he judged the precise moment to flip, the single lemon, cut into wedges, the sound of the spatula sliding yet another pancake out of the pan. It was impossible to imagine a morning coming without that familiar, buttery smell, my glass of milk, my napkin laid. But now, sitting there, waiting for my food, I watched him in a different way, with a new, uneasy tolerance as if it was no longer quite clear to me which of the two of us was indulging the other.

He was a quiet person. My mother called him cynical. I didn't know what she meant by that, only that he seemed separate from other people, as if his personality, the demands of his work – whose details were kept from me, but which I understood involved quite terrible things – had placed him between two different worlds, understanding something of both, but belonging to neither.

'The Fen Rapist!' he said abruptly, shaking the newspaper. 'That's what they're calling him now. Like some kind of bird. The Marsh Wader, the Lesser Spotted Beach Plover, The Fen Rapist.'

My mother continued to plump up the cushions on the sofa without comment.

'He's a celebrity,' my father said.

'Well they've got to call him something,' my mother said. She glanced at me rather strangely. 'I don't want you going out and hanging around anymore. I want to know exactly where you're going. Every time. Do you understand?'

'I don't have anywhere to go,' I pointed out.

'Aren't you going to change?' my mother asked my father. 'And Sophie, you need to comb your hair.' She was suddenly very urgent, her cheeks flushed. I didn't know why she was making such a fuss about a few people coming over seeing as she saw them every day at work.

'Do I *have* to stay?' I said.

'Yes. It will be good for you. You can pass around the peanuts. I had to keep reminding you last time.'

I said nothing. I was dreading the peanuts. I had a vision of myself, bowl in hand, hovering by the coffee table, horribly unsure of the correct time to present. Then the sudden lunge forward – propelled more by a sense of my own foolishness than anything else – interrupting the conversation at always the most inopportune moment and eliciting the kind of smiles that made me certain I was being laughed at.

'Why can't they just help themselves?' I said.

My mother was about to answer when there was a movement from the street outside. She ran to the window. 'They're here!' she cried.

My father put down the paper reluctantly and stood up.

'Christ,' my mother said in a changed voice, 'I don't believe this. Ivy's at the gate again. She's just standing there, staring.' She rushed to the door to greet the three guests crowding up the tiny path from the garden gate. 'Hello! Come in!' she cried out hastily. 'Let me take your coats . . .'

'Nice evening,' I heard Ivy say in a reproachful voice.

'Yes, yes, isn't it?' my mother said, apparently ignoring the leaden sky.

'Lovely.' Ivy said. There was a long, awkward silence, broken at last by my mother.

'This is my neighbour, Ivy,' she said, her voice bright with desperation. 'Erm, George Collins, one of my colleagues, his wife Sylvie . . . Marjorie from the English department . . .'

'Nice to meet you,' a man said in a loud, breezy voice. 'How are you doing?'

'I've got diarrhoea,' Ivy said.

I left the gathering well before everyone sat down to dinner, but I could tell even at that early stage that the evening was not going to be a success. My mother seemed to take a long time to recover from her mortification at Ivy's comment. She was flustered and distracted. My father, too, appeared tense, although the source of this was harder to define. I thought perhaps it was something to do with the manner and general appearance of George Collins.

George taught German History at the Tech. He was short, balding slightly, with an eager look about him. He came in, a few steps ahead of his wife, taking off his hat, a curious, checked affair, with a brim front and back. 'Something smells good!' he said, rubbing his hands together and looking around him. 'Love the decor, Margie. Very eclectic.'

My mother normally hated to have her name shortened. She thought it sounded over-familiar. But she didn't seem offended when George did it, taking his hat with a pleased smile. Behind him, his wife Sylvie tugged half-heartedly at her scarf. 'I'll keep my jacket if you don't mind,' she said, as if my mother was about to rip it from her by force. 'It's this terrible damp in the air.'

'Don't you hate the weather we get in Cambridge?' my mother said. 'You wouldn't know it was June. Sometimes I think we live in a kind of meteorological Bermuda Triangle. Summer comes sailing in and then just vanishes, never to be seen again.' She spoke jokingly, but there was an undercurrent of bitterness in her voice and nobody laughed.

While they were talking, the third guest, Marjorie, stood silently in the background holding a bottle of wine in a hesitant fashion. I could tell she wasn't quite sure when to proffer it and felt a rush of fellow-feeling. She wasn't very old, I thought, although she might just as well have been fifty, with her shapeless brown corduroy skirt and flat shoes.

George Collins came forward, hand outstretched. 'Ah!' he cried, 'the social worker. I've heard a great deal about you.'

My father narrowed his eyes.

'Would you like some peanuts?' I said.

My mother gave me a look. 'Wait until we're *sitting down*.'

They milled around for a while as if finding seats was a challenge they were unprepared for. My father opened Marjorie's bottle of wine and poured everyone a glass. I didn't pay much attention to the conversation, partly owing to extreme boredom, and partly due to the demands of my task. I was also thinking about Julia. Her parents had just told her she could take over the shed at the bottom of their garden to use as a meeting place for friends. I was lost in envy at this generosity. Julia's parents let her do anything she wanted, I thought. The shed was wired up with electricity and she could put chairs in there. Perhaps a small table . . .

'. . . Immeasurably superior,' George Collins was saying. 'No question . . . the rubbish on the small screen these days . . .' He broke off as I offered the peanut bowl, flashing me a look of annoyance. 'You can't call it an art form. When you think of the written word . . .' He shook his head. 'Without exception, the written word is better.'

'Better?' my father said.

Marjorie's fingers fumbled slightly as she fished for a nut. She slid one up the side of the bowl, dropped it and searched for another. 'I'm not sure you can really . . . well, different media . . .' she began tentatively.

'We haven't owned a television in years,' George interrupted. 'Never watch the thing.'

'There are some quite good things on,' Marjorie said, stumbling over her words, 'I mean, from time to time . . .'

'Of course there are,' my father said.

'I'd better check on the beef,' my mother said, standing up and giving him a sideways look. I sat on a chair in the corner. My bowl was half empty and I wondered whether I was meant to do the circuit again. Sylvie Collins had refused the first time around. But did this mean she didn't want any at all, or simply not at that particular moment? She was sitting on the edge of her chair, not taking part in the conversation, sipping her wine rather fast. My father had already refilled her glass once. I rattled the peanuts half-heartedly in her direction.

Julia's mother had suggested we might brighten up the inside of the shed using left-over paint. 'Make it into a real den!' she'd suggested, in that brisk, jolly way of hers. She always talked like that, like a mother out of a story book. Like the one who packed provisions for everyone in *Swallows and Amazons*. Of course, the shed wouldn't be a *den* exactly. More of a clubhouse, I thought. Dens were what children made behind the back of the sofa.

George Collins was still talking away. 'Quite ridiculous,' he said. 'Inept. I don't see why . . .'

'He's obviously rather cunning,' Marjorie suggested. 'I mean, cunning in a . . . well, I don't mean to suggest anything flattering by that . . . perhaps simply very *elusive*. And after all, he could be anyone really.'

'That's what the police are for! That's what we pay them for.'

My mother came back into the room. 'I agree with George. The police don't seem to be doing anything. How many attacks do there have to be before they take it seriously?'

'I'm sure they're already taking it very seriously,' my father said.

Sylvie broke her silence. 'George thinks he could crack the case himself,' she said abruptly, her gaze fixed on a point somewhere below the coffee table. 'If he had all the facts.'

'Well,' George said, chuckling modestly, 'I wouldn't go quite *that* far, but I'm sure the application of simple common-sense . . .'

'Really?' my father said.

'That explains the hat, the deerstalker look. It's obviously the detective in you coming out.' He spoke lightly, but George Collins seemed unamused. He stared at my father coldly.

'It is a Bavarian mountain cap,' he said, dragging out the syllables with offended emphasis. 'It was purchased in Bah-var-ia.'

There was a short silence. 'Well,' my mother said at last. 'If everyone would like to come through to the dining room . . .'

★

The others were already in the shed when I arrived. It was smaller than I had imagined and it smelled of earth and mildew. A little, I thought, like the smell of our clothes when my mother forgot to take them out of the washing machine. The only light came from a single, hanging bulb and it gave the place a strange, subterranean atmosphere. As if it was always in the middle of the night there, no matter how brightly the sun shone above ground.

Julia and Nancy sat on a couple of cardboard boxes, discussing what colour the walls should be.

'Stripes!' Julia said. 'It'll look fucking brilliant. Each bit of wood a different colour.'

I sat down beside Nancy. 'What's that scent you're wearing?'

'It's Charlie,' she said, 'I got it from Watson's.'

'You must have put on half the bottle.'

'I told my mum it was yours,' Nancy said. 'So remember that, if she asks.'

'Why would she ask?' Julia said. 'I mean, I know your mum's got a nose like a bloodhound, but she's not constantly sniffing your neck is she?'

Nancy's eyes narrowed. 'I wouldn't put it past her. She's always snooping around.'

'You make out like she's in the Gestapo or something,' Julia said. 'I know she's banned me and everything, but I quite like your mum. I mean, at least she's out working most of the time. My mum's always *there*. She doesn't do anything. It's totally depressing.'

Nancy shook her head. 'You don't know what it's like.'

'I hate Charlie anyway,' I said.

After we cleared all the cardboard boxes and old gardening tools out of the shed, it looked a little larger and more welcoming. 'We could fit a sofa in here,' I said. 'Where could we get a sofa from?'

'Charity shop,' Nancy said. 'That's where all our furniture comes from.'

I turned to Julia. 'Your parents are amazing. I can't believe they just gave you this place.'

She rolled her eyes. 'They're so *organized*. I hate that. I hate the way Mum has a day for everything. The linen cupboard, the way she stacks the dishwasher. One night I'm going to get up and set fire to the house. I mean it. Just watch it burn. I like chaos. I *dream* of chaos.'

'I don't,' Nancy said. 'I'd like to live in a country that was completely flat, so flat that if you stood on a box you could see for a hundred miles in every direction. My house would be completely quiet. All you'd hear is the wind blowing across the land.'

'Boring,' Julia said. 'Why would it be so quiet anyway?'

'Because my husband would be sick,' Nancy said. 'He'd lie in bed, not moving, not even talking. I'd buy a colt for him and bring it up to the window so he could see it. He'd turn his head on the pillow and see it standing there outside. In the wind.'

'You're totally obsessed with that Badedas advert aren't you?' Julia said.

'I wasn't thinking about *that*,' Nancy said, sounding offended.

'You can't call that a plan anyway,' Julia pointed out. 'The whole thing would only last thirty seconds.'

'What would you name it?' I asked. 'The colt, I mean.'

'Nothing. It wouldn't have a name.'

'Boring,' Julia repeated. 'Why do you want to look after somebody sick anyway?'

'I don't know,' Nancy said. 'I just thought of it like that.'

We went outside and poked around for a while rather aimlessly. Julia's garden was pleasant and well kept. But between the shed and the fence at the far end was a small unkempt area, invisible from the house. It was dark there; a tangle of brambles and mallow. If you kept your gaze low, avoiding the sight of chimney tops from the houses beyond, it was possible to imagine yourself in an enclave of some neglected forest; an accidental opening, unlovely and unknown. In the centre of this space stood a small, dead shrub, held upright only by the creeping grip of bindweed around its trunk. Nancy went over to it, fumbling in her pocket.

'A memento,' she said, pulling out a potato masher and hanging it from one of the bare twigs.

'What's that for?' I asked.

'Ivy. I got it from her house. When I went to apologize. I took it out of the drawer in her kitchen. I had to choose something nobody would think I'd take. She'll just think she lost it.'

'Poor old bag,' Julia said. 'What did you do that for?'

'She kept making me tea. She wouldn't let me leave till I'd finished all the biscuits.'

'But why did you do it?' I persisted.

'I don't know. I hate her.'

'You should take it back,' Julia said.

'You take it back if you're so worried about it.'

Julia shook her head. They both looked at me. '*I'm* not doing it,' I said. 'Why should I do it?'

'Poor old bag,' Julia said again. We stared at the potato masher dangling from its miserable perch.

'It's a hating tree,' Nancy said suddenly. 'That's why it's dead.'

It was a little strange, what happened then. Even at the time I couldn't explain it properly to myself. Something possessed us; a mysterious fury without precedent or future, but belonging only to that time. How easily we called it up and how readily it came. The whole world nothing more than a fine, containing skin around it, broken in an instant. I don't remember who began the thing, only that we were suddenly walking around the shrub, taking it in turns to call out the names of the people we hated. It would have looked ridiculous to an observer. I thought it was ridiculous myself, but still we kept on, around and around, beating down a small track in the weeds with our feet.

We called out so many names. We hated everyone: teachers, parents, casual acquaintances. The names flashed through my mind in an unbroken ribbon. Nancy's voice was a fierce mutter, Julia sang, the ground hummed with the sheer force of our spite.

'Mr Watson,' I said.

'Mr Watson,' Nancy repeated.

'Mr *Watson*!' shrieked Julia.

We continued for an hour, perhaps longer. It was quite dark by the time we finally stopped, tired, a little embarrassed, strangely exhilarated.

'I can't believe we just did that,' Julia said. 'That was completely sick.'

We smiled at each other with secret triumph. The wind had died down, taking part of the cloud cover with it, and the dark lay in pools; deep and stocked with stars. For the first time in weeks, I felt light, myself again. I walked back up the street to home, my step careless, my heart floating in calm seas.

IV

Immediately after school broke up for the summer, we had a spell of warm weather. Julia, Nancy and I went to the open-air swimming pool on Jesus Green almost every day. No matter how long the sun had warmed the water, it was always shriek-ingly cold. Only the hardiest – small children and the occa-sional old man in goggles, ploughing along with the speed and endurance of a turtle – could stand the temperature for long. Everyone else went to the pool merely to sit around its edges. It was enclosed by a thick line of trees on one side and changing huts on the other, and sometimes, if you could ignore the smell of chlorine, and the sounds from the play-ground beyond, it was possible to imagine yourself some-where quite different; somewhere almost exotic. The south of France perhaps, I thought, although I had no idea what the south of France was actually like.

On the side which caught most of the sun, next to the huts, young women in their late teens and early twenties lay stretched out on their towels. They wore bikinis, their skin smooth and already tanned. They lay very still, but there seemed to me a kind of tension in their bodies, as though they weren't resting at all, but rather waiting for something. From time to time they would shift, flicking their hands over their legs or hair with careful, apparently pointless move-ments, their eyes glancing briefly at the young men who walked by and then returning to contemplate themselves anew. I didn't think I would ever look like these women. And I didn't think they had ever looked like me.

Nancy and I sat on the grass, on the further, shadier side of the pool, counting our money to see how many penny chews we could buy at the refreshments kiosk and watching Julia climb up the ladder to the highest diving board. She stood at the top for a moment, evaluating the height, one toe curled over the edge, her arms easy at her side. Then the leap upwards, confident, almost leisurely, the sun flashing on her wet skin as she twisted in mid-air, her body falling with such controlled purpose that it made gravity itself seem optional.

'I don't know how she can do that,' I said. I was wearing my swimsuit from the year before; a black one-piece that dug into the tops of my legs and around my arms. I thought I looked terrible in it, like an overweight nine-year-old. When I wasn't actually in the water, I kept my towel draped around my waist at all times. I was beginning to regard my body as if it only partially belonged to me. Sometimes, at night, the smell of my own skin seemed unfamiliar, as though I was no longer alone, but lay with a stranger of uncertain loyalty in the bed beside me.

I watched as Julia rose up through the water, her sleek head breaking the surface. 'I couldn't do that in a million years. I can't even dive from the side of the pool.'

Nancy wasn't listening. She was staring into space, her gaze transfixed, her mouth hanging slightly open. Every few seconds, the pupils of her eyes ranged from left to right and back again.

'What *is* that stuff?' she said.

'What stuff?'

'When it's really bright. That stuff you see floating just in front of your eyes. The minute you try and look at it, it sort of drifts away.'

'It's just eye crap,' I said.

Nancy blinked a couple of times then resumed her inspection. 'I don't know,' she said, cross-eyed with effort. 'They sort of look like amoebas. Stringy ones. They're just sort of swimming around.'

'Julia's going up again,' I said.

'I think they're alive. Millions of them, swimming around on the surface of my eyes. It's probably like a great big ocean for them. When I blink it's probably like a tidal wave or something. I probably kill thousands every time I blink.'

There was a small scattering of applause as Julia executed

another flawless dive. She swam to the side of the pool, lifting herself over the edge with a single movement. 'Aren't you slugs coming in?' she called.

She stood over us, dripping. 'What's wrong with *her*?' she asked, looking at Nancy.

'She's trying not to blink.'

'Come on,' Julia said, pointing to the sunbathing women on the far side, 'Let's get them wet.'

We followed her around to the other side until we were standing in a line on the very edge of the pool, just in front of a particularly large group of sunbathers. Julia stood between us, holding each of our hands in a firm, wet grip.

'Are you ready? After three.'

We jumped all together, tucking up our legs for maximum impact, the sky breaking into sharp pieces above us, our shrieks joined by the distant, outraged cries of bystanders. Our feet touched bottom and we rose, still holding each other's hands; a trio of avenging mermaids, come up from the deep.

I put my jeans on over my swimsuit and cycled home damply. When I got there, the house was empty and I drifted upstairs, glad of the quiet. My bedroom was in its usual state of clutter; my clothes – both clean and dirty – piled in a great heap over the chair by the desk. It had been days since I'd been able to sit down there and weeks since the desk itself had been of any use, beneath its layers of school files and papers. Even my bed, strewn with towels and discarded books, offered little in the way of space. I shoved the duvet aside and made a small trench for myself, settling down with a copy of *Frenchman's Creek* by Daphne Du Maurier and a large packet of salt and vinegar crisps.

I had taken to spending most of my available money on food. I was hungry all the time, quite capable of consuming a couple of Bounty Bars and then sitting down to a large supper. But I was secretive about my eating, ashamed of the betraying rustle of crisp packets in my pockets, the empty chocolate wrappers stuffed under my bed, the furtive speed with which I ate, fearful of my mother's scorn.

I was deep into my book when I first heard the intruder. I had read it perhaps three or four times already and thought it was the saddest, most lovely story I had ever come across. It flooded me with longing, made everything that belonged to the moment of reading – my still wet swimsuit chafing my legs, my fingers smeared with illicit crisp grease, the narrow view of the street from my bedroom window – not shameful and unimportant things, but part of the profound, impossible wonder of eternal love . . .

At first I thought that the sound downstairs meant one of my parents was home and I almost called out, not wanting them to come upstairs unknowing and find me there. But the noise didn't seem as though it was made by anyone familiar with the interior of the house. It sounded clumsy, footsteps heavy and uncertain. I put down my book and stood up slowly. The footsteps stopped abruptly and there was a clattering from the kitchen as if someone was going through the drawers, violently and impatiently.

I went to my desk, rummaged for a pair of scissors and then stood by the bedroom door, listening. It occurred to me that I was perhaps better off hiding somewhere, but the only place to go was under the bed and that was always the first place that people like the Fen Rapist looked. Just the day before, the newspaper had printed a picture of him, or at least the mask he wore. A black woollen balaclava with the mouth hole stapled shut in a long, crooked line. Anyone wearing such a thing, I decided, would be almost certain to look under the bed.

The clattering sound from below broke off and there was

silence. Gripping the scissors in my fist, I opened the door cautiously and crept slowly down the stairs. The telephone was in front of me, on a table in the hallway, but I passed it by, knowing I would have no time to complete dialling for help. A chair scraped in the kitchen and there was a thud as though someone had fallen heavily onto the seat. I paused. Even with the vision of the balaclava firm in my mind, it struck me as odd that the intruder should be so very unstealthy; almost as if he didn't care if he was caught or not.

'What are you *doing*?' I said.

He was sitting slumped over the kitchen table; a large man, very red in the face, with a despairing expression on his puffy features and a dirty handkerchief in his right hand. Even from ten feet away, the thick, breath-stopping smell of him filled my nostrils.

'Cah fin it,' he said incoherently. 'Iss gone, iss gone.' He looked up, blinking, not seeming at all surprised to see me there. 'Not in the ri place. Iss not there. Looking for tha . . . tha . . . tha . . .' He stopped, tried to gather himself. 'Tha . . . tha . . . ke-ell.'

'The kettle?'

'Yeah!' he said, suddenly excited.

'You're in the wrong house,' I said loudly, spacing out the words. 'The Wrong House. You Don't Live Here.'

He looked at me with sudden cunning. 'Makus a cuppa. Nice cuppa tea.'

I put down the scissors. 'All right,' I said. 'But you have to go home after that.'

I put the kettle on and found a mug while he sat there, wiping his eyes with the handkerchief. Julia was right, I thought. He wasn't really crying. His face was just wet, although the impression of sorrow still remained even after you realized this fact.

'Do you want sugar?'

I put down the tea cautiously and then stepped back, as though proffering nourishment to some shy, wild animal. 'You'll have to drink it quickly,' I told him. 'My mother will be back very soon.'

He gave his face another slow wipe. 'Wha . . . wha . . . time is it?'

'Nearly ten to.'

'Ten two?'

'Ten to five,' I said.

'Ten to five,' he repeated, nodding. 'Yeah. And after . . . it'll be five to and then five o clock.'

'I suppose so,' I said. He hadn't touched his tea.

'After five, it's six. It's six o . . . o . . . o . . .'

I waited while he floundered, searching for the word.

'Clock?' I said finally.

'Yeah! Six o clock. And after, it'll be seven. Evening time, evening time. It will, won't it?' His face had an urgent look suddenly. As if he had a story of utmost importance to relate.

'Then night. Night already. I'm right about this, aren't I? Aren't I?'

'Yes,' I agreed, weakly. He craned his neck towards me. 'After that, tomorrow. It'll be Sunday then. After Sunday comes Monday and Tuesday and Wednesday. All one after the other. Just like that. Halfway through the week. Feels like halfway through, but soon as Thursday comes, just one day later, it changes doesn't it? Doesn't it? Starts to feel like the week is nearly over. Weekend coming up again. Now, we're getting into July here . . .' He paused, staring at me fixedly.

'You haven't drunk your tea,' I said. 'My mother will be home soon.'

'July, July, July,' he repeated in a fast, loud voice. 'We're talking August next month. August. Almost the end of summer. September next and October. We're knocking at Christmas before you know it. Winter. Then it's a new year already. A new year. But winter is halfway through already isn't it? New year and spring just around the corner. January, February, March . . .'

I nodded helplessly, wondering how long he was going to talk. But his train of thought seemed to have become derailed. He slumped forward once more, burying his face in the grubby creases of his handkerchief. It was very quiet. I could hear the clock on the wall ticking. Out in the garden, a blackbird sang with hidden, innocent voice. I stepped forward uncertainly.

'Are you all right? Are you feeling okay?'

His voice was muffled; still urgent, but softer this time.

'Wha . . . wha . . . time is it? Wha time is it then?'

I looked up at the clock automatically. 'It's five to now.'

He took the handkerchief away from his face and looked at me very sadly and wisely. 'I thought it would be,' he said. 'Didn't I tell you this would happen?'

I nodded silently.

'It's all turning out exactly like I told you,' he said.

There was a bang as the front door opened and suddenly my mother was in the doorway, looking very tall, her face rigid.

'What the *hell* are you doing in my house?' she said. She stared at us for a second or two. 'I can't take this place,' she cried abruptly. 'I can't take it any longer.'

Julia had a jam-jar three-quarters full of a thick, brownish concoction, containing a splash from every single bottle in her parents' large drinks cabinet. We sat on the thick foam wedges in her shed, staring at it with a mixture of horror and delight. The wedges – salvaged from a skip – were a recent addition to the shed, as was the table-lamp on the floor which Julia was decorating by burning a pattern of cigarette holes in the paper shade.

We took it in turns to sip from the jar, holding our breath and forcing the liquid down. In a very little while, all three of us were drunk.

'Weeping Tom came to see me,' I said slowly, squinting a little. Everything I looked at seemed to have a fine, buzzing line around it.

'Oooh, lucky you,' Julia said, smirking.

'I thought he was the Fen Rapist.'

'Whatever gave you that idea?' Julia said, giggling. 'His air of quiet menace?'

'Was, was he wiping his ma-ma-mask?' Nancy burst out.

'I didn't think he was the Fen Rapist when I *saw* him, only upstairs, when he was walking around. I got the scissors. I was quite brave actually.'

'Scissors?' Julia spluttered. There was a long pause while the pair of them shook and gasped.

'What did . . . what did you do?' Nancy finally managed.

I began to laugh too. The kind of laughter that perhaps only fourteen-year-old girls are capable of: violent, unstop-pable, propelled by its own absurdity and carried to the point of torture. Each gasp and sob from the other two prompting another spasm in my own throat, my eyes watering, my gut aching, my whole body convulsed and helpless.

'I made him a cup of tea!' I managed to shriek.

Julia writhed on the foam sofa. 'How'd he drink it? Through the . . . the . . . *staples?*'

We stopped at last, sighing, sucking in air. The room swam around me. 'I think I'm drunk,' I said. 'Really, really drunk.'

'He'll die soon,' Nancy said suddenly. She lay very still, looking up at the wooden ceiling.

'Who?'

'Weeping Tom. He'll die soon.'

'Well, we've all got to go sometime,' Julia said. 'Up to that big doss-house in the sky.'

'Not everyone,' Nancy said. She turned her head and looked at us. 'They go somewhere different, the people who die young.'

'Like where?'

'I don't know.'

'You're drunk,' Julia said.

'You mean like people who die in car crashes or who kill themselves?' I asked.

'Killing yourself doesn't count,' Nancy said. 'That's cheating.'

'What about all those people who drink themselves to death,' Julia said. 'Like the men across the street. Like Weeping Tom?'

'That doesn't count. You can't take yourself. You have to be *taken*.'

'You're weird,' Julia said. 'God, I wish I hadn't put the crème de menthe in. I think the crème de menthe was a step too far.'

'Did you know,' Nancy said, in a low, distant voice, 'that Wilfred Owen died only a week before the end of the war? Only one week. He was in France. They were trying to get across this canal, only the bridge was broken and Germans were firing at them from the other bank. With machine guns. But the British just kept going. They had to repair the bridge, even though they knew they were going to get killed. Can you believe that? They just kept trying to repair it and getting killed. Wilfred Owen was one of the officers. He was down by the water, encouraging the men, when he got hit.'

Julia and I looked at each other uncertainly, numbed by the alcohol and the steady, unemotional tone of Nancy's voice.

'I just keep thinking,' Nancy continued. 'What if the war had ended one week sooner? Just one week. It wouldn't have happened then, would it? He'd have survived. He'd have been able to go home. Why did it have to end then, and not before? It could have. Easily. He'd have lived then. Why didn't they stop it?'

Julia lay back and rested her head on Nancy's stomach. It was one of her gifts; this ready physical affection. A kind of generosity expressed through touch, easy and unselfconscious.

'I suppose they just kept going too,' she said, slurring her words slightly. 'Like the men trying to get over the canal. Everyone just going and going and going.' She stroked Nancy's leg. 'Don't be so weird, don't think about it. S'all right, you know, s'all right.'

I lay down beside them, not touching, but close enough to see the slow rise and fall of Nancy's chest and smell the faint, sickly scent of left-over Charlie on her skin. We stayed like that for a long time without moving or speaking, in a dim stupor. The kind of sleep which does not know itself, full of broken thought and uncertain dream, that holds us dazed until we wake, staring, bewildered by the clock.

V

It was mid-July and the funfair was setting up on the Common. Over the trailer-muddied grass, the dinosaur bones of the Big Wheel and Dodgems lay stretched out, waiting for assembly. I glanced at them quickly as I cycled past. Last year, Julia and I had spent all our money at the fair, riding the Twister at least a dozen times, our bodies plastered to the sides, our teeth bared in a centrifugal howl. In the evenings, the lights, the sudden music, the heady smells of toffee and machine grease, had transformed the Common into a place of glamour and mystery, to be enjoyed as long as our ten-pence pieces lasted.

But now the funfair seemed changed. It looked thinner, far more shabby. In the back of a lorry, the nylon bodies of hundreds of cheap soft toys – prizes for the rifle range or hoop-toss – lay stuffed in dustbin bags like rubbish waiting for collection. Around the trailers, the men of the fair stood glum-faced, smoking and staring at the convoys of foreign students wheeling past them. I felt their gaze on me too; indifferent, evaluating, their eyes sliding away after a brief moment. Almost with scorn, I thought, pedalling a little faster. As if I had failed some kind of test.

When I got home, Miss Pemble was in the front room, talking to my mother.

It was well known that Miss Pemble had two passions in life. The first was genealogy. For years – nobody was sure quite how many – she had been toiling on her family tree. But the work – a homage to the reproductive capabilities of countless ancestors – must have carried its own reproach. For Miss Pemble, lone product of all those centuries of painstaking begetting, was the last of the line, both chronicler of its success and agent of its failure. It was perhaps this fact that had turned a mere hobby into something of an obsession.

I had never seen inside her record book – an important-looking volume, bound in dark leather – but I had glimpsed it many times, wedged into her bicycle basket as she made her way to various local record offices or to Somerset House in London. She had, she told my mother proudly, taken it even further afield – to France and Holland and once, many years ago, even to Argentina – in her unflagging pursuit of the Pemble name. My mother was predictably dismissive of the enterprise, never exhibiting any curiosity as to the book's contents. People were always confiding things to her in which she had not the smallest scrap of interest.

But it was not family trees that concerned Miss Pemble on that particular day. She was gathering support for the formation of another committee, neighbourhood affairs being the second of her great enthusiasms. There was no local cause to which Miss Pemble had not devoted time and thought. She sat on several council boards, organized jumble sales for the church, wrote letters to the paper, knew down to the last millimetre how much space there should be between a parked car and the kerb. More than one resident of the street had had their plans for a kitchen extension foiled by her intimate knowledge of planning permission and her feud with the landlady of the house across the street was legendary.

'. . . A group of concerned neighbours, meeting once a week to pool information . . .' she was saying as I entered the sitting room.

'Once a week?' my mother said. 'Surely . . .'

'Anything out of the ordinary, anything at all. The idea being to maintain *vigilance.*'

'But the police . . .' my mother said. 'One would surely report anything to the police.'

Miss Pemble leaned forward. 'Somebody knows this man. Somebody knows what he is up to *without even being aware they know* . . .' She broke off, noticing my presence in the doorway. 'Well, perhaps another time,' she said quickly. 'One doesn't want to alarm the children.'

My mother looked relieved. 'Well, quite,' she said, taking Miss Pemble by the arm in an effort to usher her to the door. 'I'll certainly give it some thought.'

The phone rang. 'I'll get it,' I said, purposefully ignoring my mother's meaningful look. 'It's probably for me.'

It was Julia. 'You've got to come over,' she said, speaking

very fast. 'Nancy's mum's just been here. You've got to come right now.'

'She's in the shed,' Julia's mother told me when I rang the doorbell. She looked at me rather sympathetically. 'I know you didn't have anything to do with this, Sophie. I told Mrs Packenham I thought so. That it was all some kind of mistake. And Julia, it's just not like Julia. Well, perhaps . . . but it's the age, I told her. One has to be careful not to overreact. I thought she should sit down for a bit, have a cup of tea, but she went rushing off.'

'Oh.' I said, carefully. It seemed rude to point out that I didn't have the slightest idea what she was talking about.

'I said I thought perhaps simply returning the items . . . Anyway, Julia's in the shed.' She paused. 'It's coming on very well. Polka-dots!'

Julia, it turned out, had grown tired of painting the shed with stripes and was standing on an upturned tin, covering one wall with a haphazard pattern of blue blotches in an effort to be done with the job. She threw down the paintbrush when she saw me.

'Has Nancy's mum been round your house?'

I shook my head. 'Well, she's been round here,' Julia said.

'Why? What did she want?'

Julia paused dramatically. 'I knew she was going to come round. Nancy told me. On the phone. She called me a couple of hours ago. She couldn't talk long. I don't think her mum even knew she was on the phone. They had a terrible row.'

'What about?' I asked, feeling a small dart of jealousy that it should have been Julia rather than myself to whom Nancy turned. But of course it would be Julia, I thought. She was the one I'd have called too.

'Her mother found half of Watson's shop under her bed,

didn't she? She was cleaning out her room and found the whole bloody stash.'

I stared at her in appalled silence. 'I told Nancy not to keep it. I *told* her,' Julia said. 'Bottles and bottles of stuff. Soap, nail varnish . . . you name it.'

'What did she sound like? Was she crying?'

'No. She sounded weird though. Talking really, really fast. She said she couldn't live there any more, not with her mother spying on her the whole time.'

'Where is she now?'

'Home, I suppose. Her mother yelled at her for *hours* . . .'

'What are we going to do?'

'I've got to have a cigarette,' Julia said, sitting down. 'Keep an eye out for my mum, will you?'

'She thinks those crappy blobs on the wall are polka dots.'

'My mum doesn't have a clue,' Julia said, lighting up.

'You don't think . . . they'll find out about us do you? I mean, we did it too. Okay, so I only did it that one time, but I was *there.*'

Julia shook her head. 'It's not going to happen. My mum believes everything I tell her. I told you, she doesn't have a clue.'

'Do you think her mum will make her take it all back? She can't do that, can she?'

'Why? So fat old Watson can give her a good spanking? He'd probably enjoy that no end.'

I laughed, a little uncomfortably. 'What are we going to do about Nancy?'

'We've got to get her out of there,' Julia said. 'She can come and live here. Just for a bit, until her mum calms down. My parents won't mind.'

'I don't know, Julia . . .'

'You'll see. What we need is some bin liners.'

'What for?'

'To put her clothes in. She's probably going to have to leave in a hurry. Her mum's not going to let her go without having another fit is she? There's got to be some law or other against keeping people in houses against their will. We should get your dad onto that.'

'I don't know,' I said again. 'I think you have to get *battered* or something before my dad would get called in. There were these parents who kept their kid in the attic with the cats. I heard my parents talking about it. They never let the kid out or let her see anyone else but the cats. Right from when she was a tiny baby. They just put food in for her when she was asleep.'

'What happened?' Julia said with great interest.

'I'm not sure. I think she turned into a cat. Not a real one. I think she was kind of crawling around meowing or something when they found her. Lapping up milk with her tongue, stuff like that.'

'Jesus. Cat Girl. I wonder if she could jump really far and land on her feet.'

'I don't think so,' I said. 'I think she was just crawling around the whole time.'

'Anyway,' Julia said, dragging her mind with evident reluctance away from this vision, 'we've still got to get Nancy. We should go now. She can put her stuff in the bags and climb out of the window. I've climbed out of the bedroom window here and it wasn't that hard.'

If I'd thought about it for two minutes, I would have known that nobody was climbing out of the window, but I was in that excited state where anything seemed possible. We walked down the street to Nancy's house, hearts thumping, full of the rightness of our cause. Julia threw open the gate and marched up to the door, while I followed a little behind her. I had already decided that she was going to do the talking.

'I'm just going to ring on the door,' she informed me.

I looked up at the bedroom window. The curtains were pulled back, but there was no sign of Nancy. 'What are we going to do if her mum says no?'

'We'll just tell her she's got to let Nancy come over to my house,' Julia said with bravado, pressing her thumb hard against the bell. 'We'll tell her it's the best solution for everyone.'

Steps sounded in the hallway and the door opened.

'What do you want?' Nancy's mother said. Her face looked rather puffy, her eyes small. Almost as if she'd been crying, I thought, although the idea was confusing. What did she have to cry about? It was Nancy who was in trouble. I looked at Julia, waiting for her to declare herself. But the same thing must have struck her too, because she hesitated before answering.

'Is Nancy in?' she finally asked.

'Yes, yes of course she's here,' Mrs Packenham said, sounding angry. 'I'd like you to know I'm very . . .' she paused, closed her eyes for a second or two. 'I'm very . . . disappointed.' There was a moment of silence, broken only by the faint tinkle of Mrs Packenham's charm bracelet as she tugged at the frayed neckline of her cardigan. 'Can't you girls just see . . .'

'Is it possible to talk to her?' Julia ventured.

Mrs Packenham stared at the two of us, taking in our air of self-importance, our nervousness. Her eyes travelled over the bin bags clutched in my hand and then returned to my face.

'Go home,' she said. 'Both of you.'

I glanced at Julia and then up to the bedroom window once more. Nancy was standing there looking out at us, her body

obscured by shadow, one hand pressed hard against the glass.
I expected her to open the window, or at least tap against it
to attract our attention. But she never moved.

Julia shuffled a little. 'Okay then,' she said dismally.

Nancy's mother shut the door and we trailed off, not
speaking to each other. 'I thought you were going to tell her,'
I said at last.

'I would have done, but you were just standing there like
a spastic. You weren't any help.'

'Do you think she'd been crying?'

Julia shrugged. 'I don't know. It'll all blow over anyway.'

'You think so?' I said, thinking of Nancy's still figure in the
window.

'Course it will.'

Later, at home, I took my wooden jewellery box and tipped
out its contents. I went to Watson's and bought a small bottle
of Charlie and a Mars Bar, trying not to meet Mr Watson's
eye as I handed over the cash. I put the bottle and the chocolate in the box together with my battered copy of *Frenchman's
Creek*. Then I looked through my drawers for other items to
add to the collection. I put in a plastic hair slide, a rubber that
fitted on the end of a pencil and – as an afterthought – a
rather crushed poppy, left over from last year's Poppy Day. I
closed the box and Sellotaped it shut, then went outside. There
was a light on in Nancy's bedroom. The rest of the house was
dark. Her mother must be in the back, I thought.

'Nancy?' I called out softly. She appeared immediately.

'Open the window,' I said. 'Have you got any string up
there? Tie some stuff together.'

She nodded and disappeared, then came back with her
hands full. 'Let it down so I can get the other end,' I told her.

She had tied her dressing-gown cord, a skipping rope and

three belts together in a long rope. I took the end of it and wrapped it around the box, using one of the belt buckles to make it safe and tight.

'Lift it up *slowly*,' I whispered. 'Try not to let it bang against the wall.'

I watched fearfully as it rose, swaying from side to side. It reached the window and she leaned forward to grab it, her hair falling over her face.

'It's for you,' I told her. 'It's a Feel Better Box.'

She held it in her arms, not looking at it.

'It used to have my jewellery in. But I don't need it. You don't have to give it back or anything.'

She nodded again, still not saying anything, and I stood for a moment, looking up at her. Perhaps it was a sense of premonition that kept me lingering there beneath her window. There are some people, who through no fault of personality or behaviour seem marked for catastrophe. As if they stand closer to the edge of things than the rest of us, the muffled guns of the enemy always in their ears.

'The poppy's for Wilfred Owen,' I said.

3 Peter

I

Andrea lived in a flat in an expensive neighbourhood. Everything inside it was either white or cream, including Andrea herself in her pale palazzo pants and wispy scarf, the colour of breath on a cold day. She kissed me on the cheeks three times. Unless you knew she was going to do this, you could find yourself caught off-balance. I'd seen it happen with other people, the pulling back after the first two kisses and then the correcting neck lunge as they realized, an embarrassing fraction too late, that yes, she was coming back for another.

'I haven't seen you in *ages*,' she said.

'I'm sorry,' I said. There was something about Andrea that never failed to inspire a vague sense of guilt in me. She was one of those fragile women that manage to stay looking waif-like even into old age; all cheekbones and wide eyes. Rather like Mia Farrow might have looked if she'd smoked all her life. Andrea was rarely without a cigarette but I'd never actually seen her remove one from a packet. Instead she kept them stored in a dozen or more elegant little onyx boxes scattered around the flat.

'You must have some tea,' she said. 'You will stay for tea won't you?'

I sat down on the white sofa while she made it.

'That terrible business with Simon,' she said, emerging finally with a tray, 'I've been having nightmares ever since. It's been quite dreadful.' She sat down beside me. 'So much death,' she said. 'So much *destruction* in the world.'

'Yes,' I said. 'His parents came into the shop the other day.'

'Oh dear. The mother. It's so hard being a mother you know.' She cast her eyes up to the ceiling as she often did when referring to Lucien. The gesture always accompanied by a small, wistful smile

'We need to think about getting a replacement for him,' I said. 'Placing an ad somewhere.'

'Oh dear,' Andrea said again. She took a sip of tea. 'The truth is, even before this happened, I was thinking of well . . . letting him go. His salary . . . the sums just don't add up, I'm afraid.'

I got a sudden picture of Simon's face as he was being zipped into the black plastic bag. 'Did he know this?' I asked. 'Had you told him?'

'Oh no!' she said, sounding shocked. 'Of course not. It was only a thought. But now, with things . . . turning out the way they have . . .'

'But if we don't get a replacement, I don't know how I'll manage. I can't do all the work by myself, Andrea. I've let such a lot slide just in the last couple of weeks. We have to have *someone* working there.'

She touched my knee. 'You do such a marvellous job,' she said. 'Really marvellous.'

'I didn't know you were thinking of letting Simon go.' What I wanted to say was that this was a decision I should have been party to right from the start, but Andrea was patting my leg so gently that pointing this out seemed churlish.

'It's a numbers thing,' she said.

'But the shop is making money,' I pointed out. 'Profits are up for the second year in a row.'

She shook her head sorrowfully. 'It's more of a big picture

thing. I'm not very good with finances, but I'm told a cut has to be made somewhere.'

'Oh, I see. I had no idea . . .' Andrea's money situation had always been something of a mystery to me. I knew she must have some because she'd hinted at a settlement that Lucien's father had made when they divorced, years ago. And she appeared to live in some luxury, with her glass coffee-table scattered with copies of *Harpers & Queen* and her bathroom always stocked with new, expensive face creams. On the other hand, Lucien's father – a professional blackjack player – was a shadowy, rather nefarious figure, the sort of person one might easily imagine being financially unreliable . . .

'Look,' I said, making one last effort, 'if we put money *in* rather than taking it out, the shop could really take off. If we expanded next door we could do some amazing things with the extra space. Bring far more people in.'

She shook her head. 'I'm sorry, Sophie,' she said, looking utterly downcast. 'I'm really sorry.'

'It's okay. Don't worry. It's just that if we don't replace Simon, I'm not sure how it's going to work.'

Andrea finished her tea and lit a cigarette, her lips pouting fastidiously around the filter. 'Well,' she said, 'perhaps there's a solution. I wasn't going to bring it up, but since you seem in some need of help, it could be just the thing.'

I thought she was about to suggest we hired someone part-time, but Andrea had other plans.

'It's my best friend,' she said. 'My oldest friend. She lives in Scotland and her daughter . . . well, she's rather worried about her daughter . . . she needs a fresh start, something like that. I don't know, in my day, young people migrated to London, but apparently the daughter's coming to Oxford and needs somewhere to stay. I said I'd help, but honestly, she can't stay *here*. I don't have the space.'

'You've got the spare room,' I pointed out.

'Well, yes, but my bathroom is so tiny. It's hardly bigger than a telephone box. I thought instead perhaps you'd like to have the company.'

'Me?'

'It would only be for a short time, a week or so, until she found her own place. She's about your age. A bit younger actually. Twenty-two or three I believe. It might be nice for you.'

'I've only got the two rooms. Plus the kitchen . . .'

'I promised her mother,' Andrea said, looking as though she might start to cry. 'She's my oldest friend.'

'I don't see where she'd go. She'd have to sleep in the living room.'

'What I thought,' Andrea said, 'was that she could help out at the shop. In return for having somewhere to stay. She'd be helping you see, and we wouldn't have to . . . well, obviously some nominal payment would be appropriate . . .'

I stared at her, momentarily speechless.

'Of course it's up to you,' she said, leaning forward to stub out her cigarette in the marble ashtray. 'You'd be doing me such a favour. And really, Sophie, I don't know what else we can do. Hiring someone on a full-time basis is out of the question at the moment. Perhaps in a month or two . . .'

'When's she arriving?' I asked.

Andrea clapped her hands together. 'Oh, you're such a darling. Next week.'

'Has she worked in a shop before?'

'I don't know, I really don't know, but I'm sure she'll pick it up in no time. The Scots are so resourceful aren't they?'

'Are they?'

'Her name's Michaela,' Andrea said, already reaching for another cigarette.

II

Every morning, before opening the shop, I spent some time picking up pieces of litter from the street outside. There was always enough to fill at least one plastic bag; old newspapers, cans, the odd condom to be poked into the gutter with the toe of my shoe. It wasn't the most salubrious of neighbourhoods but I felt I had to make the best of it. The morning I met Peter Byrne for the first time, I was stuffing my bag with kebab wrappers and thinking about the Hating Tree, wondering whose names I would call out if I was faced with the thing now.

The fact was that I didn't hate anyone any longer. I hated various things of course, certain situations, but the word no longer seemed to apply to any of the individuals in my life. I should have been relieved by this and I was. But my relief was tinged with a kind of vague regret, as though I'd lost something and was the lesser for it.

A man came walking down the street towards me, looking up at the shop signs in a searching kind of way. He was in his mid-thirties, solidly built, not particularly tall, dressed conventionally in jacket and blue tie. I stood quite still and watched him approach. Although there was nothing in his appearance to suggest it, I knew that he was looking for me. I couldn't explain how I knew this, only that the certainty brought with it no surprise. As if the present moment – the short space of time that I stood there, bag in hand, waiting for him – was simply the retelling of a story already told.

He stopped when he came up to me and stood for a second before speaking.

'I'm looking for Sophie Barrett.'

He had a regular, well-proportioned face, his eyes very dark and serious.

'That's me,' I said. He put out his hand with an easy, natural gesture, like someone who made a habit of politeness.

'Dr Byrne. Peter. We spoke on the telephone a few days ago.'

'Yes,' I said

'I wasn't sure which shop was yours,' he said. 'I wasn't even sure this was the right street.'

'You had to hunt then,' I said.

He smiled suddenly, with great warmth. 'Yes, a little bit.'

He paused. 'I'm glad I found you. After we spoke, I felt, well, that I'd been rather rude to you. I was at the end of a chaotic shift.'

I shook my head. 'It's okay. It really doesn't matter.'

'You caught me at a bad time,' he said. 'I just wanted to say sorry for that. And sorry for . . . for the rest.'

'Yes,' I said. 'Thank you.' We looked at each other solemnly. 'Do you want to come in?' I asked. 'I've got some coffee. It's only instant I'm afraid.'

'Instant's fine. Actually I never drink anything else. Never have the time.'

We went into the shop and I could see him looking around with what I thought was a certain pleasure. He followed me down the stairs where I kept the kettle and coffee mugs. 'I was the one who found him,' I said suddenly, when we were standing in the room below. 'It was right here.' It felt easy to talk to him like this, quite directly, without any hedgings or qualifying statements. He nodded slowly, without saying anything, his eyes on my face.

'I realized afterwards that I did completely the wrong thing. I didn't call for an ambulance at once. I tried to lift him. I thought he might still be alive.'

'What makes you think it was the wrong thing?' he asked. 'I'd have probably done something very similar.'

'Yes, but you're a doctor.'

He smiled slightly, but said nothing more. 'I still don't really know why he did it,' I said. 'He didn't leave a note or anything.'

'Sometimes they don't,' he said.

'When I called you, I didn't know whether . . . if you'd had any contact with him after the attack.'

'We met for a drink. Just once, very briefly. I think he regretted it once he got there.' He smiled again. 'I got the impression I wasn't who he was hoping for.'

'I didn't know him very well either,' I admitted. 'Although I should have done. I saw him almost every day for two years. You'd think you'd get to know a person in all that time.'

I half expected him to say something in response to this; something quick and reassuring. But he said nothing. The kettle boiled and I made us each a cup of coffee. He drank his slowly, as though he had nowhere else he needed to be. My own I left virtually untouched. I kept glancing at him. At first sight, I'd thought his face fairly ordinary, but up close it looked different; stronger, far more arresting. The kind of face you'd have no trouble remembering even if you'd only met him briefly . . . He looked up suddenly and caught my eye and it was so quick I had no time to rearrange my features, to pretend that I was doing anything other than simply staring. No time to look away, to prevent that sudden, piercing exchange of gaze. I turned abruptly to my coffee, too abruptly; making an awkwardness of the moment, making it seem, perhaps, as if I thought it something that it wasn't.

'This is a really good cup of coffee,' he said.

I couldn't help smiling. 'You don't have to be polite. I don't think the kettle had even boiled properly . . .'

'No, I mean it. I'm enjoying it.'

'I'll give you the recipe then,' I said, making him laugh.

'It's quiet down here. What time do you open?'

'Ten. Although people don't start coming in until a bit later. We get a lot of students and they don't often emerge until the afternoon.'

I asked him what sort of a doctor he was. He was an oncologist. Not the sort of person you'd ever want to see professionally, although if you had to have cancer, I thought you could do a lot worse than him. He had a steadiness, a kind of certainty about him. I found myself bringing the conversation back to Simon.

'I'd never seen a dead person before,' I told him. 'I'd never actually seen a body.'

'It must have been very frightening.'

'It was the way he looked. Like himself but not. Like an object that just happened to look exactly like him . . . a kind of horrible trick . . .' I felt tears rise in my eyes. 'I'm sorry,' I said, surprised and ashamed. 'I'm so sorry . . .'

'Please. Don't be.'

'I don't know why I'm crying now,' I said. 'I've spent so long thinking and thinking about it and it's the first time I've actually cried.' I sniffed, lifted my hand to wipe my eyes, thought suddenly of my mascara and changed my mind. 'Oh God, I'm going to look like a mess when I open the shop.'

He looked at me carefully, examining my face. 'You look just fine to me,' he said.

'You must have seen a lot of dead people,' I said. 'You must be used to it.'

'It's different when you expect it. There's a place for death in a hospital. Even then, you never quite . . .' He broke off. 'I think what you did, how you feel, is very natural.'

'Would you like another coffee?' I asked, noticing his empty mug.

'Actually I really do have to go. I have to be at the hospital fairly soon. Are you all right?' he added.

'Yes, much better. I'm okay now.'

'Do you mind if I take a quick look around? I love book-shops.'

'Do you?' I was a little surprised. 'It's pretty small. There's a lot of stuff I just don't have the space for . . . It's getting hard to compete now, with people buying off the Internet and everything.'

'But there's nothing to compare with a bookshop.'

'Well, I don't think so. No. I mean, buying books online is alright if you know what it is you want. But it doesn't really give you a chance to . . .'

'Not know what you want?'

'Yes, exactly. They do try to encourage you to browse a bit. They do that "customers who bought this item also bought . . ." thing. But it isn't the same at all.'

'I hate that "customers who bought this item" thing,' Peter said.

'Me too.'

I watched him as he wandered around the shop, glancing at everything in an appreciative kind of way. I remembered how I'd torn up his card and wondered if I should ask him for another one, whether that would seem . . . too eager or perhaps just the opposite – rather too formal. As if we were simply business associates.

'I wish I had more time to look around,' he said, coming up to me. 'But I have to get going.'

'It was nice to meet you,' I said.

'I'm glad I came.' He shook my hand again, looking at me rather intently. 'We didn't have enough time to talk,' he said. 'Perhaps we could go out. One evening.' The suggestion came quite seriously, with none of the lightness that would have made refusal easy. I thought of Lucien and his talk of pair-bonding and something froze inside me.

'I can't really. It's . . . rather difficult,' I said automatically.

He nodded. 'Of course. I understand.' He smiled and turned for the door.

'It was really nice to meet you,' I said again. I didn't want him to leave. I thought of all those patients of his, waiting to talk to him, to be listened to, helped, and I felt something strange; something that seemed like envy.

'Perhaps we *could* go out,' I said hastily, feeling stupid. 'I mean, why not? I think it would be nice.'

After he had gone, I was possessed with a kind of agitation. I kept turning the encounter over in my mind, replaying what had been said and how I must have seemed to him.

I shouldn't have cried, I thought. Why had I cried? I went into the bathroom to tidy myself up, staring at my reflection in the small, stained mirror above the sink. My hair looked good, I thought. It was shiny, almost luxurious. I'd washed it that morning and for once taken the trouble to dry it properly. If only there was something I could have done about my cheeks, which always looked far too round, almost fat. 'Baby cheeks' Lucien had called them once, pinching them with both hands until I pulled my face away. I shouldn't have cried, I thought again. It must have made me look even more infantile. But he'd asked me out . . .

I wasn't at my best when confronted with the unexpected. It filled me with the sort of anxiety, that, lacking any clear attachment, makes itself part of everything. I told myself that although it wasn't every day that a person got asked out, it was still an ordinary enough event. Anyone else would have been cheered by it, rather than thrown into this state of dim worry. But I didn't think I was like other people. I sometimes thought that I carried my life out in front of me like a person holds a bowl of water, careful to avoid spilling even a single drop.

It was at least an hour or two before the routine of work

was able to restore my self-possession. And I had other things to occupy my mind. Michaela, the daughter of Andrea's friend, was due to descend that evening. I had to buy a new duvet cover for the sofa bed. Andrea might have offered to pay for things like that, I thought. But the idea didn't seem to have occurred to her.

III

Michaela turned out to be one of those people whom one finds both extraordinarily annoying and yet impossible to dislike. She was older than Andrea had said, in her late, rather than early twenties, with long, sandy-coloured hair and a friendly, open face that sloped towards a disproportionately small jaw, giving her features a shelved, rather hapless look.

'I won't get in the way, I don't have much stuff,' she said, flinging a small rucksack down on the sofa bed. 'I left my other bag in the taxi.'

'Did you? We should call. Find out where it is. Do you remember what company the taxi was?'

'Not really. I just got into it. It doesn't matter. It was just sweatpants and stuff.'

'Are you *sure*?'

'I'll be all right,' she said with a cheerful shrug. I offered her a drink and she followed me into the kitchen as if I might disappear unless she kept me within arm's reach.

I made her a gin and tonic. 'I'll be under the table if I drink that,' she said, taking a vast gulp. 'I'm really glad I'm not at Andrea's. I was dreading going to stay with Andrea.'

'I don't think there was much chance of that,' I said.

'I'm always breaking everything,' she continued, 'and her stuff is all so posh isn't it?'

I wasn't sure how to respond to this. 'I don't know how she and Mum ever got to be friends in the first place. My mum's not like that at all. She thinks Andrea's great. My dad doesn't. He sees right through her, he says. He's good at seeing through people. It was his idea for me to come down here. To get sorted out, he said.' She paused. 'Although it might have been just because he was sick of me hanging around.'

'Oh no, I sure that's not . . .'

'He likes things to be sorted out, my dad,' Michaela continued, taking another gulp of her drink. 'You don't have any bread or anything do you? I forgot to have supper.'

'I'll make you a sandwich. It's just cheese, I'm afraid.'

'That'd be great. Perfect. I get like that, you know?'

'Like what?'

'Like I could suddenly eat the table. That hungry.'

'Well, if you go for hours without eating . . .' I began, uncomfortably aware that I was already sounding like her mother. 'But you must be very tired. Perhaps I should show you where you'll be sleeping. You'll be wanting some rest. In the morning, when you're fresh, I can take you into the book-shop and show you around.'

'The bookshop!' she cried. 'I can't wait to see it. I'm going to work *really* hard. I can be really organized when I want to be.' She followed me through into the sitting room and I made up the sofa bed with the new sheets and duvet cover while she rummaged with increasing frustration through her rucksack.

'I thought I put my toothbrush in here! It must have been in the other bag.'

'I don't have a spare one, I'm afraid.'

'Oh well. Don't suppose it matters just the once. You can't get a cavity in one night, can you?'

'Unlikely,' I said.

I settled her finally and went to my own room, beset by

gloom. It had not been established quite how long Michaela was planning on staying with me. I was already beginning to think that it might be longer than the 'week or so' that Andrea had talked about. But giving her a deadline to leave seemed out of the question, even at this early stage. I sensed that rejection would be especially hard for her. She seemed so entirely unprepared for it. I could already tell that she was one of those people who move through life in a kind of oblivion, deaf to all hints, suffering the exasperated cruelty of others with dim-witted stoicism. No, telling Michaela I didn't want her around would be impossible. Besides, I needed the help in the shop.

I sat down on my bed, thinking about Peter and wondering when or if he would call. The phone rang and I reached for it, half expecting to hear his voice, but it was only Lucien.

'Just wondering when you'd crack,' he said.

'You're the one calling *me!*'

'True,' he said.

'And you came into the shop, remember? If that's not cracking, I don't know what is,' I said, wondering if I could ever have a conversation with Lucien without first having to plough through this kind of sparring that never seemed to tip over into proper argument, but always remained at that maddening, uncertain point where joke meets insult and leaves you looking humourless if you show frustration.

'I just popped in on my way past. It was a detour, not a destination. There's a difference.'

'So why are you really calling?'

'Do I have to have a reason?'

'I suppose not.' It occurred to me that Lucien, unable to commit to a relationship, was equally incapable of *uncommitting*; that he couldn't leave me be any more than he could get down on one knee and propose. But I had always known this, I thought suddenly. Perhaps that had been the real attraction for me. For years I had idled along in a relationship that I knew would never become one thing or another.

I thought of the first time I had told him I loved him. We were in Wales, walking along the beach at Aberdovey. It was evening, the tide low, and the distant town stretched like a ribbon on the edge of the sands. Something very beautiful and calm filled my heart. Lucien was walking ahead, with his back to me. I called out to him and without even waiting for him to turn, told him I loved him. Even at the time, I wondered a little at the impulse, uncertain where the true source of my feelings lay. In the dusky gleam of the sand, perhaps, or in the small, friendly lights of evening coming on one after another in the row of houses beyond. For a fleeting second or two it seemed as though the love I felt had nothing to do with Lucien at all, but had always been there, waiting for this moment of happiness, for a chance to fasten itself upon something. But once spoken, the words became true. He walked on a few paces, then half turned, frowning a little.

'Do you?'

I nodded. 'You know I feel the same way too, don't you?' he said.

I nodded again, although up until then, I hadn't known at all. But disagreeing with him might imply doubt in his sincerity and besides, Lucien claimed that people who really loved each other didn't need to say it. It was one of his many beliefs, like the fact that Valentine's Day was nothing but an excuse for florists to make money and that women looked better without make-up.

'It's been a crazy day,' I told him on the phone. 'That daughter of your mother's friend turned up without a toothbrush. I'm not sure it's going to work out. She seems rather . . . fragile.'

He snorted. 'Friend my arse. My mother doesn't have any friends. So what else is new?'

I thought of telling him about Peter, and then rejected the idea. There seemed something vaguely disloyal about it. As if I was somehow betraying Peter by taking Lucien into my confidence; or worse, as if I was trying to make Lucien jealous.

'Nothing really. Same old stuff,' I said at last.

'You know,' he said, 'this separation thing has a lot going for it. Absence really does make the heart grow fonder, not to mention sexier . . .'

'Lucien, it's not a *separation*,' I said. 'I mean, not in that way . . . It's an ending. I thought that's what we decided.'

'You mean I can't even phone?' he said, pretending to sound hurt.

'You know I'm not saying that. Of course you can.'

'Well, that's a relief. For a moment there I thought you'd gone all bitter on me. I only wanted to tell you I'd been thinking about you.'

I didn't know what to say to this. It was as if we'd never discussed going our separate ways at all, or as if the conversation had just been another of his games.

'That's nice. Thank you,' I said at last, feeling like an idiot.

After a week of living with Michaela, I knew more about her than many people with whom I'd been friends for years. I knew about her struggles at school, the exams she had taken and retaken, the job applications that never resulted in interviews, the time she was fired as a waitress because nobody could read her orders, her troubles with a succession of inexplicably hostile room-mates and all the ups and downs of her relationship with someone called Jervis who was either a policeman, or training to be one.

'He dumped me,' she said, through the door of the bathroom where I'd gone for a pee. Unless I closed the door in her face, she was prone to wander in after me, still following the thread of her own conversation. 'I never really knew why. But that's men isn't it? They won't talk about anything will they?'

'No,' I said, rattling the loo-paper dispenser rather desperately.

'You have to move on, don't you? He wasn't really my type anyway. Physically I mean. He wore glasses. He had these shoulders that kind of went downhill. It made his neck look really long, although it wasn't that long in actual fact. It just looked that way.' She paused for breath. 'I'm more into the Brad Pitt type. You know, like in that film when he's fishing the whole time.'

'Yes,' I said, emerging from the bathroom. 'Although thigh-high leather waders might look a *little* odd on your average high street.'

'I know what you mean,' she said. It was her favourite expression, always uttered with the same earnest look on her face as if she was trying very hard to comprehend some profound, yet elusive truth. 'It's all about fantasy isn't it? Do you want a cup of tea?'

'That would be nice.'

'Someone called for you,' she said. 'While you were out. I've forgotten the name.'

'Oh, *Michaela* . . .'

'I wrote the number down,' she said. 'I did do that. It's on the table somewhere . . .'

'I can't really phone it if I don't know who I'm calling, can I?'

'Why not? You'd soon find out. I do that all the time. Write down numbers and then ring them back to find out who it was who gave me the number. Everyone does that.'

'No they don't.'

'I do know it was a woman,' she said.

'Never mind. I suppose if it's important, they'll call back.' I paused. 'Try to get names when you take messages. Especially in the shop. You really have to do that when you're taking messages in the shop.'

She nodded very vehemently. 'Got you. Yeah, I'll do that.' Privately, I thought it didn't really matter if she took names or not, since she usually misspelled them to such a degree that they were worse than useless. It was some kind of intractable dyslexia. Michaela was hardly the employee I'd been hoping for.

But I couldn't deny that a large part of me welcomed her company. She was so undemanding, so eager. If she talked too much it was because she was lonely, because she thought you could make friends that way; by the scattering in great handfuls of all her thoughts and secrets, no matter how stony the ground.

She was the same when it came to personal possessions, unable, it seemed, to contain even her small hoard in one space. I moved around the flat, constantly retrieving items: grubby hair scrunchies and odd socks beneath the cushions on the sofa, the stub of an old eye-liner pencil on the stairs, slips of paper with addresses written on them lying like leaves under the kitchen table.

In the end, tired of trying to find places for all of her scraps, I bought a plastic lost-and-found bin and put it at the bottom of the stairs, dropping in items as I passed by.

'You're so organized,' she said admiringly when she saw it. 'I'd never think of something like that. I'm going to get a felt-tip and write my name on the side.'

'You don't have to,' I pointed out. 'There's only one of them.'

'No,' she said firmly. 'I'm going to take a leaf out of your book. I'm going to start being really *organized*.'

But I think the real reason she wanted to mark it was because it had been a long time since anyone had afforded her even this small amount of space. Being entirely without territory, even a plastic box with her name on seemed like a gift.

'My dad's a very tidy person you know,' she said. 'He has a little library, all in alphabetical order. We used to get things like bookmarks in our Christmas stocking. One year, I got a filing cabinet for my birthday. I didn't really know what to do with it.' She paused. 'That's a funny thing to give a ten-year-old isn't it? Although it was a very nice cabinet. Sort of a reddish colour. Two drawers. Don't you think that's a funny thing to give? Like he didn't really know me. Or perhaps did know, but wished I was somebody different . . .'

'Michaela,' I said cautiously, 'have you thought about . . . well, some kind of therapy? Perhaps not therapy, more like counselling. It might be really helpful, you know.'

'Why would I do that?'

'Just to have a place to talk. To get ideas.' I reached for the magic phrase. 'To get sorted out.'

'Oh,' she said. 'I didn't know it was for that. I thought it was only if you were a bit loony or something.'

'Lots of people use counselling,' I persisted. 'You know, to deal with issues, get advice, that kind of thing. You can go on a one-to-one basis, or find a group. A friend of mine went to one when she was, I don't know, at a bit of a crossroads, if you like. I think it helped.'

'Did it? Honestly?'

I nodded. 'It wasn't you, was it?' she said, giving me a cunning look.

'No. I told you. A friend.'

'Oh, okay, only sometimes people say "a friend" when they mean themselves, don't they? It's like a code or something.

Like at school when you say, a friend of mine fancies you when you really mean you fancy them but you don't want to come right out and admit it.'

'*No*, Michaela. It was my friend, all right? If I wanted to go to a counsellor, I would. I mean, if I felt I needed it. Which I might, sometime in the future, but in the meanwhile . . .'

'Okay, I get it,' she said, giving me a startled look.

'I can get the number for you, if you like,' I said. 'From my *friend*. Sarah. That's her name.'

'All right, although I don't know what I'm meant to say. I don't know what there is to talk about really.'

'I'm sure you'll think of something,' I told her.

IV

I met Peter at a restaurant in town. One of those over-designed places – all sparse lines and shiny surfaces – that make you feel vaguely unkempt no matter how much care you've put into your appearance. I was a little early and had already finished a glass of red wine before I saw him at the door. I turned my head away automatically – a nervous response, I suppose. I sometimes pretend I haven't seen people, even when I know them well. There's something about greeting a person across a certain distance that has always unnerved me.

'Hello,' he said, 'I hope I haven't kept you waiting.'

I looked up, feigning surprise; a trick I suspect I never pull off very successfully.

'Oh, no,' I said, 'I just got here. Just this minute.' I looked down at my empty wine glass. 'I drink quite quickly,' I said.

He looked a bit startled. 'I mean, well, not in *general*,' I said, 'Just this particular glass . . .'

He was dressed the same way as at our first meeting, minus

his tie, and I wondered fleetingly if he had any other kind of clothes. In the trendy surroundings of the restaurant he looked out of place, almost awkward, an impression enhanced by the seriousness of his expression; something in the relationship between his eyes and the width of his broad forehead giving him a grave, almost solemn look. He didn't scan the room, but glanced at one thing and then another, holding his gaze for a beat or two longer than expected, with controlled, rather wondering intensity.

We settled in at our table, the waiter bringing us a bottle of wine and the menus. I forget what I ordered. In restaurants like that, the description of each dish takes longer to read than actually eating the thing. He didn't mention what had happened at our first meeting, for which I was grateful. Instead, we talked about the usual subjects. The areas of town we lived in, the length of time we'd been doing our particular jobs, brief accounts of how we spent our days. He wanted to know more about the bookshop, what sold well, how I made my selections.

'It's hard at the moment. I'm getting behind with everything. I don't think I realized, until he was gone, how very, very organized Simon was. Unless you're on top of things, the books can get completely out of control . . . why are you laughing?'

'Nothing, nothing,' he said, 'just the thought of hordes of marauding paperbacks.'

'Well,' I said, thinking of my list of orders, the unpacked boxes piling up, the way Michaela flapped her hands whenever a customer asked her a question, 'well, you'd be surprised. Marauding's not a bad description at all. But it'll be all right. Andrea will come through eventually.'

'Andrea?'

'The . . . owner. She's rather grand. But a terrible ditherer.'

'One of the things I regret about working these long hours is how little time it leaves me for reading,' he said. 'I used to read far more.'

'What kind of things?'

He shook his head. 'Bits of everything really. Quite a lot of poetry. Yeats, Wordsworth, the First World War poets.' He smiled a little sheepishly. 'Nothing terribly adventurous. The usual schoolboy stuff.'

'I knew this girl once,' I said. 'She was kind of in love with Wilfred Owen. She was a strange girl. I don't think I realized quite how strange she was until I got older. That's the thing about being very young, isn't it? You have nothing to measure anything against. It's like those pictures you sometimes see of empty deserts or glaciers. You don't know the size of the thing you're looking at because there's nothing in the picture to give you a sense of scale. I think that's what being very, very young is like. You have no idea whether you're standing in the middle of the Sahara or on Blackpool beach.' I stopped, a little embarrassed by my volubility, by my sudden need to communicate a rather confused train of thought.

'I never thought of it that way before,' he said. 'But I think that's true. The way the extraordinary can seem quite normal.'

'Or the other way around. I think we spent most of our time back then thinking everyone else was completely mad.'

'Wilfred Owen,' he said. 'He was a favourite of mine too. I don't think I'd ever read anyone who could make rage sound so lyrical. *Bitter as the cud of vile, incurable sores on innocent tongues . . .*' He smiled. 'Perhaps that was the line that got me into medicine.'

'Do you like being a doctor?' I asked him. 'I can tell you're a good one.'

He leaned back in his chair. 'Now, how can you tell that?' he asked in an amused voice. Was it my second glass of wine, or my third? It must have been my third. 'I don't know,' I said. 'I can just tell. You have . . . it's sort of a theory of mine . . . you seem to have a very clear outline. I know that doesn't make any sense . . .'

I fully expected him to laugh, but he didn't. He simply gazed at me, very thoughtful. 'You have a lot of faith in people,' he said finally. 'I like that. It's rare.'

I feigned a great interest in my bread roll, my cheeks suddenly hot. 'So you memorize verse,' I said to break the awkward pause. 'I'm impressed.'

He shook his head. 'No. I just have one of those memories. The kind that sort of works independently of you. I could just as easily have recited the Coca-Cola jingle I'm afraid.'

'I wish I could do that,' I said.

'It's easy,' he teased. 'There aren't that many words . . .'

'Not the *jingle*. I wish I could remember things better.'

There was a short silence. 'What happened to her?' he asked finally.

'Who?'

'Your friend. The strange one.'

I took a sip of wine, looking away for a second or two. 'It's a long story,' I said.

He waited, not saying anything.

'There was something about her,' I said, unable to quite leave the subject. 'She believed in a kind of . . . magic, I suppose you could call it. She thought her wanting could change things. I'm not sure I can explain exactly what I mean. She used to read *The Lord of the Flies* over and over. I think she must have read it ten times. And she always cried when Piggy died, even though of course she knew it was going to happen. She said she always hoped it would turn out differently. That she would turn that page and the rock would somehow miss him. And he'd be saved.'

I paused. 'She used to think that the stuff you see floating on the surface of your eyes was . . . what *is* the name for those floating bits by the way?'

He smiled. 'Floaters.'

'Is that it?'

He nodded. 'They're not on the surface actually. They're tiny particles inside your eyeball that you can see in bright light.'

'Oh.' I said. 'Trust a doctor to know stuff like that. I think you would have liked Nancy. Both of you into saving people.'

'Doctors don't save people,' he said, rather shortly. 'Occasionally . . . certain childhood leukaemias . . . surgical interventions . . . But on the whole, no. Not in the way you're thinking about anyway. Most medical treatment just keeps people going for a bit longer. You try to minimize the suffering. That's all you can really do.'

His voice had changed. It sounded almost angry. I should have changed the subject, but my perceptions were dulled.

'Oh, but surely that can't be right,' I said. Later, replaying the scene in my mind, I thought of how foolish I must have sounded. 'I mean, what about when you find something at an early stage and can treat it. Or those premature babies that they keep in incubators. Car-crash victims who get put back together again . . .'

He was silent for a second or two, as if he was gathering himself. 'I'll tell you something,' he said, in the same tight, charged voice. 'People sometimes ask me what's the worst thing I've ever seen as a doctor. They think I'll tell them about seeing children die, about what certain diseases can do to the body.'

He stopped, his dark gaze fixed on the bottle of wine in front of him, as if he was regarding something quite different, beyond my sight. 'I came around a corner in a hospital once,' he continued. 'There was a man lying on the floor in the corridor. A patient, in purple hospital pyjamas. There was blood coming out of his mouth. It was everywhere. Huge puddles on the white tiles, his clothes, everywhere. There were medical staff all round him, handling catheters and central lines, thumping on the side of the suction machine, trying to get a tube in his airway.'

I said nothing, not knowing where this was leading, a little frightened by his fierceness.

'He was dead,' Peter said. 'I could see that at once. His stillness and all this movement around him. All this frantic effort to resuscitate. They were kneeling and tugging at him, their clothes covered with his blood. As though they were praying to him.' He paused. 'Or eating him. Some kind of terrible feeding frenzy. It was the ugliest thing I've ever seen.'

'Perhaps they thought there was still some hope, something that could be done . . .'

'Yes, of course,' he said, abruptly, as if I had said something annoyingly obvious. 'But too often there's a refusal to accept that the best you can do is not good enough. A kind of arrogance. As if Lazarus is going to walk out of the tomb at the touch of your hands.'

I didn't know what to say. He spoke so bitterly and I thought how easily one can be lulled into a false sense of intimacy with a person. All it took was a bottle of wine, a few shared thoughts. I looked at Peter and realized I did not know him at all. I did not know what judgements he had formed about me or even whether he wished me well.

'It must be very difficult for you,' I said.

Perhaps he saw a kind of wretchedness in my expression because his face changed suddenly. 'I'm sorry,' he said. 'I was being rather too . . . vehement wasn't I?'

'No. No, it's okay.'

He looked down at our plates. 'I shouldn't have been so graphic. I've probably completely spoiled your dinner.'

'I've finished anyway. There wasn't that much to eat actually.'

'No,' he agreed. 'The portions *were* a bit minuscule, although they seem to have taken a lot of care over curling this strip of carrot . . .'

We smiled at each other but there was a new restraint between us. Our conversation returned to neutral topics and I was almost relieved when it was time to go, feeling as though I'd failed somehow. He didn't say anything about meeting again, not even a hollow promise to give me a ring.

'Come into the shop if you're ever in the area,' I said as we parted, unsure how to end the thing gracefully. 'We've got a really good poetry section, you know.'

He held out his hand. 'I'll do that,' he said.

I shook his hand awkwardly. 'The thing about Piggy . . .' he said suddenly.

'Piggy?'

'In *Lord of the Flies*. The thing about him is that he has to die. For the story. Don't you think so?'

'Yes, I suppose he does.'

'Didn't she realize that, your friend?'

'She must have done,' I said. 'But I think that made it worse for her. The unfairness of it, you see. It wasn't just the rock she wanted to save him from. I think she wanted to grab Piggy right out of the whole book.' I smiled at him a little uncertainly.

He nodded, his face very serious, almost sad. 'Yes,' he said, 'yes, I can understand that.'

It wasn't until much later, when I got home, that I realized with a stab of guilt that we'd barely mentioned Simon at all. I'd had questions I thought Peter might be able to answer.

Whether Simon had appeared depressed at their meeting, for example, whether he had seemed the kind of person who might take their own life. Whether, in short, there had been signs of mental anguish that I'd completely missed.

I told myself it was unlikely. If there had been anything, Peter would have mentioned it already and the reason we'd not talked about it was because there was nothing new to say.

Michaela was in the living room, watching television, the lights off, the curtains still drawn wide. I saw the dark shape of her head, lit by the flickering screen and the softer glow of street lights. She was half asleep, I thought, or wrapped in trance. I went to the bathroom to remove my make-up and get ready for bed, still thinking of Simon.

Why did it matter so much to know exactly why he died, to hold the map of his despair? For his sake, I thought; an act of loyalty, of friendship. Wouldn't anything less be a kind of failure? But he had left no note. He hadn't wanted me – or anyone – to know his reasons. I wiped my face slowly with a cotton wool ball, dragging at the skin below my eyes.

For myself then; to confirm something or maybe simply to . . . From the other room, the sound of a thud, Michaela calling out, confused, excited, 'I fell asleep!'

I sighed, tossed the cotton into the wastebasket, turned to find her standing in the doorway, all hair and trailing duvet.

'I know,' I said, 'I saw you. It's okay.'

4   *Christopher's Snail*

I

It was a day or so before we saw Nancy again. I took my bike down to the river and cycled for miles along the towpath, passing the college boathouses, the Common on my right giving way to houses and then open fields. I turned off down a long, straight sandy pathway that ended far off, at an old railway bridge. Nobody, I thought, had been there for a very long time. Nobody had walked up the stairs and stood on the bridge, looking down at the weeds growing over the railway tracks for years and years. I was the first, I thought, or perhaps the last. The sky was grey, utterly flat, without break or texture. 'Cambridge sky', my mother called it. The kind that neither brightened with the passing of the day nor ever developed into rain, but remained as it was; as blank as a painted wall. Even surrounded by empty space, it hemmed you in, that sky. It was so low, you could almost reach up and touch it. It would feel hard, I thought, and a little scratchy. Rather like polystyrene; the kind they used on *Blue Peter* to make models of landscapes.

I was worried about Nancy, unsure what her mother would do to her, or what Nancy herself might have revealed under pressure. I tried not to think about what my own mother would say if she found out about the cherry lip-gloss; her anger, her overwhelming scorn. But I needn't have been concerned. I should have known that keeping heroic silence would be a matter of the utmost pride to Nancy.

When she finally emerged, she looked thinner than ever, all knees and jutting shoulder blades. 'Your mother didn't *starve* you did she?' Julia asked, her mind still revolving hopefully around the possibility of bringing child cruelty charges against Mrs Packenham.

Nancy shook her head. We were sitting around my kitchen table, drinking cup after cup of sugary tea and discussing the situation. My mother was down in the basement with the door locked, working in her dark room, my father out in the Fens somewhere, visiting a client.

'So what did she do?'

'She talked mostly. She just went on and on. For hours. She said I had to make up for what I'd done. Get back on the right track.'

'How are you meant to do that?'

'I don't know. By doing good things, you know, helping . . .'

I stared at her, wondering if she was joking. Her head was down, fingers pulling at the hair already dragged tight behind her ears.

'Like collecting money in those envelopes?' I asked. 'Stuff like that?'

'No, not that. It's meant to be harder than that. It's meant to be something really good.'

'Yeah, but *why*?' Julia wanted to know.

'My mum says when you help other people it stops . . . it stops you thinking so much about yourself. She's always going on about it. She says it helps you forget yourself.'

'Why would you want to forget yourself?' Julia said with incredulity. 'I mean, how is that even *possible*?'

'I don't know. Anyway, she decided I have to go and visit Ivy . . .'

'Well that's not so bad . . .'

'Every other day.'

'What's so good about that?' Julia burst out after an aston-ished silence.

'My mum says she's old and she's depressed and it will give me something better to do with my time. I'm meant to help her with stuff. And keep her company.'

'She's not depressed,' Julia protested. 'She just depresses everyone else. What does she need help with anyway?'

'I don't know. Reaching things, I suppose.'

'I bet it's worse than that. They'll have you wiping her arse,' Julia said. 'You'll have to wipe her wrinkly old arse.'

'You're completely disgusting, Julia,' I said.

'I bet she has that useless bog paper,' Julia continued relent-lessly. 'The crinkly sort that doesn't absorb. I bet she has that kind.'

'It's not funny,' Nancy said. 'Don't you get it? I have to do everything Ivy says. Everything. My mum's told her already. That I'm meant to come every other day and help her.'

'But it's the school holidays,' I said. 'She can't *do* that.'

'Well, she's doing it isn't she?'

'Jesus,' Julia said, in a bitter tone that seemed to encom-pass the complete idiocy of parents everywhere. 'I don't know about you, but I can't wait until I leave home.'

They had a large bin full of old *Bunty* comics in the library at Lion Yard, and if you sorted through them carefully you could read them in order and follow all the story lines. Julia, of course, despised *Bunty*. She had graduated long ago, to the stickier, more complicated pleasures of *Jackie* with its free gifts of lip-gloss and advice on how to kiss.

The photo stories were – I privately decided – the most impressive part of *Jackie*. It was true that they were shot in black and white and someone had added speech bubbles and usually, when one of the characters was lost in thought, they showed her looking up towards the ceiling, with a finger on her chin. But these were mere details, easily overlooked. The stories felt utterly authentic. It was almost possible to imagine that they were not stories at all, but simply episodes of real life, mysteriously captured by the camera.

I read Julia's copies of *Jackie* willingly enough, but in my heart, I was still in secret, shameful thrall to *Bunty*. Comics were safe haven. Magazines, by contrast, seemed to demand something from me; an adherence to certain, mysterious standards. I was not reassured by advice on how to kiss. It seemed to imply that this was an activity I should already be engaged in. *Dear Cathy and Claire*, readers implored on the problem page, *I kissed a boy and now he doesn't seem to know I exist. Did I do it wrong?* These letters filled me with anxiety. The problems outlined seemed so much more important than my own.

Bunty, on the other hand, required nothing from me but continued devotion. I loved the stories. The suffering hero-ines, beset on all sides by misunderstanding and injustice; their innate goodness, or talent or superior birthright eventually triumphing over all obstacles. I loved the cruelty of their setbacks, their stoicism. I wanted to look like them, clear-edged, all pony tails and large, attractive tears.

I perched by the window on the second floor of the library, avidly following the dismal fortunes of the heroine of 'No Tears For Molly', and glancing down every so often at the Saturday shoppers below. Lion Yard was a new addition to the city. An enclosed area of chain stores, partly roofed by glass, the kind of thing that would spring up all over the country in later years, but which was still a novelty at that time.

My mother thought the place was hideous and seemed to take this fact personally. She had a theory that everything that had to do with the city – as opposed to the university – was purposely unattractive, so as not to compete with the beauty of the colleges.

But I thought she was right about Lion Yard. It *was* ugly and the ugliest part was the lion itself: a bright red, life-sized statue of the animal, perched on a pole, right outside the library. From my vantage point, I had a clear view of the top of its head. It was angular of line, almost crude, and even though it was fairly new, had a raw, shabby, depressing air. I thought it was the kind of thing someone might produce who wanted to make a realistic-looking lion, but wasn't quite good enough.

I was missing my friends. Nancy was being kept busy with Ivy and Julia was on holiday in America for three whole weeks. Just that morning, a postcard from San Francisco had arrived, informing me she had bought a Levi's denim jacket and two pairs of Converse High Tops. I had no idea what the latter actually were, but was nevertheless filled with envy.

I was not going on holiday that year. There had been some talk of Cornwall, but the plans had not amounted to anything. This apathy was not like my parents, who had always been enthusiastic about holidays in the past. A memory – fragmentary only, but rich in sensory detail – came to me of sitting in the back of the car combing my mother's long hair with my fingers; plaiting and unplaiting it as the miles passed unseen. She made no sign either of pleasure or annoyance at my touch, allowing it as a horse accepts the attentions of its groom. It had been a long time since I had touched her in this way. She had cut her hair short and besides, she was not the sort of person who seemed to welcome physical affection. Not like other mothers, I thought. Not like Mrs Packenham, forever snatching at her daughter's hand as they walked down the street together, as if she could, by the very suddenness of her advance, prevent Nancy's inevitable and immediate pulling away.

During the increasingly rare times that we could be together, Nancy and I had taken to meeting at the rec three streets away. It was a small place, overshadowed by tall trees. There were benches there and a couple of swings and a roundabout that probably hadn't been repainted since I was a small child. It was hard to believe that at one time I'd had the energy to seize that thick metal bar and run around fast enough to get the thing in motion. I felt tired just thinking about it. The whole rec made me feel tired. But there was nowhere else to go. We could hardly use Julia's shed while she was away and Nancy never wanted to spend more time than she had to at her own house. I felt the same way about my home. There was a new drabness to it. Something old and frayed about everything that belonged there. Even the lighting was wrong. It was too bright, almost harsh, allowing for no shadows. Like a house on a hill that you could see right through from miles away.

We sat on the swings, our bodies slumped forward, our feet idly brushing the dirt. 'What do you do with Ivy all the time?' I asked. 'What do you talk about?'

She shrugged, kicking a little against the ground. 'It's not really talking,' she said. 'It's mostly her saying things and me listening.'

I thought of the pair of them, sitting together on the yellow sofa. I'd only been inside Ivy's house once or twice, but I remembered what it was like. The dark entrance hall with its skin of ancient wallpaper, the dreary front room. There was nothing in that room that held the eye or drew the attention. Two mud-coloured armchairs, matching the sofa only in their state of general dilapidation, and a coffee-table made up the sum of the furniture. A small television set and an electric-bar heater sat in opposite corners and the mantelpiece supported nothing but a cheap-looking china dog, a box of matches and a yellowing lace doily that hung over the edge like something spilled.

'She tells me things that are going wrong with her. Like her eyesight. And her legs.'

I backed up my swing, my face towards the sky. The day was overcast, the clouds yellowish, stained like an old smoker's fingers.

'What's wrong with her legs?'

'Veins,' Nancy said. 'Really thick ones that kind of stick out. She showed me.'

'That's disgusting.'

'They're all blue and purple and sort of . . . stretched. Like they could just pop or something, any minute.'

'I think I'd be sick,' I said.

'The other thing she talks about is how nobody ever comes to visit her. Even though I'm sitting right there. But she really means her brother and his wife.'

'I forgot she had a brother,' I said.

'The other day she went upstairs and came back with a box of Quality Street. I thought she was going to open them, but she just wanted to show me the box. Her brother gave it to her for Christmas last year. She kept on and on about how it wasn't even a two pound box. I kept thinking she would open it and give me some, but she never did. She just took it back upstairs again.'

'The chocolate's probably mouldy by now,' I said.

'She's got a nephew who comes sometimes,' Nancy said. 'He's not her real nephew. He's adopted. He doesn't come much though.'

I had heard about Ivy's nephew before. According to my mother, there was something wrong with him; some kind of retardation, although she was vague on the details. 'Twenty-three years old and still living at home!' she had told me, as though this in itself was evidence of mental disability. 'It's a disgrace, the way they send him over there instead of going themselves. I expect they only do it because they're scared of being cut out of her will and losing that house. They don't even live that far away. You would have thought . . .'

'What's his name?'

'Christopher,' Nancy said. 'They got him from an orphanage.'

We swung for a while in silence. 'So how long do you have to go on doing it?' I said at last. 'When can you stop seeing her?'

'I don't know. Not yet.'

'It's so unfair.'

'It's not too bad,' she said. 'I mean, I do help her with things a bit. Yesterday I opened four tins of baked beans for her. She lined them up in the kitchen for me.'

'Four? How's she going to eat four?'

'I don't know. I didn't think of that.'

'It sounds awful,' I said.

'It's not too bad,' Nancy said again. 'Most of the time when she's talking, I just make my head go empty. It's easy. You look like you're listening, but you're not. You can think about all sorts of other things and nobody even knows.'

'I wish Julia would hurry up and get home,' I said. 'She's been gone for ages.'

II

I was walking down the stairs from my bedroom when I saw my father standing in the hallway below. It was late afternoon, the sunlight making bars across the wall and casting his body half in shadow. I had the feeling he had been there for a while, quite still, one hand resting on the banister.

'Are you going out?' he said. I nodded.

'Anywhere in particular?'

'Not really,' I said. 'Just out.'

He stared at me with an intent, distant gaze as if he was looking at someone quite different from the person I saw each day in the mirror. 'It's a shame about the holiday this year,' he said suddenly. 'I'm sorry about that.'

'It's okay,' I said. 'I don't mind.' His mouth twisted slightly, as if he wanted to say something further but couldn't find the words.

'Yes,' he said. 'Yes . . .'

A feeling came over me then, standing on the stairs. I had always secretly taken his side against my mother's anger, her dreams that did not include either of us. Why did I find myself blaming him then, for the helpless way he stood there, so clearly wanting something, so unable, it seemed, to find it?

'We've had some good holidays,' he said at last. 'Do you remember the camping trip to France?'

I rolled my eyes. 'That was ages ago. I was about *eight*.'

'It was good though, wasn't it? We had a good time. We should do that again one year.'

I said nothing, thinking of the three of us now, crammed together in a single tent.

'Do you remember the fireflies?' he said, ignoring my silence. 'You'd never seen a firefly before. I caught one in the plastic cup from the top of the thermos and brought it into the tent to show you. Then we went outside and the whole field was covered with them. The sky full of stars. Do you remember what you said?'

'No.'

'You said you couldn't tell where the earth ended and the sky began.'

'I don't remember that.'

He was silent for a moment. 'Well,' he said, removing his hand from the banister, 'well, I suppose I should let you go.'

'It doesn't matter about the holiday,' I said, coming down the last few stairs. 'Honestly. Julia's coming back tomorrow.'

He smiled at me, his lips tight. 'That's good,' he said. 'I'm glad about that.' We stood there silently for a second or two, although it seemed longer.

'I think it was blue,' I said suddenly.

'What was?'

'The top of the thermos. It was definitely blue. I remember that.'

Was it after this conversation or sometime before that I found George Collins' hat lying on a chair in the sitting room? I have no way of knowing.

I was home alone as was often the case in those days. Sometimes it seemed to me that the house was nothing more than a stage from which my parents were forever just exiting, leaving their props lying around for me to stumble across and construct from them what little information I could.

I knew the hat belonged to George. Who could forget that peculiar checked object? But still I hesitated, my unwillingness to acknowledge the fact disguising itself briefly as uncertainty. A faint smell came off it; an aroma of aftershave and otherness. I left it there, untouched, and sometime later it was gone.

I didn't tell anybody about the incident. I don't think I even thought much more about it myself. It seemed easy at the time to know a thing and at the same time not to know it. Safer too, of course. Perhaps that was the real reason I kept my silence.

III

On Saturdays, they turned the old Corn Exchange building in town into a roller-skating rink. I had never been, although Nancy claimed she used to be a regular when she was younger. 'I got quite good at it,' she said.

'No you didn't,' Julia said.

'How do you know?'

Julia shrugged, her disbelief clearly needing no explanation.

'I've been on roller-skates a couple of times,' I said. 'I'm hopeless.'

'I can go backwards,' Nancy said. 'And do spins.' She wasn't boasting. Nancy never boasted; a fact that Julia, herself a great braggart, seemed to find mysteriously aggravating.

'So you *say* . . .'

'What's the matter, Julia?' I asked. 'Can't you do it yourself?'

'What? Roller-skate?' She made a face. 'It's not that hard, is it? I mean, anyone can keep their balance . . .'

Nancy and I looked at each other. 'Okay then,' I said, 'if it's so easy, let's do it.'

Julia led the way and so took the long route round, the better to test out her new bike, an ice-green racing model, with dropped handlebars. She powered down the leafy stretch by the backs of the colleges, body low, only lifting her head from time to time to remove her hands from the bars, the bike kept upright by the strength of her legs alone. I followed as best I could, with Nancy some distance behind, the warped mudguard on her own bike making a dismal clattering as she ploughed along. A long ride, I thought resentfully. I normally never went near the Backs, except to accompany my parents on dull sightseeing strolls with visitors from out of town. Julia turned left on Silver Street and doubled back past King's towards the market square. By the time we arrived at the Corn Exchange, she was already securing her bike.

'Aren't you going to lock yours up?' she asked Nancy.

'If anyone wants it,' Nancy said, her face sweaty, 'they can have it.'

The moment we walked into the skating rink, I regretted it; immediately intimidated by the loud music, the thundering of wheels against wood and the sheer speed of the other skaters, who seemed to be a good deal older than I had expected. I could tell by their clothes that they were mostly 'townies'; the boys in wide lapels and trousers stretched over their backsides, lifting their feet and thudding them down again as they hurtled around each corner. The girls in tight shirts with tiny ornamental pockets over each breast – bought from Tammy Girl no doubt – gliding along delicately, indifferently; as if the whole enterprise was somewhat beneath them. Everyone, apart from two or three children clutching haplessly at the rails, looked utterly expert.

'I don't know about this . . .' I said.

'You get your skates over there,' Nancy said, shouting to make herself heard over the noise.

'Maybe I'll just watch for a while . . .'

She grabbed my arm, half dragging me to the booth. 'Put them on. No, *over* your shoes . . .'

'I don't like these skates,' Julia said, fiddling with the straps. 'They feel funny to me. Why can't we get what she's wearing?' She pointed to a girl with white ankle boots. 'I want some like that, like real ice skates.'

'You can't borrow that kind,' Nancy said. 'She brought them. They belong to her.'

'It's not fair,' Julia said. 'I can't get these tight enough . . .'

'I used to have some like that,' Nancy said. 'Ages ago. My mum bought them for me from a sports shop. Brand new . . .'

'It wasn't even my birthday or anything,' she added.

I stood up tentatively and then sat down again. 'I think I've forgotten how to do it,' I said. But Nancy had gone. She stood at the edge of the rink, one hand on the rail, waiting for a break in the stream. A slight turn of her body and she was suddenly in the midst of the throng, weaving her way towards an opening up ahead. I shoved at Julia, still fiddling with her straps.

'I didn't know she was *that* good,' I said. She skated as I might have guessed she would, without the smallest pretence or ostentation, her face rapt, unsmiling. As if there was nobody else in the entire place, I thought.

'She's not really keeping time with the music though,' Julia said, after a moment of silence.

I stared at her. 'Well, she isn't is she? She's all out of rhythm . . .'

'Are you going to do it then?'

'In a minute.'

'Come *on*.'

'I'll catch you up.'

I clomped unwillingly towards the rink and found a space on the very edge, my back to the skaters, my two hands clamped to the rail. I loosened my fingers, tottered slightly and instantly tightened them again. The floor vibrated. A pair of boys, moving at speed, were suddenly upon me, swerving at the very last minute with a terrifying scraping of wheels. It took me several minutes before I recovered myself enough to remove my hands from the rail.

I pushed myself forward with the smallest movement possible short of standing still and found myself rolling – feet together, with no means of stopping even at this ridiculously slow pace – out towards the centre of the rink. I turned, saw the rail already out of reach, leaned backwards and then abruptly forward to keep my balance and petered to a stop, paralysed before a horde of skaters bearing down on me.

Nancy was suddenly at my elbow.

'Keep going.'

'I can't,' I muttered. 'I just can't.'

'Bend your knees a bit.' I shifted obediently into a half squat. 'Bend your knees *and* move . . . here.' She offered me her hand and I took it gratefully. Her fingers were very dry and firm against my wrist. 'Did you see those two boys,' I said. 'They almost knocked me over. I think they did it on purpose.'

'Don't think about them.'

I stumbled forward, clutching her hand, found a way to push off from my right foot and managed a tiny glide. 'I'm doing it! Oh God, here's the corner . . .'

'Just roll around,' Nancy said. 'I've got you.'

'What's Julia doing?' I asked a second or two later. 'I can't see anything except my feet.'

'Still sitting there.'

We made a few circuits of the rink together. 'I think you've got the hang of it,' Nancy said. 'Do you want to try on your own now?' I hesitated, hearing the familiar sound of wheels coming up fast behind me. 'It's those boys again,' I said, turning to watch. They were the best skaters there, I thought; the fastest, the most aggressive. When they turned corners it didn't look as though they were skating at all, but simply running, charging, bodies low, arms relaxed. And always that insolent, last-minute swerve to avoid other skaters in their path. As if they hadn't seen them perfectly well from miles away . . .

'They're just showing off,' Nancy said.

'I know,' I said, still looking. They must be at least eighteen, I thought; probably even older.

★

Julia had ventured out from her seat to buy a coke. She sat sipping it slowly, eyes fixed on a spot on the ceiling.

'Aren't you coming on?' I stood on the edge of the rink with Nancy circling idly around me.

'I just got thirsty,' Julia said.

Nancy and I exchanged a look. It didn't happen very often that we had Julia at our mercy. 'I thought you said you could do it,' I said.

'I can.'

'Go on then.'

'Okay.' Julia said, *Okay.*'

She put down her drink and stood up. I hadn't expected her to actually get onto the rink at this late stage. I thought that having to sit out the entire morning would be the extent of her ignominy and I couldn't help feeling a shamefully gleeful anticipation at the possibility of further humiliation. If Nancy shared any of this, she gave no sign of it, although there was, I thought, a subtle eagerness in the way she hovered close by, skating leisurely backwards and forwards, her eyes fixed on the ground.

Julia went over to the rail, moving with a confidence that gave me a moment of doubt. She looked around her briefly, head up and then, without the smallest pause, shoved herself forward. For a second or two, the sheer boldness of the movement made my doubt seem justified. Only an expert skater, I thought, would take off like that. And then I saw that it was not superior ability at all, but something perhaps even more impressive: a stubborn, overriding pride that sent her hurtling forward, lost to all sense of self preservation, arms already starting to flail, legs veering in opposite directions, towards the very centre of the rink.

'Oh god,' Nancy said.

There was a split second when Julia tried to turn, lost

control entirely of her left leg, leaned desperately – low and lower still – recovered slightly, tipped, right leg rising high above her waist and finally fell – violently, spectacularly – to land with a thud on her backside.

Nancy and I stood frozen for a moment.

'She can't get up,' I said. 'She's going to have to crawl back to the side or something . . .'

'She's hurt. Is she hurt?'

'We've got to help her.'

I started to wobble across the rink, Nancy quickly overtaking me. But it was already too late. Neither of us had time to reach Julia. The boys were there before us. Of course it would be the boys; the pair of them barely breaking stride as they bent briefly to seize an elbow each, lifting her effortlessly between them and bringing her swooping back – all flying hair and amazement – to the safety of the rail. I stared at them. They wouldn't have done that for me, I thought; nor for Nancy. They'd have just kept going, probably not even caring if they ran over our fingers. Laughing probably . . .

'You should be more careful out there,' the taller of the two said.

'Yeah,' Julia said, apparently quite recovered. 'Problem with the skates.' She smiled. 'Thanks anyway . . .'

'Hey,' the boy said. They skated away backwards, still looking at her, turned finally, and were gone.

'Well,' Julia said, glancing at us with triumph. 'That was dramatic wasn't it?'

Nancy and I were silent. There seemed absolutely nothing to say.

'Told you I needed proper skates,' Julia said.

IV

There was something particularly ungraceful about the way summer gave way to autumn that year. There was no gradual ebbing of the season. Instead a long period of rain set in during which time it became clear – through some unspoken, but universal understanding – that all hopes of further warm days were over. A new school term started, the clocks changed and it was suddenly dark. In a single night it seemed, the leaves fell without flame, drifting into sodden layers across the muddy Common. Down the long, central avenue, the trees acquired a new presence, each branch blackened by rain, dark against the low sky.

I was outside one afternoon, looking for the last of the windfall apples under the tree at the bottom of the garden, when I saw a man standing in Ivy's empty yard, by the fence that divided our two properties.

'Found anything?' the man asked.

'No,' I said. 'I thought there'd be some left, but there aren't.'

'I'm Mrs Gerrit's nephew,' he said. 'She's my aunt.' I looked at him carefully. He was neatly dressed in a blue shirt tucked into pressed jeans and a pair of startlingly white sneakers. 'I was just looking around the garden,' he said.

'Oh,' I said.

'Not much to look at though is there?'

I cast my eye over the lawn; so thin it hardly needed to be mown, even at the height of summer, over Ivy's drooping washing line and the long, perfectly straight concrete path that ran from the back of the house to a dead end at the bottom of the garden.

'I suppose not,' I said, 'just the grass really.'

'Want to see something?'

'What?'

'I can't show you over there, can I?'

'What is it?' I said, not moving. He had a thin face with a transparency to his skin that seemed to match the unguarded quality of his gaze and gave him a naked look, like something that had been very delicately peeled. He waited expectantly, his body pressed close to the fence, one cupped hand held out towards me.

'It's in my hand,' he said. 'Look.'

I approached unwillingly. 'I just found it,' he said, 'right there on the path.' His hair was cut like a small boy's; parted on one side and trimmed in a straight line high on the pale nape of his neck. 'It was just lying there,' he said. He opened his hand and showed me a snail, its shell half crushed, its wet body smearing the skin of his palm. 'It's broken,' he said. 'I found it like that.'

'A bird must have got it.'

'Yes.' His thumb gently explored the jagged edges of the snail's shell. 'I'll put it down in the grass here,' he said, bending carefully.

'It might be all right,' I said. 'You never know.'

We stared rather solemnly for a moment or two at the spot where he had placed the snail.

'Not much of a place to end up in, is it?' he said at last.

'No, I suppose not.'

'Even for a snail.' He paused. 'I'm not staying here myself for long. I'm joining the army.'

'Oh,' I said.

'They send you all sorts of places when you're in the army. You never know where you're going to end up.'

'When are you leaving?' I asked. But his gaze had returned to the snail. 'It was a bird,' he said. 'They crack the shells on the path. I heard it from the house.'

'Yes. I hear it sometimes too.'

'I hate that sound,' he said.

The toggle loops on Nancy's old duffle had frayed apart, preventing her from fastening the coat higher than her waist, and she was moving quickly in an effort to keep warm. We were walking past Magdalene College and the pavement was too narrow to allow the three of us to remain abreast. Every so often, Nancy had to dart ahead or behind us to avoid being run down by traffic. The tourists were long gone; replaced by groups of students wearing bright college scarves and uncertain expressions. Julia was particularly scornful of these newcomers, casting them disdainful looks as we marched along.

'What are we going into town for?' Nancy asked.

Julia shrugged 'I don't know.'

'I need to get some stationery,' I said. The statement wasn't strictly speaking true. I had no practical need for more stationery. I already had a whole drawer full of items, many still in their packaging. But it always felt as though I could use more. There was something about standing in Heffers, fingering those virgin notepads and crisp binders that provided me with deep satisfaction. The assortment of pens and pencils was almost as pleasing. I was particularly attached to biros that wrote in unusual colours, especially the kind that had several refills of different hues bunched within a single chunky cartridge and tiny buttons on the top so you could make your selection. The fact that I would never use even half of my collection seemed beside the point. For me, the value of stationery lay mainly in its contemplation. Each clean, blank page sharp with possibility, each punch-hole strengthener a tiny halo of purity . . .

'I think I'll go and have a look in Miss Selfridges,' Julia announced. 'I might buy something.'

Envy kept me silent. Julia had the extreme good fortune to have a small clothes allowance, an indulgence that my own mother seemed to find both extraordinary and somehow shocking. When I thought about it, which was fairly frequently, it seemed to me a terrible injustice that I should have been born to my parents instead of to Julia's.

'I can't be out for long,' Nancy said. 'I have to be back by three.'

'Your mum's a complete *fascist*,' Julia said.

'It's not her. I have to do Ivy's kitchen.'

'What, *clean* it?'

'Just the floor. She can't get into the corners.'

Julia clenched her fists in outrage. 'You're a slave. She's treating you like a slave.'

'It's better than having her talk to me,' Nancy said. 'She's always telling me how her life is nearly over and what a waste it's all been and then she starts crying. She says my life's all ahead of me and that makes her cry too.'

'What do you do then?' I asked, appalled at the thought of Ivy's tears.

'I don't know what to do. I just stand there. The first time she did it, she got biscuits for me afterwards. Chocolate digestives. She kept saying sorry. She doesn't do that anymore.'

'I'd stop going,' Julia said with confidence. 'I'd just refuse.'

'It's okay sometimes,' Nancy said. 'Christopher helps me with some of the jobs. He's been coming round a lot.'

'I saw him,' I told her. 'The other day. He was in the garden . . .'

'Who's Christopher?' Julia wanted to know.

'He's her nephew,' I said. 'He's a bit . . . my mum says he's a bit slow. He kept going on about this snail he'd found . . .' I broke off. Nancy had stopped short, her body rigid. 'What? What did I say?'

'He is *not*. You can't say that. He is *not*.'

'I didn't mean . . . he just seemed a bit . . .'

'Everyone says that about him and it's not true,' Nancy interrupted, her head jerking in agitation. 'They only say that because he was adopted.'

'But Nancy . . .' I broke off. Julia was giving me a warning look, reminding me that argument was pointless. One could no more separate Nancy from her convictions than one could part bone from flesh. Even to attempt it seemed an act of needless savagery.

'He's joining the army,' Nancy said. 'I've got to stop him.'

Julia made a face. 'The army? Don't you have to pass tests for that?'

Nancy had begun walking very fast again, head down. 'He doesn't know what he's getting into,' she told the pavement. 'I have to talk him out of it. That's why I have to keep going round to see Ivy. That's the real . . .'

Behind her back, Julia rolled her eyes. 'It's really getting to her,' she whispered. 'She's losing it.'

I nodded, my eyes on Nancy's retreating figure, noticing for the first time the awkwardness of her walk, the rigid way she held her arms, as if they were incapable of independent movement, the hunch of her back. And for a moment I was grateful that she was walking ahead of us and that nobody would know we were friends. I looked at Julia quickly, but she was already hurrying to catch up. Julia didn't care what others thought, any more than Nancy did. But why it should be a strength in Julia and merely an embarrassment when it came to Nancy seemed a matter beyond my understanding.

V

During the summer, Julia had picked a plastic bag full of strawberry leaves from her garden and laid them out on sheets of newspaper under her bed where they had remained for several months. Now she brought out the shrivelled scraps to show us. 'I think they're dry enough,' she said with satisfaction. 'I'm pretty sure they're ready.'

'For what?' I asked.

'You can get high smoking these. But you have to leave them until they're completely dry.'

'God, Julia, what if your mum found them?'

'Why do you think I keep my room like this?' Julia pointed out, sweeping her arm over the chaotic piles of clothes, shoes, books and various items of sports equipment that surrounded Nancy and I on all sides. 'My mum hasn't been in here for years.'

'How are you meant to smoke it?' I asked.

'How do you think?' Julia said, waving a packet of Rizlas in my direction. 'What's wrong with you?' she said suddenly, looking at Nancy.

'Nothing,' Nancy said, squeezing her hands tightly between her knees.

'You look like you think you're going to catch something. My room isn't *that* bad. It's not dirty or anything.'

'How would you know?' I asked. 'You can't even see the floor.' I looked at Nancy for support. 'I mean, there's probably things *growing* down there.' But she wasn't listening. Julia was right, I thought. There was something odd about her. A kind of concentration in the way she held herself. As though she was afraid she might break apart if she made the slightest movement.

'Ivy's budgie escaped,' she said abruptly.

Julia paused in her task of crumbling strawberry leaves. 'So what? It'll come back. Birds are fucking stupid. Anyway, why do you care? I'd have thought you'd be pleased.'

'I don't care,' Nancy said.

'How did it get out?' I asked.

'She let it out. She does that, once a year. Lets it out to move around a bit in the front room. She's had that budgie since her husband died.'

'I didn't know she was married,' Julia said. 'God. Who'd marry *her*?'

'He had a heart attack,' Nancy told us. 'In the bath. It took three people to get him out of the tub.' We were silent for a while, absorbing this image.

'She's always telling me stuff like that,' Nancy said. 'Even when I don't want to hear.'

'Who'd marry her?' Julia repeated. 'I mean, have you seen the tops of her arms? They sort of move like they're not properly attached to her. You know, kind of *flapping*.'

'She probably wasn't always like that,' I said, trying – and failing – to imagine a younger, firmer Ivy.

'If she ever tried to put a belt round her waist, her tits would get in the way,' Julia continued, starting to laugh. 'She'd have to sling them back over her shoulders or something.'

'You're disgusting.'

'But right. You've got to admit it.'

'She couldn't have any pets when her husband was alive,' Nancy said. 'He was allergic. Always wheezing, she said. She had to hoover the house twice a day or else the dust would give him another spell. She only got that bird after he died.'

'She could at least have got a dog,' I said. 'Budgies don't do anything. They just hang there.'

'She lets it out once a year,' Nancy said again. 'On its birthday.'

'Budgies don't have *birthdays*,' Julia protested.

'It's called Bruce. That was the name of her husband.'

Julia had finished crumbling the strawberry leaves and rolling them up in the cigarette paper. She licked the edge delicately. 'Who wants to be the first to try this stuff?'

We were both silent. 'Well, here goes,' Julia said. She lit the end and took a deep drag. *'Jesus!'* she screamed. 'Burned my fucking lungs!'

'I still don't understand how the budgie got away,' Nancy said. 'Ivy never opens any windows . . .'

'Maybe it just sort of hopped out of the door,' I suggested.

'Who the hell cares?' Julia interrupted, still clutching her throat. 'I can't believe you're still going on about it.'

'Is it working?' I asked her. 'Do you feel any different?'

Julia looked around the room, squinting. 'I don't think so. Not *yet* . . .'

'How many fingers am I holding up?'

'I don't get it,' Julia said, taking another, far more cautious puff. 'I did everything that girl said . . . Jesus, Sophie, stop waving your hands in my face.'

'Maybe there's a delayed reaction,' I suggested. 'It'll probably start working later.'

'No it won't,' Nancy said. 'It's only strawberry leaves. You can't get drugged on strawberry leaves.'

There was a slightly shocked silence as Julia took in the fact that it was Nancy rather than I who had spoken. Her eyes widened in astonished fury.

'What do you know?' she said viciously. She gathered up the bundle of leaves and newspaper and jammed it into the already overflowing waste-paper basket under her desk. 'What the fuck do you know about anything?'

'Julia,' I protested. 'She's upset . . . don't . . .'

'She's always upset,' Julia said. 'If it's not one thing, it's another.'

'The leaves were worth trying,' I ventured. 'Perhaps you just need to use a pipe or something . . .' But Julia was not to be distracted.

'What is it with you?' she asked Nancy. 'Why are you such a complete pain in the arse?'

If Nancy had been a different person, she might have cried then. I feel certain that I would have done so, sensitive as I was to even the slightest assault upon my feelings. But Nancy never cried. It was one of the things about her, as fixed as the colour of her eyes. It would have been better if she had. It would have been better than seeing that expression on her face; that empty look. As if she had, with no more effort than it takes to pass through a door, already removed herself to a place beyond our reach.

'Maybe you're meant to mix it with tobacco,' I pleaded. 'From a cigarette. We could try that, couldn't we?'

VI

Something was happening to Nancy which Julia and I could not quite find the words to describe. The closest we came to it was that she was 'in a mood'. But that seemed far too petulant to convey whatever it was that gripped her. All we knew was that it made us uneasy and strangely unsympathetic.

We watched her at the rec, swinging higher and higher, possessed with furious energy. Her face had a raw look to it, her tiny mouth compressed, the muscles under the lower lip bunched slightly as if she was trying to swallow something unpleasant.

'You're going to be sick if you don't stop,' Julia said coldly.

But Nancy seemed incapable of rest. She talked as she swung; her words trailing after her, scissored by the relentless movement of her body. It was Ivy of course, who had set her off. Nancy's trick of sending her mind elsewhere was clearly starting to fail her. It was the weeks of enforced intimacy with the old woman that had done it, I thought. Those long afternoons held captive while Ivy recounted – in unsparing detail – all the miseries and discomforts of her life. I didn't know if anyone who had choice in the matter could have borne it for long.

'I asked her if I could come less often,' Nancy said. 'So I'd have more time for homework. I just *asked*.'

'What did she say?' I asked.

'Nothing. She didn't say anything. She just looked at me.' I knew that look well, having seen my mother on the receiving end of it more than once. Full of reproach it was and secret gratification. As if it brought her pleasure to add to her miser's hoard of grudges.

'Then she told me about the smell,' Nancy said.

'Stop swinging,' Julia said. 'I can't talk to you when you're up in the air half the time. What smell?'

It was coming from the kitchen. Ivy made her bend over the sink and sniff. It was a disgusting smell, both alien and oddly familiar. A wrong sort of smell, Nancy called it. The scent of something you might once have found tempting – might have even wanted to eat – but which now you would die rather than touch.

'I thought it was rotten food,' she said. 'You know, all those tins she keeps making me open . . .'

Ivy said she thought it was coming from the U-bend. Nancy knelt down on the kitchen floor and opened the cupboard under the sink and for a moment or two the scent from the bleach and cans of furniture polish that Ivy kept down there

provided her with some relief from the stench. She took everything out of the cupboard – petrified J-cloths, an ancient scrub-
bing brush, three tins of some substance to remove mould
from tiles, all with their lids rusted shut – and pushed her
head and shoulders in for a closer look.

'It wasn't coming from the U-bend,' she told us. 'I didn't
know where it was coming from.'

'Look in the drain,' Ivy said. 'Outside. It's been blocked for
a couple of days now.'

The old woman handed her a pair of orange rubber gloves.
There was a hole in the tip of one of the fingers and when
Nancy put them on, they felt wet inside. By Ivy's back door,
the water from the blocked drain crept in dark, leaf-thickened
rivulets across the concrete yard. Nancy squatted down and
peered into the brimming opening.

'There's something down there all right,' Ivy said eagerly.
'Go on, get your hand in.'

Nancy held her breath. The smell was suddenly very strong.
'Deeper,' Ivy commanded. 'You want to get in really deep.'

For almost the entire time that Nancy remained there with
her right hand trawling the black, clotted depths, her fingers
shrinking against strange texture and the foul, icy trickle of
liquid seeping inexorably through the hole in her glove, she
kept her gaze averted from the task. Instead she fixed it on
the thick legs and drooping fabric of Ivy's lower half planted
at a safe distance a few feet away.

'She kept wiping her hands on her skirt,' Nancy said. 'Over
and over.'

'What have you found there, then?' the old woman asked
with an odd tone to her voice that Nancy could not properly
describe. 'Like she wasn't asking a question,' she told us. 'Like
she already knew.'

'Knew what?' Julia asked.

'She would have called the plumber,' Nancy continued. 'She was going to. It was only when I said I didn't want to come any more that she made me look there.'

'How do you know she was going to call the plumber?' I asked, confused by this detour in Nancy's story. 'Did she say that?'

'Knew *what*?' Julia cried.

'I didn't know what it was for a minute,' Nancy said. 'It just looked like . . .'

It was small, no bigger than her fist; a clotted mass of what seemed to be merely debris, but with a certain sodden structure to it, a revealing quality of shape. 'I could see the beak,' Nancy said in a wet-sounding voice, as if her mouth had filled with saliva. 'Then the body sort of . . . fell apart in my hand. I thought . . . I thought it had escaped. But it was in the drain the whole time.' She got off the swing abruptly. 'I don't feel very well.'

She went over to the large bin in the corner of the rec and gripped the edge with both hands, then bent her head and made a choking sound, her back arched in a small, rigid hump. I stood and watched her, fascinated and rather frightened. It was Julia who went to be with her, standing very close and patting her back with a firm circling motion, not seeming at all repulsed.

'That's it,' Julia said. 'You'll feel better soon.' She raised her hand and lifted Nancy's hair away from her face. 'It doesn't matter,' she murmured. 'You'll see . . .'

Her gentleness shamed me. For the first time it occurred to me that I lacked something; the ability to forget myself perhaps, to make myself a part of a larger world. I went to the bin and put my hand on Nancy's shoulder in a hesitant way. She sniffed and wiped her mouth on her sleeve. 'Sorry,' she said. 'Sorry to be so disgusting . . .'

*

Being without a swimming pool of its own, my school took advantage during the winter months of its proximity to the public one on Parker's Piece; the large green expanse in the heart of the city. I was still at the age when I enjoyed swimming, not because I was particularly good at it or for the pleasure of the exercise, but simply for the childish joy of water itself. The pool was always filled with light, even on the greyest of days, because one wall – the one facing out over the green – was made entirely of glass. It gave you a strange feeling to be swimming there, in the warm chop of the water, surrounded by liquid reflections, while outside – separated from you by only a single pane, but seeming a world apart – traffic moved and people crossed the Piece, heads bent grimly against the rain.

I was out of the water, on the side of the pool nearest the glass, when I saw Nancy one afternoon. We weren't meant to get out during the lesson period but Charlie Hudson had just pushed my head underwater and I needed time to recover. It was the first time it had happened to me, although some of the other girls were always being similarly attacked by various boys. I had not known Charlie was close until I felt his hand on my shoulder, strangely gentle at first and then more rough as I flailed and splashed in desperate protest. Now I sat with my legs dangling over the side, watching his tall, white body moving through the water and wondering whether I had committed some gaffe by resisting his onslaught so vigorously. It occurred to me that perhaps the other girls knew something which up until then had escaped me: that serious struggle from them was not expected, was not, in fact, part of the game at all . . .

Something made me turn my head and I saw her, standing on the side of the road nearest the pool building, and for a second or two, I didn't recognize her. It was the surprise of her being there, during school hours, in a place she was clearly not meant to be. I went and stood by the glass, pressing one hand against it as though to greet her, although I knew she couldn't see me. Instead she was looking down, at Ivy's nephew Christopher, half kneeling by her feet. I knew him instantly from his sneakers, still mysteriously white, as though he had taken them from the box only half an hour before. He was tying the laces, head bent in concentration. The wind blew Nancy's hair into her face. She might have been speaking, it was too far away to tell. I tapped at the glass helplessly. Christopher lifted his face suddenly. He was saying something, something perhaps about his shoes, for he kept returning his gaze with what seemed to me a kind of eagerness, to the laces still held between his fingers. She turned then, very abruptly, and walked away, leaving him crouching alone on the wet pavement.

I tapped at the glass again, harder than before, but then the whistle blew behind me and I had to return to the pool and so never knew how long he had remained in that spot, if he had tried to follow or whether Nancy herself had turned back, relenting perhaps and sorry for him there.

I forgot the incident quite quickly, only remembering it again much later. I think it was the sheer oddity of the thing that caused this lapse. As if, by its very lack of explanation, its unexpectedness, it made no easy lodging in my memory but had to wait before it found its place.

5   The Bookshop

I

I never quite grew out of my obsession with stationery. I simply transferred it to the bookshop. I loved the substance of books, their smell, the way they stacked up together. I loved the order they conferred. In books, life did not come at you piecemeal; a confused shambles of things half understood and barely remembered. Events did not scatter themselves like unmarked stones on a beach, resisting, in their very multitude, all but the most arbitrary of patterns. Instead they followed one another, each in its place, none without purpose or connection.

Working in the shop, my thoughts had a freedom not found elsewhere and my mind made connections of its own. I thought of Simon and Nancy and Wilfred Owen. It had been one of Nancy's foibles to speculate on what the poet would have done with the rest of his life if he had not died trying to cross that canal in France, one week before Armistice. According to one version of her fantasy, the fatal bullet had not, in fact, killed Owen, but simply caused him to lapse into a coma from which he awoke, having completely forgotten his identity.

'That's stupid,' Julia protested. 'They had name tags. They'd have told him. They'd have informed his family.'

'They had name tags on their *jackets*,' Nancy explained, lying on her back in the grass, her eyes on the sky. 'But he'd taken his off you see. Just before he got hit. To cover up this man who'd been wounded right beside him. That was the kind of thing he was always doing. Looking after his men.'

We were sitting on the edge of the Common, opposite the boathouses on the other side of the river. The crews were out that day, the air full of the cox's barking cry, the rowers leaning and stretching, the surface of the water raised in thin veils as the oars went through their motions. Like insects, I thought; long legged and swift.

'They had their tags around their necks,' Julia argued. 'All soldiers do. Metal ones. So they can be identified even if they lose all their clothes. Even if they're burned to a crisp or crushed under a tank or blown into tiny, tiny pieces.'

But Nancy said nobody had known who Wilfred Owen was and he had walked out of hospital with all memory washed clean. He had gone to live in a small cottage with a garden, somewhere in Wales. He had been alone, but not unhappy. He had never written another line of poetry again, but had spent his time growing vegetables and flowers.

'Didn't he *ever* remember?' I asked her.

There was a moment, many years later, she said. He was kneeling in his garden, weeding, his mind drifting. And in an instant, it all came back to him. His name, the war, all the words to 'Strange Meeting' and 'Dulce Et Decorum Est'. His whole former life, laid out in front of him. He stopped what he was doing and looked up for a moment at the sky.

'What did he do then?'

'He went on weeding,' Nancy said. 'He just went on with it.'

'Have I ever told you you're weird?' Julia said. 'You re-define that word.'

Simon, of course, probably wanted Wilfred Owen for the gay section, but even he must have realized the whole system would collapse if we had bits of poetry here and bits over there. I used to tell him he should get a life, a joke that in retrospect seems appallingly inappropriate. But he seemed to take it in good part. 'Ditto,' he'd say, in that knowing, yet still utterly polite way of his.

'I've got a life,' I told him.

'Yes,' he said sadly, 'haven't we all?'

II

'How's the counselling going?' I asked Michaela. She was hard at work on the new arrivals table, attempting to create an air of irresistibility by piling all the volumes up into a single, teetering pyramid.

'It's great,' she said. 'It's *great*.'

'Feeling any better?'

She paused. 'I don't know . . . I still don't know whether I have a problem really, not compared with other people, but Sally said suffering can't be quantified. Something like that anyway. She said you have to be the owner of your pain.'

'Sounds sensible.' Sally, the counsellor, rarely seemed at a loss when it came to suitably profound comments, although it was sometimes hard to fathom out their meaning, filtered as they were through the patchy logic of Michaela's thought processes.

Michaela put the last of the books on the very top of the pyramid and stood back to admire the result.

'I hope you realize that if anyone takes a single one of those out, the whole thing's going to come down,' I told her.

'When there is no water, you have to row,' she said, ignoring me. 'Sally said that.'

'Are you sure? Isn't it, "when there is no *wind*, you have to row?"'

She stopped to think. 'No,' she said. 'It wouldn't make any sense then, would it?'

'Well, more sense, surely, than the water thing,' I said, wondering why I was bothering to argue with her, but unable to help myself. 'I mean, why would you be sitting in a boat on dry land in the first place?'

She gave me a look full of sorrow. 'But that's exactly what it's like, Sophie. That's exactly what it feels like, when you don't know what to do next. When you don't know what to do with yourself. Like the tide's just gone out and left you there . . .'

I nodded, thinking how forlorn she looked, standing there, with a book in either hand, her ears red, her shirt not ironed. 'Michaela,' I said, 'if the counselling isn't working out, you don't have to keep going. It's completely up to you. You do know that, don't you?'

'I know,' she said, sounding doubtful. 'But it's great, honestly. Sometimes when I wake up, first thing in the morning, just for a minute, it sort of all comes together. I can feel it.'

'That's good,' I said. 'That's . . .' I turned suddenly at the sound of the typewriter, clacking away in the corner with some speed. It was Peter. He looked up from what he was doing and smiled at me a little sheepishly. 'Hello,' he said. 'I was just . . . I used to have one of these when I was a kid. It was ancient even then. The letter "o" always punched straight through the paper and when you took it out, you could see sky through all the holes . . .'

'I didn't see you come in,' I said. 'What were you writing?'

He pulled the paper out of the roller and handed it to me. It was a verse of poetry. *If I'd been born without a mind/I would be happy, tame and kind/People came, saying good things/So many people saying good things/I hid my eyes under my skin/And so they never saw right in.*

I finished reading and stood there for a second or two, just looking at him.

'Adrian Mitchell,' he said.

'I think I'll frame this,' I said at last. 'You should see what we usually get from that typewriter. 'We're lucky if it's only gibberish.'

'Often stuff about sex,' Michaela interrupted in a loud voice. 'Have to keep chucking it in the bin all the time.'

'Yes, well, I was thinking of getting rid of the thing,' I said. 'This is Michaela, by the way. She's helping me out for a while.'

He shook her hand in that formal way of his. 'Do you have a few minutes?' he asked me. 'I wondered whether you'd like to go for a cup of coffee.'

I put the piece of paper down carefully beside the till. 'Yes, I'd like that.'

'I can hold the fort,' Michaela chirped, giving me an excited, meaningful look. 'Stay out as long as you want. I'll be fine!'

We didn't go for coffee. I could tell that he had no real intention of it. Instead we simply walked, silent at first, taking no particular direction. 'I want to tell you about something,' he said at last, not looking at me. 'I want to tell you about my wife.'

'Your wife?' I kept walking, my face still turned to his in an effort to convey friendly interest, determined to show nothing of my sudden dismay, the humiliation of an unvoiced – unfounded – hope abruptly dashed. He stopped short in the street, his eyes on my face. 'It's not like that,' he said. 'Please don't think that.

'I'm not married any longer,' he said. He'd met his wife at college. She wasn't a medical student, but a musician, a pianist. She played wonderfully, he told me, although what she really wanted to do was compose. They were married in Cornwall when they were both twenty-five. It was a grand wedding, with a marquee and six bridesmaids and a famous cellist who performed a solo after the ceremony. They didn't have a honeymoon. They were saving money for a house.

'We should have gone,' he said. She'd always dreamed of Costa Rica. The jungles, the black, volcanic beaches.

Her cancer wasn't diagnosed until it was at an advanced stage. He'd known she didn't have much of a chance, although he'd kept this fact to himself.

'Cancer?'

'Ovarian.' He was walking faster now. I had to stride to keep pace. 'A small percentage of patients have a type that's not necessarily fatal, given treatment.' He paused. 'She wasn't in that percentage. She went fast. Even slightly faster than I thought she would.'

He spoke steadily, without emotion, in a manner that seemed to convey, far more than faltering words, of a depth of feeling incapable of all but the most basic expression. Was it bitterness I saw on his face? He had not been able to help his wife. All his medical training amounting to nothing more than the ability to predict, with clinical accuracy, the length of time left to her.

I kept silent as he talked. Any expression of sorrow I might have made seeming quite pointless. And I didn't want to interrupt him. There is something about the action of walking that frees conversation, gives words and thoughts a certain rhythm. I have found it is easier to say things when one is not looking at the other person; easier to listen too.

'I don't think she knew what was going to happen,' he said. 'Not really. Or she knew but didn't totally believe it.' I could tell that it distressed him, this question of knowing or not knowing, although I wasn't sure why. Some sense of failure on his part, perhaps. That he hadn't said the right things to her and suspected he may not have given her what she'd needed. Or maybe it was not this at all, but simply grief for her.

She'd been released from the hospital so that she could die at home, he said. He had been there when it happened. We walked a little further in silence. I didn't know what to say.

'She wasn't . . . in any pain at all?' I asked finally. 'At the end, I mean.' Of course she wasn't, I thought. She'd have had enough drugs; he would have made sure of that. It was a stupid question.

He shook his head, giving me a lost, absent, look. I wanted to touch him, to hold him, but I didn't have the courage. I felt strangely insubstantial; as if my hand, on contact, might pass straight through him. As if I was the ghost, not her.

'When did it happen?' I asked. 'When did she die?'

'Two years ago.'

'Not long then.'

'It seems like a decade,' he said.

It was a breezy day, although at first we had not been fully aware of this, having the wind at our backs. Then, turning a sharp corner, it was suddenly full in our face and we stopped for a moment or two, gathering ourselves, the mood abruptly broken.

'Why did you write out that poem?' I said, on impulse. 'Just now, in the shop.'

He hesitated for a second. 'It reminds me of you.'

I didn't know what to say to this. I wanted to ask him why, but the question seemed over-eager. As if I was too interested in myself and what others thought of me.

'That part about hiding under your skin,' Peter continued, looking at me. 'You don't do that at all. I'm not sure you can. There is something about you that's quite . . . skinless.'

'You make me sound like a supermarket chicken breast,' I said, trying to sound light, amusing.

'No,' he said, without smiling. 'That's not what I meant at all.'

I looked down at the ground. 'We've been out for ages. I should get back. Michaela is hopeless, you know. I sort of love her, but she's hopeless. She turned up on my doorstep and now she's my responsibility.'

'Thanks for the walk,' I said, 'and for telling me about . . .'

'Do you want to go on a trip sometime?' he interrupted. 'The South Coast perhaps. Birling Gap.' He paused. 'Just for the day.'

'That's a long way,' I said.

'I know. It's a bit of a drive.'

'Why Birling Gap?'

'I like it there. It's one of my favourite places. Do you want to go?'

I hesitated, thinking suddenly of that famous cellist and the big marquee. Peter's long fingers placed with tender precision against a slender wrist, the counting in his eyes. 'Well . . . won't it be rather cold . . . ?'

He turned to me abruptly and put his hand on my arm. 'Just for the day. You'd enjoy it.'

'Yes, perhaps . . .' I was about to say more, but just at that moment, bringing my hand up to brush a strand of hair away from my face, I accidentally caught the blue-bead necklace I was wearing and snapped the string. Beads shot all over the pavement and into the street and we had to scramble to retrieve them. I never did get them restrung. They stayed in the pocket of the coat I was wearing that day.

III

I needed to talk to Andrea about the situation in the shop. We were short-staffed, overcrowded and, in my opinion, there was nothing much about the place that distinguished it from any other small bookshop. In the midst of my frustration, I imagined how different it would be if I had more control. The main problem was with the ordering system. In a shop that size it was easy to miscalculate, to order too many of one book and not enough of another. And it meant that customers simply went somewhere else if they couldn't find what they were looking for. What I wanted was to be able to order a small number of a wider range of books and then replace volumes almost as soon as they were sold.

The only way to do this, I thought, was to have an arrangement with a warehouse nearby and have daily, or even twice daily, pick-ups. I needed a van and at least two more members of staff. I wanted to be able to stay open later, perhaps until ten or eleven at night on certain days of the week. In my more fanciful moments, I imagined the shop as more than just a venue to sell books. Instead, a kind of meeting place, with events and readings and special discounts for regular customers. I thought there was value to be made from not being part of a chain, of giving people the feeling that their reading choices were not shaped by mass marketing, by those monumental piles of certain, selected books one saw in the larger book shops.

I knew that Andrea would never agree to even half of these proposals, but I thought I should at least ask about finding a permanent replacement for Simon. Since Lucien and I had split up, I'd not had much contact with Andrea and I wondered whether this was because she blamed me in some way. But on the phone, she was her usual self; the warmth of her words as always offset by a certain disconcerting vagueness of tone that suggested you were not to take them entirely personally.

'Darling, how lovely . . .' she said, pausing to inhale on a cigarette. 'What a lovely surprise.'

I told her we needed another member of staff as a matter of urgency. I was quite forceful about it. I think I also mentioned the van idea, although with rather less conviction. She could refuse the van, I thought, but refusing would mean she would have to capitulate on the member of staff issue. I talked for several minutes without interruption, rather pleased with the firm stance I was taking.

'I don't quite know how to say this,' she said, after a brief silence. 'We've had an offer. Rather a good one actually.'

'An offer?'

'One of those mobile phone companies. You know the sort.' She paused. 'They get smaller and smaller, don't they? Phones, I mean. It's like having a conversation with a matchbox . . .'

'An offer?' I repeated.

'Darling, it's just business. We were always going to sell sooner or later. You knew that.'

'I didn't. I didn't know that. You're going to *sell* the shop?'

'It's not a good location for books. Not with Blackwell's and the chains . . .'

'But it's my shop,' I couldn't help saying.

'I didn't think you'd want to stay on, not after the . . . horrible thing that happened. And anyway, it's not for ages. You know how long these things take. It's not for months and months.'

'I don't believe this, Andrea. I would never have left because of Simon. I don't know how you can think I would . . .'

'If you don't mind me saying,' she interrupted, in the manner of people who know very well you *will* mind and don't particularly care if you do. 'If you don't mind me saying, from time to time, Sophie, I think you need a little *nudge*. Do you know what I mean?'

'A nudge?'

'Before you can move on. It's important to recognize when

you have to move on, you know. I don't think you . . . well, I'm not going to get into all that right now.'

'You don't think I'm what? I thought this was about the shop.'

She sighed. 'Well, of course it is. Of course. And I'm sure, if you think about it for just a moment or two, you'll see that it could be very good for you. Get you out of . . . well, your *rut*, if you like. Who knows what new opportunities . . .'

I cut her off mid-sentence, not roughly at all; my finger creeping to the receiver button almost absentmindedly. I imagine she kept talking for several minutes before she realized that nobody was listening.

I sat there for a while, my hands quite still on the desk, thinking about what Andrea had said, her heartlessness. I hadn't owned the shop, but I'd thought of it as mine. And in some ways, Simon's too. When it went, it would take him with it, carrying away the small marks of his existence there, the product of his labours. And it seemed to me that my link with him – however slight, however undeserving of friendship's name – would be lost too.

I kept returning to the way Andrea had spoken about his death and then about moving on. As if the correct, the healthy response to all unpleasantness was simply a matter of relocation. The furniture loaded into the back of the van, the front door closed for the very last time. But perhaps she was right. Perhaps this was what everyone who understood the rules of survival did.

Was it what Julia had done? And had it been an easy thing for her?

Quite suddenly, without giving myself a chance to reconsider, I decided to call her. I knew that finding her would be simple – merely a matter of calling the newspaper where her most recent articles had appeared – and I told myself I didn't have to mention the agreement to meet that we'd made all those years before. In fact, it would be better if I pretended to have completely forgotten about it and my calling simply a coincidence. Perhaps later, if we met, I could feign some dim recollection of the episode. As if seeing her again had triggered the memory. It would be something we could laugh about over our drinks and then forget again.

But as it turned out, I needn't have worried about what I would or would not say, since it didn't seem as if the woman on the newspaper switchboard had ever heard of Julia. 'I think she's freelance,' I said, at a sudden loss. 'She's one of the writers . . .'

'I'll put you through to the news desk,' the operator said, sounding rather angry.

For some reason, the thought of the news desk filled me with vague alarm. A man picked up the phone sounding in a great hurry. But he knew at once who I was talking about.

'She's in Baghdad,' he said.

'Ah yes, of course. Yes, I should have remembered that. Can I leave a message?'

He took my name and number. 'I don't know when she'll get this. Will she know what it's about?'

'I think so,' I said, trying to inject confidence in my voice. But I didn't think so at all. In fact, it occurred to me that Julia might have forgotten quite a lot more than our agreement. It was the way the man on the news desk had sounded: his impatience, his apparent importance. After I put down the phone, I wondered whether Julia would even recognize my name.

6 The Postcard

Mrs Packenham was worried about Nancy. She rang our doorbell one Saturday morning, not long after Nancy had vomited at the rec, and told my mother she wanted to speak with me.

'I just need a quick word,' she said hesitantly, her arm bracelets jangling. I stared at her mutely, instantly wondering whether I was in some kind of trouble. She was dressed even more terribly than ever, I thought. A pair of white jeans stuffed into long, black boots that made her look as though someone had cut her off at the knees.

'I wanted to ask your opinion about something,' she told me, still standing on the doorstep.

'Oh,' I said, caught off-guard by the implication that I could provide any insight that might be useful to her.

'It's Nancy,' she said, grimacing slightly. 'Of course it is, yes.' She paused. 'Is she eating enough do you think?'

'Eating?'

'You girls aren't on some . . . diet are you?'

'No, Mrs Packenham. It's the first I've heard about it.'

Her face seemed to collapse slightly. 'She's skipping breakfast and I don't know what she eats at school. It doesn't seem to matter what I cook for supper, she just picks at it. I thought you'd . . . well, you might have noticed something.'

'Not really,' I said, thinking of the three of us sitting around Julia's kitchen table after school. Julia's mother always provided food. Toast and biscuits and homemade fruit cakes cut into vast, dense wedges. We congregated there most days for half an hour or so before the demands of homework needed to be met, eating and drinking tea and talking. The kitchen was always very clean, with plates arranged in a rack and little hooks for the mugs and a shining array of copper pans hanging from a metal grid on the ceiling. They didn't use a plastic washing-up bowl, but instead had a double sink with one side for cleaning and the other for rinsing, and instead of a normal oven, a large, dark blue affair which my mother referred to as an 'Aga' in the respectful tone of voice she reserved for particularly envied objects.

Julia's mother never intruded on our gatherings. She stayed in another room doing something or other. Ironing sheets perhaps, I thought.

Nancy's duties with Ivy had meant she had not been able to come to many of our recent meetings and now that I thought of it, I could not remember her eating anything during the days she had been there.

'Well, perhaps she has cut back a bit . . .' I said.

Nancy's mother put her hand on her throat. 'I don't know what to do,' she said in a small, strained voice. 'I just don't know.'

I was unsure how to reply to this, disconcerted by her tone which seemed to suggest that I could somehow help her, that we were suddenly equals.

'Try to get her to eat,' she said at last, 'will you try?'

'All right, yes.' She turned to go. 'Mrs Packenham . . . ?'

She looked back at me. 'I think Nancy . . . I don't think she likes going to see Ivy. I think it's making her a bit upset.'

Her eyes left my face abruptly. 'Nancy doesn't always know the best . . .' she said sharply, cutting me off. 'It's not something I'm about to stand here and discuss with you, Sophie.'

I watched her go down the front garden path, her high-heeled boots making an agitated clacking sound on the wet concrete and felt sudden pity. But whether it was for Nancy or Mrs Packenham herself, I couldn't tell.

'What did she want?' my mother demanded.

'Not sure. She wanted to know what Nancy was eating, stuff like that.'

'There must have been a bit more to it than that, surely.'

'I don't know,' I said, 'I don't think so.'

My mother looked away, irritated.

'I told her about Ivy,' I said. 'I did tell her, you know. About how she hates going there. Not that she paid any attention. Nobody else seems to realize how completely evil Ivy really is.'

'Oh honestly, Sophie. I'm not saying the woman isn't a nuisance and doesn't go on about her health the whole time, but there's nothing sinister about her. She's lonely and anxious like a lot of old people. I don't know why you have to be so melodramatic about everything. Half your life you seem to exist under a kind of thick blanket and the rest of the time you're seeing something nasty in the woodshed.'

'I'm not,' I said. 'And anyway, Ivy doesn't even have a wood-shed.'

November 4 came but Nancy didn't light a candle for Wilfred Owen and when I looked for his postcard on her bedroom wall, it had gone. I went over to the spot where it had been and touched the plaster. But the only sign of him was a small, grubby scrap of Sellotape.

'Where's Wilfred?' I asked her.

'I threw it away.'

'No you didn't,' I said. 'You've put it somewhere. You wouldn't chuck it out.'

She shrugged obstinately. 'It was looking messy so I tore it up.'

'No you didn't,' I said again.

'I don't know why you're so bothered about it anyway.'

Something came over me then, a kind of panic out of all proportion to the moment. Sourceless, without shape or edge; part fear, part desperate longing. I couldn't explain why I felt this way, nor why everything – the grey light, Nancy's scattered books, the cuffs of my own jeans, inexpertly rolled up to fit my shorter-than-average legs – all these petty, inconsequential elements seemed bound together with new and vital significance. As if I was seeing all of it for the first – or very last – time; the whole world on the brink, about to tilt towards some still unseen but unrecoverable loss.

'Put it back,' I said, almost violently. 'Put him back.'

She made no movement apart from a sudden pinching around her mouth. 'Please, Nancy . . .' I begged, not knowing why I persisted or what would be achieved even if she did what I asked.

She didn't seem at all curious at my agitation. Perhaps she understood it better than I did myself, or maybe it was simply that being a creature of odd impulses herself, she was unsurprised by passion in others.

'Light your own stupid candle,' she said expressionlessly. 'Nobody's stopping you.'

For a good two weeks leading up to Bonfire Night, Oakville Street had been beset by the sudden bangs and low, drifting smoke of rogue fireworks. A feeling of unpredictability filled the air. Ivy had taped her letter box shut on the inside as a precaution against marauding pyromaniacs and advised my mother to do the same.

'How on earth can the postman deliver anything if I do

that?' my mother said impatiently. But apparently this was not an issue for Ivy, since the old lady never received letters anyway. In recent weeks, the scope of her fears seemed to have widened. An intruder, she told my mother. She had never seen him, but she knew he came.

'*When?*' my mother enquired in an exasperated voice. Ivy shook her head. Perhaps when she was asleep, or outside, sweeping the concrete in her front yard. She couldn't be certain.

'Took the air freshener, didn't he?' she said, by way of evidence. 'Brand new it was. Just got it from the Co-op. Came down in the morning and it was gone.'

My mother gritted her teeth slightly.

'Can't think what he wanted with *that*,' Ivy mused. 'But you never know with perverts do you? Took my potato masher too.' She paused. 'I've had that masher for years,' she added mournfully. 'Perfectly good it was.'

'I think there must be some other explanation,' my mother said. 'Honestly, Ivy, I really do.' And she came back into our house, banging the door behind her.

On Bonfire Night, a thick fog descended, preventing visibility further than a few yards. Julia, Nancy and I went to the public fireworks display on the Common. 'We're not going to be able to see a thing!' Julia announced as we made our way to the gathering. This was undeniably true, but it didn't seem to matter. If anything, the fog added to the air of excitement, mingling with the darker pall of gunpowder smoke in the little streets leading down to the river and giving the hurrying figures around us the drifting insubstantiality of ghosts.

From time to time, the muffled explosions of unseen rockets came to us and then, a moment later, the fog was lit with red or yellow light for a second or two; a silent, unearthly flare that seemed to come from nowhere and everywhere at once. Down on the Common, the tops of the trees were lost in mist and the great bonfire in the centre merely a distant, orange glow. We stood by the road, on the edges of the crowd, listening to the thumps and crackles of invisible fireworks overhead.

'I missed the Guy burning,' Nancy said. 'They've already burned the Guy.'

'You wouldn't have been able to see anyway,' I told her.

Julia lit a cigarette from my sparkler. 'It's just for kids anyway.'

'I always feel really sorry for that Guy,' Nancy said. 'I mean, what did he ever do?'

'I think it should be foggy every Bonfire Night,' Julia said. 'That way you can't see how crap the fireworks are.' She dropped her cigarette and ground it out with her foot. 'I wish we could go to the pub.'

'We'd never get in,' I said.

'Why? Josh and Gareth go all the time and Josh is only fifteen.'

I knew that the boys' mother was friendly with Julia's, but I had no idea that Julia ever talked much with the brothers, despite the fact that they lived only three streets away. I caught sight of them often, both of them tall, with the same long, almost-blond hair and effortless way of moving.

'How do you know?'

She shrugged. 'Gareth told me. They go all the time.'

I was absorbing this information when Miss Pemble suddenly appeared, pushing her bike with evident difficulty through the crowds on the pavement. She was wearing a thick coat of some shabby tweedy material and a woolly hat perched a little too high on her head.

'Are you with your parents?' she said abruptly, stopping in front of us.

I shook my head. 'It's all right, Miss Pemble, they know where we are.'

'You girls,' she said. 'You must keep *safe*, you know. Even in a crowd.'

Julia nodded solemnly. 'We'll remember that, honestly, we will.'

'Safe,' Miss Pemble said again, very firmly. She nodded a couple of times as though underscoring the seriousness of her message and then, renewing her grip on the handlebar of her bike, turned and pushed on through the throng.

She must have heard us laughing. She was only a few paces away. The three of us, bent double, not caring if she knew we mocked her. We saw her hat bobbing for a moment or two in the mist and then she was gone.

7 *Lucien*

I

I had been lying in the dark for hours, enduring the kind of wakefulness that is not soothed, but only intensified by the clock's slow march and which persists, wide-eyed until that point of no return, when the edges of the curtains turn to grey and another night is lost. In this state, I was glad of any distraction and greeted with relief the sound of the front door banging shut and Michaela's heavy feet coming up the stairs.

Over the last few days, I'd noticed a new reticence to her; a secretive, slightly sheepish aspect. This was the second evening she'd been out until late. I slipped out of bed and met her at the kitchen door. She was wearing make-up, something she was not normally in the habit of doing, and the eyeliner had spread out in rings around her eyes, giving her a dazed, baffled look.

'I didn't know you were up,' she said.

'I wasn't. I just got out of bed.'

'Oh *sorry*. I was really, really trying to be quiet.'

'I was awake anyway,' I told her. 'Can't sleep. Did you have a good time?'

'Yeah, I did actually . . .'

I looked at my watch. It was a little before two. 'Do you fancy a quick glass of wine?' I asked, suddenly wanting to talk to someone, even if it was only Michaela.

'Just a quick one then,' she said eagerly, following me into the kitchen. I opened a bottle and poured us both a glass. 'Your make-up is a bit smudged.'

'Is it?' She raised her hands to her face, patting her cheeks with alarm. 'Is it really bad? Do I look awful?'

'No. No, it's not that noticeable.' I paused. 'So who were you out with? Anyone I know?'

'Just someone I met,' she said, trying – and failing – to sound nonchalant.

'A date?'

'We just talk. I met him at Sally's. In the waiting room.'

'Oh, another of her clients then,' I said, with a slightly sinking feeling.

'No,' she said. 'He was just fixing the computer. He's a computer person.'

'He's nice is he?'

She brought her shoulders up and slightly forward, managing to convey in the single gesture a mixture of excitement, fear and hope. 'He is, Sophie, I really, really think he is. He's quite tall, brown hair. With sideburns. Not really long ones, not *funny* looking, but you know, just about an inch on either side.' She paused. 'I've never been out with anyone with sideburns before.'

I found myself rubbing at my forehead in an agitated manner. 'Anything else?' I asked. 'Anything else apart from the sideburns?'

'Well, he doesn't talk much. I suppose that's because he's good at listening. I can tell him all sorts of things.'

'Well, that's good . . .'

'Like you,' she said, giving me a pleading, slightly adoring look. 'I really got lucky landing here. I think about that all the time.'

It had started to rain. I could hear it against the kitchen window. 'When was the last time you phoned home,

Michaela?' I asked her. 'Does your mother even have this number?'

She looked down. 'I didn't want to call long distance . . . you know, the phone bill.'

'It's only Scotland. It's not the other side of the world.'

'Why couldn't you sleep?' she asked abruptly.

'I don't know, I just couldn't.'

She gave me a cunning look. 'It's that man, isn't it? Peter someone. The one who came into the shop.'

'No it isn't. I haven't been thinking about him much at all. He's just a . . .'

'He's loads better looking than Lucien,' Michaela interrupted. 'Loads.'

'That's completely irrelevant. Lucien and I . . . anyway, I'm not sure I'll be seeing Peter again.'

'Why not? I thought he seemed really nice.'

'How do you know? You only met him for about ten seconds.'

'He likes you,' Michaela said in a satisfied voice. 'I could tell. I could tell by the way he looked at you. I'm not surprised really, you're so pretty.' She stopped talking for a second or two, suddenly shy. 'Well, gorgeous really . . .'

'You've had too much to drink, Michaela.'

'I think he wants to make you happy,' she said.

I put my head in my hands. 'Oh god, Michaela, you're so . . .'

'I know it's corny. I do know that. But it's true. I could tell. The way he made up that poem thing for you and all.'

'He didn't make it up. And anyway, it's a lot more complicated than that.' I paused, not wanting to say anything further and then continued speaking, despite myself. 'He has this thing about his dead wife.'

'What thing?' Michaela leaned forward eagerly.

'She was a pianist. She only died two years ago.'

'He should go to Sally!' Michaela exclaimed. 'She does bereavement stuff as well. He could work it through there. You know, deal with the issues. Have you told him about her?'

'Of course not!'

'Why?'

'Not everything can be solved by the Almighty Sally, you know,' I said, knowing I was being cruel. 'And anyway, how would it look if I made a suggestion like that?'

'Yeah, see what you mean,' she said dismally. 'Hadn't thought of it that way.'

'He asked me out for the day. To the coast. Birling Gap of all places. I said yes, but now I don't know if I should have done.'

'Why not? I'd go.'

'I don't think two years is a long time at all. I think you need longer than that. Also, I don't know why . . .' I broke off. Michaela was staring at me with a peculiar expression on her face. 'What?'

'I don't see the problem really.'

'It's obvious, isn't it?'

'Maybe I'm just being thick,' she said. 'But . . .'

'But what?' I said, beginning to feel annoyed.

'Well, she's dead isn't she? I mean it's sad and all that, but she's *dead*.'

'Yes, I think we've established that fact, Michaela.'

She gave me a slightly nervous look. 'Forget it, forget it.'

'No, you've got something to say, so say it.'

'Well,' she said – very nervous now – 'well, it's all about the here, isn't it?

'Being in it,' she added.

'Very profound,' I said, before I could stop myself. 'That is, if it actually meant anything.'

'You're angry,' she said. 'I can tell. It's my big mouth again.'

'Don't be ridiculous. I'm not. Why on earth would I be angry?'

She hung her head. 'I don't know, I don't know. Sometimes I do that. I make people angry and I don't know what I've said. I'm really, really sorry, Sophie. You'll want me to go now, probably. I'm probably not welcome any more.'

'You're being silly,' I said. 'You can stay as long as you need to.'

'Colin – that's the name of my friend – he has this friend who has a spare room . . .'

'No,' I said. 'You're not moving in with some stranger. I'm not having that.'

She began to sob, very loudly, without the smallest warning sniffle. 'Sorry, sorry,' she cried, her voice muffled. 'It's just that you're so nice. I mean, nobody's ever that nice to me.'

I patted her a little clumsily, on the shoulder, still nettled by her earlier remarks and not entirely sure why; the confusion only adding to my bad mood. 'Come on,' I said, 'you're tired. We should get some sleep.'

'I'm not even that good in the shop, am I?' She looked up despairingly.

'You're great in the shop. Honestly, a big help.'

'Honestly?'

I nodded. 'You'll be fine.'

She sniffed deeply a couple of times. 'I'd better be off to bed then. What time is it? Actually, don't tell me. I don't think I want to know. You don't have any make-up remover I could scrounge do you?'

II

I didn't expect to find Lucien home late on a Saturday morning, but rang the bell anyway. He opened the door, naked to the waist, still in the sweat pants he wore in bed, his skin steaming slightly as it met the cold air. 'Sophie,' he murmured drowsily. 'Lovely.'

'Lucien –'

He pulled me inside, kissing me and pushing shut the door at the same time. He was very warm, his body relaxed from recent sleep; something entranced still about his urgency. I kissed him back, more out of habit than anything else. He had an unwashed, morning smell that had never bothered me when we spent the night together, but which now seemed very noticeable, almost distasteful.

'Lucien –'

'Come on,' he said, taking my hand and leading me through his short hall into the bedroom.

'I'm not here to . . .' He slept on a futon, an article of furniture that I had always thought both practical and stylish but which now appeared far too low to the ground. The thought of sinking down on such an insubstantial surface seemed suddenly absurd.

'We can't do this, Lucien,' I said. He was kissing me again, the duvet rumpled into a great heap, still warm from his sleep. 'I know,' he said, 'I know. That's what makes it so much fun.'

'I didn't mean that.' He was tugging haplessly at my coat now. 'Stop it!'

His hands fell away. 'Christ, Sophie, you really know how to break the mood, don't you?'

'What mood?'

He flopped back on the bed with a sigh. 'What do you want?'

'Do I have to want something?' I said, playing for time. It was the kind of thing he would have said to me and for the first time in my dealings with Lucien, I had the sense – rather distant, but not without affection – of having the upper hand.

'Some coffee might be nice,' I said.

He groaned.

'What happened to that fancy new espresso maker?'

'Too much fucking effort,' he said. 'You fiddle around, wait forever and all you get in the end is a crappy trickle. Complete waste of money.'

'So the novelty's worn off then.'

'You could say that.'

I sat beside him on the futon, my knees awkwardly drawn up. Everything in Lucien's bedroom was close to the floor: the cube that served as his bedside table, the cheap digital alarm clock on top, unset and blinking, the two Moroccan leather-topped stools positioned aimlessly in the centre of the room, the stereo equipment, trailing wires, the expensively framed Andy Warhol print of Chairman Mao leaning up against one wall. The room was designed to convey a certain sparse masculinity, a look Lucien was far too untidy to pull off even remotely successfully. Instead it simply looked as if he was camping.

'I'll have instant then.'

'That's what I like about you, Sophie,' he said, levering himself to his feet. 'You're so low maintenance.'

'Unlike your mother,' I couldn't help commenting. He trailed into the kitchen, yawning and scratching his back. 'I sense peevishness,' he said. 'What's she done now?'

'Do you know what she's planning for the shop?'

He paused in his task of washing coffee mugs at the sink. 'Oh I see,' he said. 'So that's what you came about.'

'No it isn't,' I said. 'That isn't it at all . . . So you know about it already then?'

'I had some idea, yes.'

'Nice of you to warn me.'

He gestured helplessly as if the whole thing was out of his hands. 'It's a business thing.'

'That's what she said. You're starting to sound more and more like her.'

That angered him, although he did his best to hide it. 'What's that supposed to mean?'

In a different, former time, I would have tried to force the matter to a head, to demand – more out of frustration than any real hope of change – some statement of support from him, or at least some acknowledgement that his loyalties were divided. But now this seemed a pointless exercise.

'Nothing,' I said. 'It doesn't mean anything. But I think you could have told me about the shop. I really do.'

'Are we having a fight?'

'No, Lucien, we're not having a fight.'

'Pity,' he said, handing me a cup of coffee. 'There's a certain, how can I put it? A certain *edge* to make-up sex I've always found rather exciting.'

'I don't believe it,' I said. 'You never give up, do you? Where's my milk by the way?'

'Run out.'

'You're completely useless.'

'Yes,' he said with enormous cheerfulness. 'Yes, I suppose I am.'

I looked around me, noticing the espresso maker gathering dust on top of the fridge and the thin film of grease clouding the door of the microwave. 'When are you going to . . . sort this place out? When are you going to actually hang up that picture of Chairman Mao for example? It's been sitting there forever.'

The question was made rhetorically. I didn't expect a serious response. But he paused, as though deliberating over his answer.

'I suppose I can't decide whether it belongs there or not,' he said slowly. I glanced at his face. He was looking at me with uncharacteristic intensity, a shadow of the expression that crossed his face when we were making love. I had always wondered at that look, not knowing then or now whether it was a revelation of the real, the true Lucien, free of all posturing, or quite the opposite, an insignificant quirk in an otherwise shallow nature. The answer to that question had once seemed of utter importance, weighted with the need to believe the best of him. Now I simply sat there, silently holding his gaze and feeling nothing stronger than amiable curiosity.

'What do *you* think?' he said at last, his words heavy with hidden meaning.

'I don't think it belongs there at all,' I said as gently as I could. 'I don't think it's right for you. You need something quite different.'

He sighed. I could see the naked movement of his chest as the breath passed through his body. 'Yes,' he said. 'Yes, you're probably right about that.'

I felt sorry for him then; very sorry and suddenly impatient to be done with the thing.

'Besides,' I said, in an effort to rescue him, 'I hope you know it's a total cliché. I mean, *Chairman Mao* . . .'

He brightened at once. 'Ah, but that's what makes it a statement you see, the fact that I *know* it's a cliché and am therefore employing a certain irony in displaying it. It's the old cool/uncool twist.'

I laughed. 'That's going to really pull the babes in, no doubt.'

'One does one's best,' he said modestly. 'You're not drinking your coffee.'

'That's because it's disgusting. Even for me.'

'So what're you going to do then, after the . . . shop?'

I shrugged. 'I don't know. I'll think of something.'

'Oh, I didn't tell you about this project I'm doing,' he said excitedly, changing the subject. 'I've got the go-ahead on it. I'm flying to New York next week.'

'That's great.'

'The Coney Island world hot-dog eating championship! You wouldn't believe it, Sophie, this thing is *huge*. They've got just a few minutes to eat as many hot dogs as they can. Buns and all. Relish optional. You've got all these massive guys who've been in training for literally months, preparing themselves for the event. And here's the kicker. The last few years, the Japanese have been sending competitors. And they've got the best techniques. It's completely amazing. They're half the size but somehow or other they keep winning. It's driving the Americans crazy. The whole thing is fantastic material . . .'

I listened to him talk, smiling and throwing in the odd question. 'I can't wait to see it when it's done,' I said finally. 'I'll be thinking of you when you go off next week.'

'Wish me luck. It's probably going to be a nightmare to organize.'

I stood up and hugged him, laying my cheek for a second or two against his bare chest, then lifting my face to kiss his neck. 'Goodbye, Lucien,' I said.

8 *The Hating Tree*

I

I don't know how Julia persuaded Josh and Gareth to come over one Saturday night shortly before Christmas. She must have exaggerated the meagre charms of our meeting shed. Or perhaps they simply had nothing better to do for a couple of hours, although at the time I found that hard to believe. Gareth, after all, was seventeen.

The three of us were sitting there when they arrived and the moment they entered – Gareth having to duck his head to get through the door – I was struck by a new sense of the shabbiness of our surroundings. It was still poorly lit and damp-smelling and all our efforts to make the shed look habit-able – the old blanket thrown over the back of the foam wedge sofa, the arrangement of plastic hooks stuck on the far wall – did nothing but underscore the general inadequacy of the place.

They had brought beer with them. Three cans. I could tell by Nancy's staring silence that she was disconcerted by this and felt suddenly intensely ashamed of her. She was wearing an old stained Mac, several sizes too large, and she sat hunched forward, making no effort to find room for the newcomers.

'Sorry about this dump,' Julia said easily, seating herself between the two boys on the large sofa. 'Anyone want a fag?' We all took one from her packet except for Nancy, and Julia performed her one-handed trick with the matches, leaning forward to light Gareth's cigarette, their two heads bent close together for a brief moment.

I sat on one of the chairs opposite, silenced by shyness and the sight of Gareth's long, thin legs stretched out in front of him. He was wearing black, faded Levis, rather tight. Josh was similarly dressed, although his jeans looked newer, I noticed. He was gawkier than his brother, with a remote look about him as if his mind was at one remove.

Gareth opened a can of beer for Julia and one for himself. He leaned across and gave the last can to Josh. 'You can share,' he said, pointing to me. Nobody looked at Nancy.

I took a small gulp and handed the can back to Josh, our fingers touching briefly.

There was silence for a while and then Julia and Gareth started up a conversation about a mutual acquaintance. A girl at Julia's school who'd had a party while her parents were away for the weekend. Gareth had arrived at the tail end of it. 'The place was trashed,' he said casually. 'Five thousand pounds of damage. Someone put the cat in the oven.'

'Jesus,' Julia said, sounding enraptured.

'There was this antique table thing in the front hall. Completely smashed.'

Josh leaned forward to hand me the can again. 'Did you go to the party?' I asked him, making an effort. He shook his head and I lapsed back into silence.

'What happened?' Julia asked.

'Suzanne Morgan passed out on the toilet,' Gareth continued. 'Someone called the police eventually. I only just got out in time.'

'How old are you?' Josh suddenly asked me.

I hesitated. 'Fourteen.'

'What about her?'

'Nancy? She's fourteen too.'

'She doesn't say much, does she?' Gareth interrupted.

'Leave her alone,' Julia said idly. 'She's in a funny mood. She gets like that sometimes.'

Nancy leaned forward a fraction, her arms tightly crossed as if she was guarding something under her coat. 'What happened to the cat?' she said suddenly in a clear, distant voice.

'What cat?'

'The one in the oven.'

'How the fuck should I know?' Gareth said. 'It got cooked, didn't it.'

'You're crazy,' Julia said, laughing. I laughed too. It seemed important to separate myself from Nancy, from her childish preoccupations, her naiveté.

'What's your last name?' Josh said, evidently fixated on personal facts.

'Barrett.'

Gareth shifted impatiently on the sofa. 'So what else do you do in here apart from sit around?'

Julia shrugged. 'It's a bit boring isn't it?' Gareth said. He rummaged in the pocket of his donkey jacket and retrieved a tobacco tin. 'Anyone want a spliff?'

Julia hesitated for a slightly stunned moment. 'Yeah, all right then,' she said.

I stared at him as he opened the little tin and poked around inside. His hair fell over his face and he blew it away impatiently, his fingers busy with a packet of Rizlas. The paper made a tiny hissing sound as he pulled it out.

'Where did you get it from?' Julia asked. I could tell by the tone of her voice that she was trying to sound knowledgeable.

Gareth didn't answer. He took one of Julia's cigarettes and licked it down its length, staring at her. Then he emptied the cigarette into the tobacco paper.

'We can smoke at home,' Josh announced, out of the blue. 'Our parents don't mind.'

'Really?' Julia said, clearly impressed by this information.

Gareth fiddled with a small black lump, crumbling off tiny pieces and mixing it with the tobacco. He rolled up the paper and lit the end, taking a deep, satisfied drag and pausing for a long time before letting the smoke out of his lungs. He passed the roll-up to Julia who took it unhesitatingly.

'Barrett,' Josh said, taking a long drag in turn. 'So your initials are S. B.' His words came out in a cloud of exhaled smoke.

'Yes,' I said, frozen at the prospect of the approaching spliff.

'S. B.' he repeated. He leaned forward to hand it to me and then moved over so that he was sitting next to me on the chair, leaving Gareth and Julia alone. I wasn't sure at the time whether this was his idea, or whether some signal had passed between the brothers. The end of the spliff was wet. I held it in my hand for a second or two, trying to look casual. 'Small Bra,' he said, 'that suits you.'

I think I tried to smile. 'Josh is always coming up with nicknames,' Gareth said.

I took a tiny puff on the spliff, still smiling helplessly, my face very hot. Josh was right. My bra was a small one. In fact, despite the general chubbiness of the rest of me, my chest remained almost completely flat, not requiring the services of even the slightest of supports. It was only at the insistence of my mother – motivated perhaps more by a sense of general decorum than actual evidence – that I owned one at all. It was from Marks and Spencer's; a white stretchy scrap, the material merely puckered in the areas where the cups should be.

There had been a time when I would have felt no more personally responsible for the shape of my body than I would for a scab on my knee. But now, for the first time, it struck me with humiliating force that my physical imperfections were not random things at all, but somehow my own fault. And more than this, that they no longer quite belonged to me, but were public matters that others were permitted to comment upon.

Josh's thigh was almost touching my own. If either of us moved even a fraction, I would have felt him actually against me. I sat very still, overcome by shame.

'Don't pick on Sophie,' Julia said in a careless voice. 'I don't even wear a bra as a matter of fact.'

Only Julia could have got away with a statement like that, I thought enviously. The boys were looking at her as if she had said something funny and daring, instead of confessing to an embarrassing secret. 'Horrible things,' she continued, 'I'm never going to wear one.'

Gareth smiled, but Josh was looking at Nancy. 'Why doesn't she take her coat off?' he said. 'She looks like a tent with a head sticking out.'

A moment before, Julia had taken my side against Josh, but she was silent now. I too said nothing. Nancy made no move to indicate that she had heard. She sat motionless, her eyes on the ground. 'Yeah, go on,' Gareth said, a touch cruelly. 'Take your coat off.'

She shook her head. 'Don't be so uptight,' Gareth said, handing her the butt of the spliff. She shook her head again. 'I don't like that stuff,' she said.

'How do you know?' Julia pointed out. 'You've never had it before.'

'Take your coat off, Nancy,' Gareth said again.

'Yeah, why don't you?' I said. 'Why don't you just take it off?'

II

I wish I hadn't said that. Even now, sixteen years later, the memory burns me.

It may seem like a small thing, but I used to think of it as somehow pivotal. I never had any real evidence for this, only the conviction that it was at that moment Nancy recognized that Julia and I belonged to a different world from her own and stepped away from us, rejecting – finally, irrevocably – any impulse she might have had to confide in us or ask for help.

I used to take comfort from this idea. If it's true that life's great events hang on certain key moments whose significance is only later fully recognized, then – not knowing at the time what these moments are – we can't be entirely held to blame for their effects. All betrayals remain small ones, even the unkindest word not without innocence. There was a tidiness to this, an ease of explanation that was hard to resist. For years I didn't even try, but clung to the telling and retelling of that moment, finding within it both evidence of my guilt and the means of my absolution.

But the truth was different from this, far quieter and less dramatic, although harder to bear. The truth was I had a hundred moments to put things right for Nancy. A hundred chances to change the course of events. And I missed all of them.

III

'I think I'll go home now,' Nancy said, in a small, tight voice. We watched her leave in silence and soon after, Josh and Gareth made their departure. They were going to a party. The entire visit to the shed, it seemed, had been nothing more than an effort to kill time before it started. Julia and I sat there for a while, plunged in gloom.

'Well, Josh was pretty weird, wasn't he?' Julia finally said.

'What do you mean?'

'I don't know. He didn't seem all there. Probably all the dope he smokes.'

'Do you think they're really allowed to smoke it at home?'

'How should I know?'

'I hope Nancy's all right,' I said.

'God, that reminds me,' Julia said abruptly. 'I've got to show you something.' She rose to her feet – a little unsteadily – and I followed her outside. It was a cold night, very clear, with a thin, icy moon carved into the sky above the rooftops and an utter stillness to the air. 'Fucking hell,' Julia grumbled, hugging herself and hopping from foot to foot as she led me around to the back of the shed.

'I just noticed it the other day,' she said. 'I don't think anyone else has seen it. I hope not.'

The sudden transition from warm shed to frigid air had disorientated me a little. I stood panting, my breath clouding the inky air, not seeing, for a second or two, what she was showing me.

'We should do something before my mum finds it,' Julia said.

Since our orgy of resentment several months before, I had not given the Hating Tree another thought. It was even more wretched than I remembered, the new absence of greenery around it throwing its puny branches into sharp relief. But now it glittered in an unexpected way, each stunted twig burdened with oddly shaped objects, impossible to identify at this distance. I stepped forward for a closer look.

'We've got to get rid of it,' Julia said.

I squatted down by the tree and fingered the items. A nail

file, a plastic air freshener, an ornamental teaspoon from the Isle of Man, a hair net, three combs – all missing teeth – a stained Chinese pincushion, a small ball with a bell inside, a glass thermometer and, of course, the potato masher that I remembered from before.

'I'm assuming they belong to Ivy,' Julia said. 'Poor old bag.'

'But how . . . ?'

'Think about it.'

'Nancy,' I said. 'It's got to be. She must have taken something almost every time.'

We stood there for several minutes, in the cold, staring at the tree. 'I knew it was bad for Nancy,' I said, 'but . . . *this*?'

'Poor old Ivy,' Julia said. 'She must think she's going completely demented.'

'She told my mum she had an intruder. Probably thinks it's the Fen Rapist who's nicking her stuff.'

Julia reached out her foot and touched the tree with the tip of her toe. 'At least it's sort of festive . . .' She swayed slightly, perhaps feeling the effects of the spliff. 'Christmas in Oakville Street,' she said heavily. 'Sums it all up, doesn't it?'

IV

It was not so much what my mother was saying, nor her tone of voice, but rather some quality of the silence between her words that stilled me suddenly.

I squatted on the landing, and peered down. From this vantage point I could see a short way into the sitting room below; a foot or two of sofa, the edge of the dining table beyond and my mother's right arm held out at an angle, playing with the phone cord, looping it away from her body and then bringing it in close as she listened.

I pressed my face against the banisters, aware both of the ignominy of my position and my need to maintain it with perfect, unbroken concentration.

'Well . . .' my mother said at last, with a small laugh. 'Well . . .' Her arm stilled itself for a second or two, then resumed its slow, twisting motion.

'I could say the same,' she said. 'Unless . . .'

She could not have known, or had forgotten, that I was in the house. I spent so much time alone in my bedroom that it must have been easy to overlook my presence. 'Of course not, George,' she said, her voice very light. 'Of *course* not. With or without. You know that.'

I stood up, grateful for the silence of my socks against the wooden floorboards of the landing. It crossed my mind to make some kind of noise then; a cough or shuffle or the banging of a door. She would hear it and her voice would change and something would be prevented. But whether this would be for her benefit or mine was a question I did not have time to ask myself.

'That's not what you were saying the other night,' she said.

I turned and walked back to my room, one finger trailing along the wall as I went. For a few moments, I was aware of nothing but this small point of contact; the flat rub of plaster beneath my skin, my own bewildered sense of the pointlessness of the movement and the importance of continuing it.

My room was exactly the same as I had left it; the curtains still drawn despite the late hour, my book face down, open on the bed, and I was caught by a fleeting disbelief that it should be so. That finding all changed within me, I should see no corresponding dislocation in my immediate surroundings seemed a mark of indifference amounting almost to betrayal.

I sat down carefully on my bed, and stared at the wall

opposite, my thoughts consumed. I had nowhere to place the information I had just received, no area of my mind where it could find containment. For the first time in my life I had the sense of knowing something about which I could not talk to anybody, not even myself.

I heard the front door close with a bang and I shot to my feet, my heart beating very hard and urgently. But there was no further noise. The house was empty.

I reached for my book, unable for a moment or two to see anything but a net of print, the spaces between words making a trapped and broken pattern on the page. Then, finding my place at last, I lay down on my side, chin snug against my shoulder, and resumed reading where I had left off.

'I can't stay,' Miss Pemble said, plunking an armful of books down on the dining table. 'I've got to be at Castle Hill in fifteen minutes.'

'Well, it's nice to see you,' my mother said, wiping her hands on a tea towel. 'How have you been, Miss Pemble?'

Watching my mother with minute attention as I had begun to do since the phone call, it seemed to me that in recent days she had lost her old dismissiveness, becoming almost light-hearted. It disturbed me, this change, not simply because I held it against her, for all that I found to secretly resent in each glance of hers or shift in tone. There seemed a new reck-lessness behind her manner, a flippancy masquerading itself as good humour that frightened me a little.

'Mustn't grumble,' Miss Pemble said.

'No, no we mustn't do that,' my mother said. 'That wouldn't do at all, would it?'

'I've come about the Vigilance Committee,' Miss Pemble said after a short, rather puzzled silence. 'We've had our first meeting and the attendance was really quite fair.'

'Oh yes?'

'Really quite fair, all things considered,' Miss Pemble repeated, in the manner of someone attempting to convince themselves of the truth of their words. 'Several important issues were established. The name of the committee . . . objectives . . . the date for our next gathering.'

'This is the rapist thing you're talking about?' my mother said. Miss Pemble shot me an alarmed look. 'Quite,' she said. 'Yes, as we discussed . . .'

My mother made a gesture in the air with her hands. 'God, the rapist. I'd forgotten all about him.'

Miss Pemble leaned in, seeming in her eagerness to ignore the irreverence in my mother's tone. 'We're convinced there's a pattern,' she began. 'The key to it is geography, you see. His choice of victim. Not a matter of picking a specific person at all, but a specific *place*. That's the key to it. Which is why we need participation from the neighbourhood. From responsible members of the community . . .'

'I'm sure the police are going to catch him any day now.'

'. . . from people like yourself, Mrs Barrett. Our next meeting is a week on Thursday. Can I put you down as someone who will be in attendance?'

'I don't know,' my mother said, 'I really can't see the usefulness of . . .'

'I'll take that as a definite maybe then, shall I?' Miss Pemble said, producing a clipboard from her bag and making a note.

'Look on the bright side, Miss Pemble,' my mother said, escorting the woman to the front door, 'he may be caught well before a week on Thursday. Then you won't need to have a meeting will you? Not if he's already safely behind bars . . .'

She came back, shaking her head, all good humour abruptly

vanished. 'Supper's in half an hour,' she said shortly. 'Lay the table will you, Sophie?'

I went into the kitchen and collected three plates and sets of cutlery, watching as she poked at the spaghetti sauce on the stove.

'Hurry up,' she said, as if the meal was suddenly a matter of utmost urgency.

I carried the plates through to the dining table and saw Miss Pemble's books still piled up where she had left them. 'She left her stuff behind,' I called. I might have simply stacked them up and left them in a neat pile somewhere, but I didn't. Instead I picked them up and took them into the kitchen. 'It's her book,' I told my mother, 'the one with her family tree.'

She stopped what she was doing. 'We shouldn't look at it,' she said, taking it from me and laying it down on the sideboard. 'She'll come back for it.'

And then, as if she had not spoken at all, she opened the cover and began turning the pages. We stood side by side, looking at the thing, momentarily deprived of speech.

Miss Pemble's book was like no other; so initially baffling to the vision that one's eyes were forced to undergo a second or two of readjustment before they could quite register what they were seeing. It was not merely that almost every single page in the thick volume was entirely covered in print, leaving not a single gap or whisper of a margin, but the quality of the handwriting itself that was so astonishing. Without the proof in front of me, I wouldn't have thought it was humanly possible to write so small and so neatly. Each word a tiny, squinting miracle, packed tight against the next without so much as a comma to give the reader breath.

'Jesus Christ,' my mother said reverently, turning the pages slowly. They made a crackling sound, like paper does when it has been written on with repeated and unusual force.

'It's a list,' she said. 'It's a list of names. Look, she started with hers.'

I peered over her shoulder as she pointed to the first page. *Caroline Myrtle Pemble, b 1918 Coventry, England.*

'Myrtle?' I said. 'What kind of a name is that?' My mother ignored me, flipping with increasing speed through the book. 'It's just names,' she repeated, her voice rising in disbelief. 'There must be thousands. Look at the dates! She's just going back and back. Where did she get this stuff?'

'*William Fitzwarren Pemble, Emily Pemble née Brand,*' my mother read in a breathless voice. '*Thomas Wallingford Wheeler, born 952 . . .*'

'952?' she said. 'That's the Dark Ages. Records don't go back . . .'

'She hasn't finished the book,' I remarked. 'There's some empty pages at the end.'

'No,' my mother said. 'No, she's finished it. She just hasn't filled in all the blanks.' She turned to the very last page. 'See, she got to the end. You can't go further than that in a family tree can you?'

And there they were, their names as carefully inscribed as all the others.

Adam & Eve, Gdn of Eden.

'You can't go further back than that,' my mother said again. She started to laugh. 'I was right!' she said, her laughter rising. 'I told you didn't I? Everyone on this street is mad. This is the street of lunatics!'

I smiled uneasily, unsure of the joke. 'Adam and Eve!' my mother shrilled, still laughing. 'Jesus Christ.' She paused for a second. 'Oh he'll be in here too I expect. *Jesus Christ, b in stable . . .*' Her words brought on a renewed attack of laughter.

'Perhaps we'd better close it,' I said. 'Miss Pemble might come back . . .'

But she didn't seem to hear me and I left her there, gasping to herself, the book still open in front of her and the supper quite forgotten.

V

There was an afternoon when my father drove us to Ely to visit the cathedral. I didn't want to go and would have refused, preferring to spend the time huddled in my bedroom in my usual fashion. But there was something in my father's manner when he made the suggestion; an edge to his enthusiasm, that persuaded me into grudging acceptance. The best I could do in mitigation against the inevitable boredom of the outing was to ask if Nancy could come along too.

Nancy didn't seem to mind whether she came or not. She sat with me in the back seat of the car, staring blankly out of the window while my father attempted to make conversation.

'Have you been to the cathedral before?' he asked her. 'It used to be one of our favourite outings, didn't it, Sophie?'

I grimaced silently behind his back. 'We must have been there a hundred times,' he continued. 'But there's something about the place that makes you feel – just a little bit – that you're seeing it for the first time. Perhaps it's because it seems so improbable. Such a huge construction in the middle of this tiny, out of the way part of the country . . .'

'It's just a *building*, Dad,' I said.

It was a cold day, the sky overcast with thin cloud. We drove down Coldhams Lane, past the wet football field and the rows of council houses, and then onto the A10 where the buildings gave way to low, thorny trees and ploughed fields beyond. Away from the town, the land revealed itself; endlessly flat, relieved by nothing but thin lines of trees, and on the far horizon a rent in the sky where the grey clouds broke and bled dark towards the earth.

I didn't like the Fens. I didn't like their solitude; the lone farmhouses with their battered trees, too feeble to afford protection, the eternal cry of the peewits circling low over the ground. At this time of the year, the famously black Fen soil lay in dense furrows, thick as meat with the mark of the blade still upon it; a treacherous substance, giving the lie to the openness of the broad horizon. Even the crops grown here were alien; dark leaves of kale bunched low to the ground and in the summer, the fields of rape, violent in colour and in name. But there was something undeniably mesmeric about the landscape, an emptiness there that silenced talk and held the eye transfixed.

Beside me, Nancy had grown very still, her face turned to the window, her hands curled motionless as though in sleep.

'We'll be at Streatham soon,' my father said. 'You turn a corner and on a clear day you can see the cathedral in the distance.' He glanced up at the sky suddenly as if aware of it for the first time. A pale sun had part broken through the cloud and was casting a watery, shifting light in scattered patches on the fields. 'Visibility's not too bad today,' he said, 'all things considered.'

He tapped the wheel a little impatiently, eager to be around the famous corner. As if that was going to make any difference, I thought.

'There, what did I tell you?'

Far off, but huge even at this distance, the cathedral floated, seeming in that uncertain light to be a thing neither of sky nor earth. 'See the West Tower?' my father said. 'We're lucky with the weather today.'

'Why did they then?' Nancy said abruptly. My father shot her a confused look in the rear-view mirror. 'Why did they what?'

'Build it here.' It was a moment or two before I understood that she was referring to my father's earlier comments. Even for Nancy, the question seemed disconcerting. As if she was quite unaware that any time at all had passed. My father smiled slightly. 'I don't really know,' he said. 'The correct answer would probably be that it was built as a demonstration of Norman supremacy but I think it was built for its own sake. Do you know what I mean?'

She nodded slightly.

'For the simple joy of it,' my father said.

Entering Ely, the trees grew higher on the sides of the road; a sensation of narrowing continued by the high, moss-covered walls that lined the way to the cathedral car park. Outside, it felt colder than it should, an effect created perhaps by the extreme dampness of the air that seemed to find its way through any amount of clothing. I walked with my arms crossed in front of me, sucking the air loudly in a suffering fashion designed to remind my father that I was an unwilling participant in the whole venture. Everything looked dreary, I thought resentfully. The low, blunt houses with their windows flush to the brick, the narrow streets, the monumental cannon in the square outside the cathedral with its barrel pointing at nothing.

'There was a monastery here long before they built the cathedral,' my father was saying to Nancy, apparently eager to capitalize on her slender interest in the place. 'It was founded by St Etheldreda, a queen of East Anglia who gave up everything to become a nun. Sometime in the seventh century I think. She was famous because although she'd been married, she was still a virgin . . .'

He shot Nancy an uncertain look. As if he'd said something she wouldn't understand, I thought; something embarrassing. 'What was so great about being a virgin?' I said loudly. 'Of all things.'

'I think it must have been a very hard thing for a woman to be,' he said. 'In the seventh century.'

I was about to respond to this, but we were at the doors of the cathedral; two vast wooden structures that didn't open themselves, but that had a smaller door, the size of a coffin lid, cut into them, to allow access.

Despite the fact that I had not been to the cathedral in a while, I would have described myself as familiar with its atmosphere and general layout. But my father was right – stepping into the place was always to see it for the very first time. Perhaps it was simply that the mind's eye could never fully contain that arching space, that particular combination of vast expanse and unswerving direction. I stood motionless for a moment, looking up at the slim, vaulted ceiling, the pillars on either side of the long nave opening out towards me like great wings.

'I think there's going to be a tour soon,' my father said, glancing at a group of people huddled by the entrance.

But I wasn't interested in a tour. I moved off by myself, down the left side of the nave, my breath tentative. All my earlier disgruntlement vanished now that I was alone. It was the weight of the place, its utter lightness, the two sensations coming together without apparent contradiction. As if, despite all signs of labour – the layers of stone, the carvings, the tens of thousands of pieces of glass, arranged just so – the place had simply grown by itself, its columns veined with living sap rising effortlessly towards the light.

It was a quiet time of day. The silence full of echoed murmur and the sound of careful steps against the stone. I walked slowly, reading the carved names of priests and princes.

Elsin, Brithnoth, Leofric, Thurstan . . .

They did not seem to me like other dead. Not as the living cither, but suspended somewhere in that space – slender as the line of the horizon, vast as the Fen sky – that lay between the two.

I followed them for many minutes down the long aisle, caught in a dream, until, close to the centre, with the high octagon opening into golden flower above, I stopped by the side of a tomb, staring at the marble figure placed on top. Some king or abbot, I thought vaguely, wondering at the way his face had been carved. His eyes, not those of death or even sleep, but open still, transfixed in gaze . . .

'There you are,' my father said. 'Have you seen your friend? She wandered off some time ago.'

I turned. He was standing slightly behind me, on the other side of the tomb, and in my state of reverie it was not his face that I saw first, but his right hand, resting lightly on the stony shoulder of the effigy. Perhaps it was the angle of its placement that caught my attention, the cathedral light falling upon it in such a way as to highlight the bones of his fingers and knot his veins with shadow. For a split second it seemed to me that what I saw was not the hand of anyone I knew, but instead the man that I would come to know, ages and ages from now. My father grown old, with old man's hands.

'Well, I expect she's around here somewhere,' he said.

I wanted to tell him then about what I had overheard; the way my mother had sounded, her words. The need rose in me, confused by pity, by an overwhelming desire to be consoled.

'Daddy . . . there's something I want to ask you about.'

'What is it?'

Now that the moment had come, I did not know how to phrase the thing. I struggled silently for a second or two while he watched me. Was it with the phone call that I should start or the discovery of George's hat? But this was to arrive at the heart of the thing with too little warning; the suspicion – so serious, so dreadful – coming more readily than I wanted to admit. Perhaps then some mention of her changed manner, her distracted behaviour . . . but surely this meant nothing unless one was aware of all the rest . . .

'What is it?' he asked again.

'I was just wondering,' I said at last. 'If you're all right. I mean, if everything's all right.'

I think if he had questioned me, if he had said, quite simply and without pretence, 'what makes you ask such a thing?' I would have told him everything. But he didn't ask. Perhaps he knew already what I meant and wished to spare himself and me.

'Of course I am,' he said lightly. 'Of course I'm fine. Why wouldn't I be?'

'I don't know. I was just asking.'

He lifted his hand towards me, hesitated for a fraction of a second and then patted my head two or three times. 'We really should get hold of Nancy,' he said. 'We should be making tracks pretty soon. I was thinking of that tea shop we used to go to. How would a slice of cake sound to you?'

I visualized it sitting on my plate. The way it would fill my throat and clot my mouth with sweetness, banishing, for a moment or two, all other thought. 'Good idea,' I said, attempting to smile. 'I'll see if I can find Nancy. She must be around here somewhere.'

'I'll be at the front entrance then. Or in the shop. I wouldn't mind seeing what kind of books there are on this place . . .'

I watched him go, my impulse towards confession already fading. Now that I had missed the opportunity to unburden myself, I think I may have even felt relief. There would have been no containing the words once spoken. Not even this vast place would have been large enough to hold them. And Nancy would no doubt have appeared, just at the wrong time, making the whole thing even more embarrassing.

I crossed and recrossed the nave, looking for her. She was not in the cloisters or the Lady Chapel, or in the dark corners of the transept. I paused for a moment by a long marble scroll where the names of war dead were carved, but these were men from the second war, not the first, and I pressed on, a little anxious now, thinking of Nancy's strange, blank face in the car, her disconnected words.

Right at the back of the cathedral, behind the choir and high altar, I found her at last. There was a small area there for candles; a basin filled with sand and a box for donations. She was lighting a candle, her face bent low over the flame.

'Nancy?'

She turned slightly, her face in shadow.

'We have to go,' I said. 'My dad's waiting.'

'I didn't have 5p for the box,' she said. 'There's a sign there that says they pray for whoever you light a candle for. Even if they don't know them. They pray for them anyway.'

'Who's your candle for?'

'Do you think they'll still pray if I didn't put 5p in the box?'

'I suppose so. I mean, how would they know if you put money in or not?'

She touched her candle with careful fingers, setting it firmer in the sand. 'I don't know . . .'

There was a statue placed next to the basin of candles, a small figure, barely taller than Nancy herself. It was simply carved; the unsmoothed stone revealing no detail but merely the outline of a robed, female form, the crowned head tilted slightly upwards, the eyes wide and unfocused, like those of a person who walks in their sleep.

'Look!' I said. 'St Etheldreda. The famous virgin.'

But she was not to be distracted. 'I think you're right about the praying,' she said. 'I think they'll do it anyway.'

'Of course they will, Nancy,' I said impatiently. 'I don't know why you're getting so het up about it.'

She turned away from the candles, hunching forward with an odd, self-protective movement of her shoulders and presenting me with that tight, closed-in look that had become so habitual with her. Tormented though it was, there was something in that expression that never failed to aggravate me; an aloofness there that brought to mind a sense of my own ineptitude, my helplessness.

'What's wrong?' I asked, half-heartedly.

But her mind was still on the subject of prayers and candles.

'What I'm thinking,' she said miserably, 'is that they're going to pray all right. But if I didn't put 5p in the box, it makes no difference.'

'Why not?'

'Because it won't work. Don't you see? No matter how much they pray. It won't do any good at all.'

9 Birling Gap

I

I had never been to Birling Gap before and at the first sight of those green, unimpeded cliffs, it struck me as being an odd – almost morbid – choice of destination for us. Perhaps there was an unconscious link in Peter's mind between this place, famous for suicides, and the death that had brought us together. If so, he gave no sign of it. After the weariness of the long drive, he seemed to have gained new energy, his face clearing, losing some of that concentration of expression that I had come to associate with him.

'There's usually at least one person with a kite up here,' he said. 'Hand gliders too.'

It seemed a good day for flight; the sky almost free of cloud, the ocean a pale, wintry blue. With the beach still hidden below us, the demarcation between cliff-edge and sky had a clarity I'd not seen anywhere else; a simplicity of line that might, I thought, make stepping off that place seem almost an easy thing for those who had fixed their minds upon it.

We found a spot in the empty car park and made our way to the long wooden stairs that led down to the beach. I was carrying the bag of sandwiches we'd bought on the way and Peter had a blanket in his arms. It had been in the boot of the car and I had no idea whether it was always there, ready for outings such as this, or if he had searched it out that morning, rolling it up carefully in preparation for the trip. It seemed like a small thing to wonder about, but I was curious.

'Do you always keep a blanket in your boot?'

'Depends what you mean by *keep*. I just found it this morning. You may have noticed that I have the sort of car you find things in.'

'Yes I did notice,' I said, thinking of the back seat piled with files, maps and assorted items of clothing. 'I kind of like that in a car . . .'

He was walking slightly ahead of me and I thought how strange it was that from a distance he looked almost short in stature, when up close he did not seem that way. Up close you would not describe him as a short man at all.

At the top of the stairs there was a sign warning people that removing stones from the beach was prohibited. 'Why would anyone want to steal the stones?' I asked him.

'You haven't seen them,' he said.

The tide was in and the beach was little more than a narrow, sloping stretch between cliffs and sea. It seemed an alien place to me; disturbing in a way I could not easily explain. There was something tactile in the oddness of it; the texture of everything strangely reversed. The chalk cliffs unnaturally soft, looking as if they might crumble at a single touch; the inhospitable stones beneath our feet, sharpened to blades in that cold, clear light; the sea itself, scarred by rock, tugging at the broken shore.

'It's beautiful isn't it?' Peter said.

'Yes, yes it is.'

'I think this is probably my favourite beach in the world.' He smiled. 'As you can probably gather, I'm not a big fan of lying around on sand. I like beaches where there's things to look at.'

'And stones to steal?'

'Yes.'

I wanted to ask him whether he had ever come here with

his wife. It suddenly seemed a matter of great significance. But I hesitated, aware of the power of his answer, how it would change everything about the place, the sound of the sea, the very light itself.

'When was the last time you were here?' I asked, hating the hedging tone of my voice, the hint of neediness beneath my words.

'Not for years and years,' he said. 'Not since I was a child. We used to live in Brighton. My mother used to bring us on the bus. Double-decker. We always tried to get the top front seats. You'd leave your stomach behind going down the hills.'

We had begun to walk along the beach, keeping the cliffs to our right, our feet slipping on the stones. 'When I was little, we used to go to Norfolk,' I told him. 'The beach at Hunstanton. It was a two-hour drive from Cambridge. I loved it too.'

'Look!' he said, bending to pick something up. 'Have you ever seen anything like that before?' The pebble in the palm of his hand was speckled like an egg and round as a marble. 'I think it's an almost perfect sphere,' Peter said, placing it carefully into his pocket.

'I could report you for that,' I said. 'Although I bet I can find another one, even better.'

We continued in silence, our eyes darting over the ground. Down by the shore, the sea, on the turn at last, revealed great boulders of pale chalk and darker stones, covered by long green weed that swirled in the water, luxurious as hair. I was growing used to the place, finding in its strangeness something almost soothing. I walked slowly, absorbed in the task of searching for pebbles, possessed by a sense of peace that I had not felt for a long while.

I stooped abruptly, straightened, held out my hand. 'This one's even bigger. Like a ping-pong ball . . . How many have you got?'

'Three.'

'It's not fair. You have more practice.'

'Perhaps we should stop here,' Peter suggested, indicating a slightly smoother area close to the base of the cliffs. He spread out the blanket, fastening down each corner with a large stone. 'Are you hungry?'

I shook my head.

'I'll show you something,' he said, wiping his hands on his trousers and moving a few yards away. 'This might take a bit of time because I've half forgotten how to do it, so be patient.'

I sat on the blanket with my knees drawn up, glad of the opportunity to watch him. He spent a while walking in a small circle, examining the ground before selecting a medium-sized rock with a long, sharp, pointed edge. 'What are you going to do with that?' I asked.

'Just wait.' He was kneeling now, fingering the flat surface of a second, larger stone as though trying to locate something. 'I think this will work,' he said, lifting the first stone and positioning it, sharp point down onto the flat one.

'You'll never balance that. It's impossible.'

'You'd be surprised,' he said, his hands making minute and careful adjustments as he steadied the weight. 'There's a sweet spot. You just have to find it. There, you see?' His hands moved away and the stone was fixed, holding itself in perfect equilibrium on a surface no larger than the end of a pencil. 'Now it gets hard,' Peter murmured, casting his eyes around once more. He found another pointed stone and then a third, positioning each in turn on top of the one below with a steadiness of hand that seemed almost miraculous.

'How did you *do* that? Could I try?'

'The trick is to be patient,' he told me. 'You have to let the rocks find their own place.'

I searched out a large, triangular-shaped stone and tried

balancing it, point down, my movements clumsy at first and then becoming gentler as I searched for the sweet spot, the precise angle of placement that would allow the thing to stand free.

'I did it! I can't believe it's staying there!'

We continued for a while in silence, building our towers until the beach around us was scattered with them. 'They look like sculptures,' I said, pausing to admire our work. 'They look like little Stonehenges . . .'

He gave me an amused look. 'I think I'll have that sandwich now,' he said, returning to the blanket and settling himself down. 'It's getting quite late.'

The afternoon light had softened, turning the cliffs to pearl behind us. 'Where did you learn to balance rocks like that?' I asked him. 'Did you do it when you were a child?'

'No,' he said. 'It was a trick of Geena's.'

It was the first time I'd heard his wife's name. The sound of it made her seem very close suddenly. Geena. A friendly sort of name although unusual, almost exotic . . . I imagined her playing the piano with slim, beautiful fingers, white as the keys themselves.

'We were on this river bank,' Peter said. 'I forget where. She just started doing it; making these towers with the river stones. "Rock ballet," she called it. Because the rocks looked as if they were standing on the tips of their toes. We ended up staying on that river bank for ages. By the end, there was a small group of people watching us. Just standing there, watching.'

'You must have loved her such a lot,' I said, with difficulty.

He didn't reply and when I glanced at him, I saw that his face had lost all expression.

'I'm sorry,' I said, 'I shouldn't be bringing it up. It's not . . .'

'No.'

'I'm sorry,' I repeated, 'it's really insensitive of me. It's far too soon for you. Two years isn't a long time. I do understand that . . .'

'I meant no, I didn't love her,' Peter interrupted, nailing his gaze to a distant point on the horizon.

I think I was too surprised to speak, alarmed by the coldness in his voice.

'I've never told anyone that before,' he said. 'I've never even said it aloud.'

'I don't understand . . .'

'In the beginning, it was different,' Peter continued, still not looking at me. 'I loved her in the beginning. Or I thought I did.' He paused. 'Is there any difference between the two? Not at the time perhaps, it's only afterwards . . . She was very beautiful, you know. And she loved me. She didn't want to wait to get married. She said she couldn't see the point of waiting. I couldn't either. It was only later . . . she started talking about having a baby. I knew it then.'

'It was something about having a baby?'

'No. It wasn't that.'

'But what had happened?' I said. 'What changed?'

'Nothing,' he said helplessly. 'Nothing changed. She was the same. I just woke up one day and didn't love her any longer. It felt as simple as that. As terrible as that. As if something had simply . . . gone. I didn't say anything. It was quite soon after that she became sick and I couldn't tell her then. It would have been pointless and cruel.'

'But you cared for her,' I said. 'She never knew anything was different . . .'

'I told myself that what I was feeling – all that sadness and pity – that it was love. I told myself that for a long time.' He stopped, unable to continue.

I didn't know what to say. I sat for a long while, staring at the retreating ocean; the movement of the water, too subtle to be detected by the eye, revealed only by what it left behind; the emerging rock, still wet, given new and lonely shape. I had been wrong about Peter. I had thought his anger, his unhappiness, was a simple thing; a frustration at his inability to keep his wife alive. Now I saw that it was deeper than that; a different kind of failure altogether. The two things, his loss of love for her and her illness, coming so close together that they had become linked. Did he hold himself responsible? Was that the true source of his guilt? I would never ask him. It was not something, I thought, for which he would ever find the words.

'You're . . . horrified,' he said harshly. 'I shouldn't have told you.'

'No,' I said. 'No. There was someone . . . I knew someone too . . .'

'Do you think they'll still pray if I didn't put 5p in the box?'

'I suppose so. I mean, how would they know if you put money in or not?'

'Peter,' I said, 'when you saw Simon being attacked on the street, what made you go and help him?'

He hesitated. 'Wouldn't anyone?'

I shook my head. 'There were three of them and they had a knife and Simon was . . . well, just a stranger really. I'm not saying that most people would have walked away, but you could have called the police on your phone, or gone into the bar to get help.'

'I suppose so. But it was all happening right there in front of me. It was . . .' He stopped. 'This'll probably sound stupid, but it felt almost like a relief. The fact that there wasn't any doubt. That doesn't happen very often, does it? That you see things so clearly like that.'

I leaned towards him and took his face between my hands. 'No,' I said, feeling the tears start in my eyes. 'No, it hardly ever happens at all.'

We kissed then. And if I lost all sense of my surroundings, it was because in that single moment, I no longer felt separate from anything else. No more aware of the sharp stones beneath me, the darkening sky, the sound of the ocean itself, than I was of the movement of my own blood.

I pulled away slightly to look at him.

'What is it?'

'Nothing.'

'Tell me.'

'Are you ever frightened? That you'll wake up one morning with somebody else and it will be . . . gone again?'

He brushed the hair away from my forehead very gently and kissed me again. 'I used to think that,' he said. 'I was frightened of that for a long time.'

Later, walking back to the car, he told me he was leaving Oxford. Months ago he'd applied for a job in a London hospital. It was a good position for him, a step up. And he'd always wanted to live in a big city.

'When?' I asked.

His hand in mine tightened slightly. 'Two weeks,' he said.

'Oh.'

'I'm sorry,' he said. 'It's awful timing.'

'Well,' I said, with a brightness I did not feel, 'it's not so far between Oxford and London is it? There's weekends . . .'

'Yes. There's the weekends.'

We walked on, a little slower than before. 'So you'll be there mid-November-ish,' I said. 'I have to go into town myself then. Just for the weekend.'

'Visiting someone?'

I shrugged. 'I haven't seen my mother in ages. I should see her. It's always a bit of an effort really. We don't have much in common . . .'

'Will you be with her the whole time?'

'Oh no. Nothing like that. We'll go out to dinner some-where. I won't be staying with her or anything. There's something else I thought I might do . . .'

'Well, perhaps we could meet up then. If you want to.'

'Yes. Perhaps, although I'm not even that sure if I'll be going at all. The whole thing's probably completely pointless.'

'You'll let me know though?'

'Yes.' We had reached the foot of the stairs leading back to the car. I stopped. 'I can't do it,' I said. 'I just can't.'

'What?'

'Take this thing off the beach.' I fished in my pocket and brought out my pebble, watched it roll in the palm of my hand. 'I'll leave it here,' I said, placing it carefully next to one of the supporting struts.

'Nobody's waiting to arrest you in the car park you know,' Peter said, laughing a little.

'I know. It's not that . . .'

'Suppose I'd better do the same . . .' He knelt down and made a careful line of our stones, arranging them in order of size. 'There. Now we're both in the clear.'

'It's where they belong,' I said.

10 *The Empty Room*

I

Our cat died towards the end of winter. It was my mother who discovered him, curled nose to rigid tail behind the sofa. She placed him in a cardboard box on the kitchen table and sat for a long time staring at him without moving or speaking.

'We should bury him,' my father said. 'I'll dig a hole for him in the garden.'

My mother shot him a ferocious look as if this suggestion – so casually, so heartlessly uttered – made my father somehow responsible for the death itself.

'He was so old,' she said. 'He was with us for so *long*.' Standing there, looking down at his familiar shape, I thought I understood something of her disbelief. It was the sense that the animal's longevity – far from explaining his death – should have qualified him for immortality. He had been a part of the family for as long as I could remember, and this fact alone seemed to make an outrage of his passing.

'We could plant something nice on the grave,' my father persisted. 'Forsythia perhaps . . .'

'Leave him be,' my mother cried. 'Just let him be, can't you?'

But of course we did bury him; my father bearing down dutifully on the spade through the winter-hardened earth, my mother standing mutely beside him, the box in her arms. They planted a shrub of some sort on the site. It never flourished, being of the kind that slugs find irresistible. Nothing, it seemed, could stop the pests' onslaught, although my mother tried with pellets and protective netting. She became convinced that the creatures were migrating – through sheer desperation – from the barren stretches of Ivy's garden, and took to flinging them, with increasing fury, over the fence that separated our two properties.

One night I woke to see the beam of a torch darting and bobbing through the darkness of the garden. I stood on the step in my nightdress and called out to her, my voice very small, uncertain. It was a long time before she came, her dressing-gown half hanging off her shoulders, her bare feet covered in mud. 'Those *fuckers*,' she cried. 'Those *fuckers*.' She wasn't talking to me. I wasn't sure in that moment, that she even knew my name, or where this place was that she suddenly found herself.

'It's all right,' I said. 'It's all right, it doesn't matter.'

'There's too many. I can't get them all. It's not . . . it's not . . .' she stopped herself abruptly.

The light was off in my parents' bedroom and I couldn't tell if my father was asleep or whether he was simply lying there, in the darkness, listening to her curse. I went to the sink and filled the washing-up bowl with warm water, adding a squirt of Fairy Liquid as an afterthought. The bowl was heavy, but she made no attempt to help me, standing numbly in the kitchen, not speaking any longer, but allowing me to lead her to a chair and then, still silent, watching as I washed her feet, very carefully, with fingers made soft by sorrow and love's brief grace.

II

The siren woke me. A sudden, single wail, so loud it seemed, in my confusion, to be coming from underneath the bed itself, or closer still, from some shrieking corner of my own head. I was up and on my feet even before it had fully died away and with its passing, I heard other noises; the sound of many vehicles in the street outside, voices, a gate banging once and then again, somewhere close to the house.

I looked outside, pulling aside the curtain carefully, almost tentatively. A sunny day, very bright. I could see each grimy stripe of the mattress leaning up against the upper window of the opposite house, the lines of the chimneys beyond, clear as drawings in a colouring book. My window had not been opened in a long time, but it came up easily enough and I leaned out, feeling the cool air on my neck and chest through the thin cotton of my nightdress. There was an ambulance parked further down the street. I twisted slightly. Two police cars and men standing there, one of them my father. With his back to Julia's neatly trimmed hedge, saying something, his head shaking. And on the street and standing on their front steps, the figures of neighbours, transfixed, uncertain, their hands clutching at the openings of dressing-gowns or flickering, with helpless gestures, toward throat and mouth as they watched.

Behind me, footsteps coming up the stairs and then my mother standing at the door. A coat thrown carelessly over her pyjamas, feet bare inside her unlaced shoes. I turned to her. 'What time is it?' I asked, bewildered. 'Is it early?'

Her long arms hung motionless by her side. 'Come here,' she said. 'You need to come with me.'

My father took my hand. 'It's Nancy,' he said. I sat beside him on the sofa, staring at his knees and his old shoes, the ones he had worn to dig the grave for our cat. His fingers tightened against mine as though they held something that threatened to escape him.

'She's dead,' he said. 'Last night.'

On the other side of the room, my mother paced. 'It's all right, Sophie,' she said, breathing heavily, 'it's all right to tell us now if you knew something.'

'Tell you what?'

'We've all been fourteen before, you know. It's not . . .'

'Stop it!' my father cried. 'For once in your goddamn . . .'

'How?' I asked.

He bent his head, pressing the thumb and forefinger of his right hand against his closed eyes. 'She wasn't in her room this morning and her mother came here to see if she could find her.'

'I didn't hear the bell,' I said stupidly.

'She was . . . very worried. I went with her down the road to see if Nancy was with Julia. She wasn't there, but then, we heard the crying, you see, and followed it.'

'For god's sake, tell her,' my mother said. 'She had a baby. In that shed of yours. On her own, poor thing. God knows what it must have been like.'

The words meant nothing to me. As senseless as hearing that Nancy had grown wings in the night and had flown off to join the birds in the trees.

'They think it came very early,' my father said, persisting with the absurdity. 'Before she . . . was showing a great deal. She must have gone to a lot of trouble to hide it. Sometimes with women . . .' He shot my mother a look, '. . . with girls that small, it doesn't show very much until the end.'

'Nancy's not *pregnant*,' I said. 'Ask Julia.'

They stared at me in silence, my father's hand still covering mine, but softer now, as if he had forgotten it was there, my mother stony-faced and motionless. 'Did Julia . . . did Julia *see*?'

My father drew in his breath as though recalling the scene. Julia already inside the shed, the three adults at the door. Not much light in there, but enough to see the slick grey twists of the umbilical cord, the girl, blue-lipped, head tilted towards the grimy window. Flat eyes, still wide, mirroring the dawn. She had the hem of her nightdress in a tight grip, the folds bunched up around her waist as if to show – to clearly demonstrate – how thick and dark the blood was that covered the whole of her lower body. There was more blood on the cheap rug and wooden floorboards surrounding the sofa where she lay. So much that there could be no cleaning of it. Only the razing of the shed itself would obliterate the stains, remove that rich, damp, dreadful smell that filled the small space.

'I'm afraid so. She came out with us. I should have known she would. I should have stopped her.'

'Where is she?'

He shook his head. 'They'll want to ask you questions,' he said, very gently. 'The police and . . . other people. To try and find out what happened. To find out why she didn't tell anyone. But I want you to know, Sophie, that nobody will talk to you until you're ready. I'm going to make sure of that. Only when you're ready. Do you understand?'

'I didn't know,' I said. 'I didn't know.'

'It seems that nobody did.'

'I thought she was looking strange,' my mother said fiercely. 'I thought she was. I said something to you about it.' My father shot her a baffled look. 'No,' she said, 'no, I thought of telling you, but I didn't.'

'Margaret –'

'I only thought of it.' She started to cry then, standing there, fists clenched. I could not remember seeing her cry before, and certainly never like this, with such grunting, violent abandon. My father grimaced slightly and looked away.

'Nobody dies in childbirth any more,' my mother said, still shaking. 'Like . . . like some kind of *animal*.'

'What about the baby?' I whispered.

'It's in the hospital,' he said. 'I don't know. It doesn't look . . .'

'What will happen?' I cried. 'What will happen?'

'This is a lot for you to take in,' my father said, either unwilling or unable to answer my question. 'I know that. But I want to tell you that nobody imagines for a moment that this is in any way your fault. And I don't want you to ever think it. Because it isn't.' He put his arm around me and drew me tight towards his chest as if to smother all denial. And I let him hold me, my body stiff, feeling nothing but the collar of his shirt against my cheek, my own arms useless in my lap.

The ambulance was gone and the police cars too. Everyone, it seemed, had been taken away. My father had left the house on some pressing errand, my mother, dressed and calm at last, was downstairs, talking on the phone. I sat on my bed, listening to the empty street. Every so often, a car passed by. Ordinary cars, with drivers who knew nothing of what had happened, on their way to places that were not here. There was nothing for me to do but remain there, in a state of misery so profound, so much a part of me already within the passage of a single hour, that it seemed carried on the tide of my own slow breath.

My mother had made me tea, carrying it up and placing it with elaborate care on the table by the bed. The police would be at the house soon, with their questions and their blank, watchful faces. At the thought, the skin on my neck burned, the heat lapping at my chin and rising to cover my cheeks. I went to the dressing table and stared into the mirror but my face was unchanged, neither flushed nor particularly pale. I picked absently at the wood of the table, noticing the way the tiny crevasses of the grain had become filled over time with lines of dirt and marvelling that I was still capable of observing such things. My eyes still pointlessly recording items of no significance whatsoever. And there seemed to me something wounding in this, a kind of indignity. As if I was no more than a collection of functions, helplessly obliged to continue operating no matter what the circumstances. Like fingernails, I thought, that carry on growing for a while, even after a person was dead . . .

Nancy bit her nails so far down, it made you almost wince to look at them. She bit the skin around them too, worrying at the splintered strands until they bled. I knew she was dead. I knew it because my parents had told me and their words had made it true. But I put my shoes on anyway and my navy school uniform cardigan lying over the back of the chair where I had left it the night before. I went downstairs and out of the house, walking carefully, so that my mother – still barricaded behind the closed door of the sitting room – wouldn't hear me.

The curtains were drawn at Nancy's house. It didn't occur to me to ring the bell. I knew, without even having to think about it that the house was empty. The front door had not been properly fastened and it opened at my touch and I entered without hesitation, given strange confidence from the certainty that it was for the very last time.

I went up the stairs and across the landing, with its shabby beige carpet and glass-fronted cabinet that held Mrs Packenham's small collection of knick-knacks. They were the kind of things adults collected: little china boxes with nothing inside them, old-looking cups and saucers, a couple of glass perfume bottles and right at the back, a child's thumb pot with a crooked lip and fingerprints stuck in the glaze . . .

At the door to Nancy's room I paused for a second then stepped inside.

If I had been expecting to see something there – some sign of disturbance, some evidence of torment – I was disappointed.

The room was exactly the same as it always was: quite tidy, her possessions carefully arranged, each in its chosen place. Nevertheless, as I stood there, I was struck by a thought that had never occurred to me before. I had been in that room a hundred times. I had lain on the bed, on the floor, sat at the desk, touched at one time or another almost every item there. But I had never noticed, until now, that in shape, size and position, it was exactly the same as my own room; that our two houses were, in fact, identical in layout. The same architect must have designed them, I thought, or perhaps it was simply that there was a standard building pattern to all houses of that time and place and kind.

Her bed had been slept in. The covers had been pulled back at one side. Not violently so, but enough to see the sheets beneath. How many feet had separated us as we lay in sleep? Fifteen or so to the wall, then the short width of the alley between Ivy's house and this one. The space taken up by Ivy's stairs and bedroom – forty or fifty feet, the stairs in my own house, the seven or eight feet to my own bed. How wide were the walls themselves? A foot?

It can't have been much more than seventy or eighty feet in total, I thought. Perhaps less. Narrow enough that we might, if nothing had been in the way, have sat in our own beds and been able to hurl a ball back and forth between us. And yet I had heard nothing, had known nothing.

I reached out my hand and touched the space where she had lain, seeing her there for a second, curled on one side, her hands on her belly. I knew what pregnant women looked like but it was impossible to reconcile this image with the Nancy I remembered. Impossible to comprehend what it must have felt like, the depth of the pain. She had had sex with someone. A man. Not just kissing and groping – those activities discussed at such great length in *Jackie* magazine – but the whole, inconceivable act. How could it have happened to her? Nancy, in her Jesus Creepers, who had never shown any interest in discussing boys, who had sat there in bored detachment while Julia and I giggled about erections. The same Nancy who did not know what the word 'lesbian' meant or why anyone should laugh at the mere mention of the number sixty-nine.

I could barely absorb the fact of these questions, let alone answer them. But the fear she must have felt was something I understood. Standing there by the bed, I felt it nudge against me, a panic-barbed weight in my loins, a sweaty prickling of my skin. The concealment too did not surprise me. How astonished my father had seemed when he had spoken of it. But I knew that kind of shame, had felt it many times in small ways; the kind that grew and fed upon itself, mortified by its very existence. It was the fact of the shame one feared revealing, that one would do anything to hide.

Concealment would have been my first instinct too. But I would never have succeeded. Sheer terror would have brought me quickly to confession. She was stronger than I was, I thought, a hundred times more implacable. What quality of will, what desperate determination could have dragged her from this bed, bent double, stifling the sounds of her pain, when help was only a single cry away?

In the hours and days to come, reasons would be suggested for her action that night. It would be all that anyone in the street talked about for weeks. She had panicked. She had been too traumatised to think clearly. She had been seeking help, but had somehow lost her way and then been overcome by the violence of giving birth. Miss Pemble hinted darkly at abduction, others who had always mistaken her outsider manner for simple-mindedness, wondered whether she had merely been ignorant of what was happening to her own body.

Even Julia, who, when we finally met later that day, would instantly clutch me in a storm of weeping, believed that Nancy's judgement had been altered by the horror of her situation. There could be no other explanation, it not being in her nature to imagine how anyone in their right mind could be so lost to all good sense.

But I knew that none of these things were the truth, although some of them may have played a part in what happened. That morning, in her room I knew the reason she had done what she did. I never told anyone about it; not the police nor any of the other officials who came to question me until my father made them stop. No doubt they thought I was hiding something, that I had some prior knowledge. I could see it in their faces, the edge of exasperation behind their show of patience. Was there an element of scorn to the incredulity they made so little effort to hide? I thought so at the time and it silenced me.

I could not tell them she had done it because she was a person who thought she held the fate of universes between each blink of her eyelids. Who believed that somewhere in Wales there lived an old gardener who was once the greatest war poet in the world. They would not have understood.

I went over to the small table that served as her desk and sat down in the chair where she did her homework. The space was as neatly organized as everything else in her room. Three or four textbooks in a tidy pile, a chipped mug holding her pens and pencils, a folder of schoolwork lying open. The first line of an essay she had been writing.

The invention of the Spinning Jenny changed everything.

History, I thought. I had done the Industrial Revolution at my school only last term. How typical of Nancy it was, that single sentence. I imagined her coming to the last word, hesitating for a moment as she considered the complexities and then brushing all aside with that impulsive, sweeping *every-thing*. My fingers flickered briefly over the page, touching the words. In the moment of writing them, she had still been safe, I thought. There had still been time for her to find help. And time for me also. To see what I should have seen.

It hardly seemed possible that I could have been so oblivious, could have failed so utterly. And behind this, a deeper disbelief: that what had happened to Nancy could have occurred at all, quite independent of my involvement. That I too was part of that great indifference that made it possible for a person to run through the whole of the rest of her life while elsewhere, others went about their ordinary business, thinking of nothing but what to eat for lunch or how their new shoes pinched.

For a long time I sat there, possessed by the sense – quite new to me then, but afterwards never to entirely leave – of my own irrelevance in the world. I was not the person who made things happen, or to whom things happened, but instead one of the extras, placed to fill out a crowd, always crossing the street in the other direction or hurrying facelessly to catch a train, obligingly gaping at the action when required, at other times invisible. Of no more consequence, I thought, than the neighbours that morning, who had stood out in the street, staring until there was nothing more to see.

The invention of the Spinning Jenny changed everything.

How easy it was, I thought, to see the significance of something after the event. All the confusion and distraction of life, all the false alarms and excitements and subtleties, in time made clear enough for summary in a two-page essay. They would assume, the people who questioned me, that I knew more than I thought I did. And they were right. I knew the one thing they seemed most anxious to find out.

'It was Christopher,' I said, with the conviction of a person who only realizes the truth of what they are saying in the moment of utterance.

'Christopher?'

'It must have been,' I said. 'She had this thing about . . . she had this postcard.' I stopped, looked at them helplessly.

'He said he wanted to join the army,' I told them.

11 *Wilfred Owen*

I

I took the bus into London. Not one of Peter's double-deckers, but an ordinary coach. I had decided not to think about the weekend ahead; my reasons for being there, what I would or would not do, but instead concentrate only on my immediate surroundings. The dark fields unrolling beyond the window, the fabric of my seat – grey plush speckled with maroon darts – the back of the driver's head.

We arrived at Marble Arch in the early evening, never my favourite time of day. There seemed something a little defeated about the light, the people trudging home, with their heads down. I walked fast through the crowds, battling my gloom, the strap of my overnight bag already digging painfully into my shoulder. I always packed too much, I thought. Clothes and shoes for all those potential situations that never actually occurred . . .

I'd arranged to meet my mother in an upmarket pizza restaurant in Soho. She often chose such places when she took me out to dinner. It was usually pizza, or fancy hamburgers or large, cheese-laden burritos. Perhaps she had a sense that she should present me with the kind of food a child would enjoy. Or maybe this was what she preferred herself. Now I came to think of it, there had always been something rather half-hearted about her forays into gourmet cooking.

It certainly wasn't because she couldn't afford more expensive restaurants. The fact that she had grown wealthy had never really surprised me. Along with her artistic aspirations, money had always been a driving force in my mother's life, although for several years following the divorce she had struggled financially, still taking portraits of small children and barely making enough to pay the mortgage.

I was at college when she made her breakthrough. A three-year-old boy came into the studio with his aunt to have his picture taken. My mother said he was the ugliest child she had ever clapped eyes on. Fat-faced, thin of hair and with an expression of ferocious disgruntlement that apparently nothing could alter. My mother tried everything. The satin cushion, the backdrop with balloons, the jaunty sailor suit. 'It was like trying to cram a warthog into a tutu,' she said. 'His awful aunt standing there the whole time waving bars of chocolate at him and grinning.'

Finally, in desperation, she had stuck him – rather roughly I imagine – into a large, containing armchair and snapped him in the split second before he opened his mouth to howl. The result surprised everyone. With his jowly face and his head thrust forward in protest, the child looked extraordinarily like Winston Churchill, an effect that seemed to utterly charm his aunt. It was only a small step to provide a cigar – plastic of course, but remarkably life-like – to complete the picture. From this unlikely beginning, my mother came up with the idea of photographing all her subjects as famous characters.

Napoleon was easy. Shakespeare required little more than a small pair of hose and a feather quill, and once she had overcome the challenges of having a Shetland pony in the studio, the creation of Lady Godiva was simplicity itself. Infant versions of Elvis, Joan of Arc, William Tell and Mohammed Ali quickly followed.

My mother's pictures were hugely successful. She had recognized that every parent secretly considers – however fleetingly – that their children are destined for greatness. And she paid attention to detail. Her sets became more lavish and expensive. She hired staff and began to create whole scenes based on famous paintings. Little girls became Pre-Raphaelite maidens and Spanish infantas. Boys strutted in silks, their hands resting on Gainsborough hounds. A glossy coffee-table book of her portraits was published and then greeting cards. Suddenly the images were everywhere. People found them adorable.

I quite liked them myself and always kept a selection of the cards in the shop. I thought they were clever and rather appealing in a sentimental sort of way, but I kept this opinion from my mother, whom I knew regarded them with more than a little scorn. It would have been another reminder to her of how completely I had been bypassed by the gene for good taste. It was telling, I thought, that none of her children's portraits were displayed in her own home, a huge, elegantly decorated house in Highgate. But she was rich and seemed happy enough from what I could tell.

She was already seated when I arrived, and I apologized for being late, even though it was she who was early. She lifted her face so that I could kiss her cheek. 'You're looking well,' she said.

'You too.' It always surprised me how little she changed from year to year. She had never fallen into the trap of having her hair cropped short like so many women in their late fifties, but kept it in a style – cut to a point below the nape of her neck and swept rather luxuriously off her face – that suggested she was a woman who was still proud of her looks. And she had, I thought, the kind of body that aged well; neither boyish nor overly feminine. The years had thickened her slightly, but she was still strong-looking, still a head-turner in her dark, beautifully cut trouser-suit and silk purple scarf.

She half rose from her seat to finger the sleeve of my shirt. 'That's nice,' she said. 'I like that.'

'Hennes,' I said.

'Really?' she said, sounding as amazed as if I'd told her I'd retrieved the thing from a skip. 'Where are the menus?' She glanced across the table. 'I can't possibly order anything until I've had a stiff drink.'

'Bad day?'

'Not really.'

As usual, with my mother, I found myself at the limits of my conversational abilities almost before I'd sat down. 'It's nice to see you,' I said finally. 'It's been ages.

'I've been really, really busy,' I added quickly, in case she thought I was reproaching her.

'That's good,' she said, her eyes roaming the restaurant in search of our waiter. 'How's Lucien?'

'Fine.' I paused. 'We've split up actually.'

'Oh.' She made a face. 'Well . . .'

'I'm okay about it. It wasn't really going anywhere.'

'No,' she said. 'To be honest, I always had that impression myself. Nice enough in his own way of course, but still, not really good . . .'

'I'm fine about it, Mum, honestly,' I said hurriedly, thereby saving her from completing the phrase 'good enough for you' which on her lips would have had a certain awkwardness, being just the kind of standard, motherly response which she felt the situation required, but which she did not necessarily believe.

'How's your father?' she said, changing the subject.

I smiled. My father was very well. In fact, he was better than well. He was living in retirement in rural Ireland, with a friendly woman fifteen years younger than him and three large dogs.

'Oh you know,' I said vaguely. 'Pottering around as usual. I talked to him not long ago on the phone. Megan wants to get a couple of sheep.'

'Sheep?'

'You know, she's a textile artist. For the wool.'

'Oh yes, I forgot about the weaving thing . . .'

Having run through her standard questions, my mother fell into a momentary silence. It always amused me slightly how her first instinct was to ask about the men in my life, seeing as how she herself had been resolutely single for years. After she and my father had gone their separate ways, she had seemingly lost what little enthusiasm she had once had for partnership of any sort. If she ever had affairs, she never discussed them with me and I doubted that she bothered with sex very much. Perhaps that dismal – and brief – encounter with George Collins had put her off for life, but I think it was more that she was that rare person who did not need the company of others for her happiness.

'How's work?' I asked.

She was putting together a large group shot, she told me; a reconstruction of one of Picasso's Blue Period masterpieces. 'You have no idea how hard it is to find *thin* children,' she complained. 'Kids are terribly fat these days. Women stuff themselves during pregnancy, give birth to ten- or eleven-pound babies and by the time they're five, the kids weigh as much as small hippos. I was so careful what I ate when I was pregnant with you. I barely gained fifteen pounds the entire time.'

I decided to let this comment pass.

'I can hardly advertise for kids with eating disorders can I?' my mother continued. 'I mean, that wouldn't be ethical, would it? But where else am I going to find a bunch of anorexics?'

'Perhaps Rubens is more the way to go.'

'Yes, but then you're talking nakedness. It's only a matter of time before someone starts screaming kiddie porn. There's a very, *very* fine line.'

'I've got problems too.' I told her about the shop, how I expected to be out of work in a matter of a month or two. She was instantly furious, as I knew she would be. 'That woman!' she exclaimed, referring to Andrea. 'I never liked the sound of her. Totally vulgar, I always thought. Isn't she married to some crook?'

'A blackjack player,' I said. 'And they're not married anymore.'

My mother snorted, as if this was sheer irrelevance. 'What do you expect from people like that?' She looked at me sharply. 'So what are your plans?'

'I don't have any,' I said, trying to sound light. 'Completely blank at the moment.'

She narrowed her eyes. 'I think,' she said, 'that this calls for champagne.'

I wondered for a second whether she was joking, but she was already gesturing for the waiter. 'I've always thought it odd,' she said, 'that people drink champagne to celebrate something, when really it should be the other way around. It should only be drunk when one is in direst need of cheering up. Don't you think?'

'I suppose so,' I said, both disconcerted and heartened by the ease with which she had seen through my air of nonchalance. *There is something about you that is quite skinless.* Peter was right, I thought. How quickly he had come to know me.

'The Moët, I think,' my mother told the waiter. 'And could you find out what's happened to our pizzas? They seem to be taking a dreadfully long time.' The waiter, who looked very young and nervous, scurried off without a word, no doubt further abashed by my mother's grand manner.

'I do think,' my mother said, 'that not knowing what to do next, being at one's wit's end if you like, can be a very good place to be.

'Interesting at least,' she added, noting my look of doubt. 'I mean, that's when things happen isn't it? That's the only time that real change can happen. When you don't know how you're going to put one foot in front of the other, let alone what to do with the rest of your life.'

'I think it only seems that way afterwards,' I said. 'When you've got through to the other side.'

'Let's drink to it then. The Other Side.' We clinked our glasses, smiling a little at each other. I couldn't remember the last time I had felt this connection with her, this moment – however small – of camaraderie. She must have felt it too, for she leaned towards me suddenly.

'I've actually been at a crossroads of sorts myself. Started working on something else. Well, I've been working on it for a while now but . . .' she gestured, rather tentatively, in the air. 'It's not commercial. Not at all. It's a departure really.'

I had rarely heard my mother sounding unsure of herself in this way. I waited, not quite knowing what to say.

'Pictures of dancers. There's this small group. You probably wouldn't have heard of them. But they're extraordinary. I've been recording them. Very simple images, very strong. Nothing high-tech. I've become interested in things that . . . bear some sign of the maker's hand. It's old fashioned, I suppose . . .'

'It sounds really, really good.'

She looked at me suddenly. 'You know, it's more along the lines of what I always wanted to do before . . . well, before a lot of things.'

I nodded. She was leaning forward slightly, elbows resting on the table, one finger rubbing against her forehead in the manner of someone momentarily cornered by their own thoughts. I had always liked my mother's hands. They were large and worn-looking, with a roughness to the nails; the hands of a person who could cut a straight line with a pair of scissors, who knew how to make things.

'I bet your pictures are wonderful,' I said.

'No. But maybe they will be. Maybe . . .'

The waiter came with our food, arranging the plates with flustered, uncertain gestures. I smiled at him encouragingly. 'This looks lovely!' I told him, as though he had cooked our meal himself.

'By the way,' my mother said, fishing through her handbag. 'I was going through some old boxes the other day and came across this. I thought you'd be interested.' She unfolded part of a page of newspaper and handed it to me.

The Cambridge Evening News. It was a photograph – grainy, yellowed by age – of the three of us, sitting on the bank of the river, our trousers rolled up to the knees, our feet covered in mud. Julia was in the middle, waggling her filthy toes at the camera, Nancy and I grinning self-consciously on either side. *Stranded!* ran the headline below. *Weir repairs put paddlers in a big mud-dle.* The rest of the article had been torn away, but I remembered that it had been about the temporary lowering of the water level along that stretch of the river.

I remembered too my feelings of outrage when the picture had first appeared. We had not been paddling in the river when the photographer had approached us. We had simply been sitting there on the bank, aimless as ever, talking about something or other that we had no doubt already discussed a dozen times already. In those days we were experts in the art of telling and retelling, of coating small events with endless layers of significance. It was the photographer's idea to shoot us with our feet in the mud and we had been happy to oblige, imagining that we were sharing in the joke. But the heading under the picture made the action seem quite different. As if we were mere children, I thought. Too foolish – or too set on our game – to notice that the weir was dry and the river half empty. And the fact that we had been tricked in this way only made me feel more foolish still.

'That must have been taken when you were about fourteen,' my mother said. 'Sometime during that summer . . .'

'I think so. Yes.'

My mother cut into her pizza. 'Julia's done very well for herself,' she commented.

'Yes.'

'I must say, I never thought that girl would amount to anything. Just shows how wrong you can be. Aren't you going to eat?'

I was still staring at the newspaper cutting, at the jumper I was wearing that day, a jumble-sale find. I'd forgotten about the jumble sales at St Luke's. How fiercely the three of us jostled among a tide of old ladies with their handbags that dug into our sides and beat against our backs. We used to joke about those bags, imagining them being loaded up with bricks in preparation for battle. We always looked for the same thing at the sales: men's V-neck jumpers from Marks and Spencer's, large enough to reach almost to our knees. Garments to shelter us, to hide ourselves within . . .

'It must have been around May,' I said. 'That was a warm spring we had that year.'

My mother put down her knife and fork. 'You'd never know from looking at this picture, would you,' I said slowly. 'What was going to happen.'

'Nobody knew,' my mother said. 'Either then . . . or later.' She paused. 'I blamed myself for it, you know. I think we all did to some extent. That whole street.'

I nodded. 'I still think about her,' I admitted, 'perhaps more than I should.'

'That was a bad time,' my mother continued, as if I hadn't spoken. 'I don't like to remember it. You know, usually time takes you forward, but back then . . . it's hard to describe. It seemed to go in the other direction for a while. Everything somehow *unravelled* itself.'

I looked at her, knowing that this was the closest she would ever come to discussing the past; this brief statement, uttered in a moment of uncharacteristic self-exposure, perhaps never to be repeated.

'Well,' she said. 'We should get on and eat.'

'You can keep that,' she added, pointing to the cutting. 'I brought it for you.'

'It was really nice of you,' I said. 'I'll make a copy of it if you like and give it back.'

'God no. I've got enough stuff piling up. Why would I want to keep it anyway?'

I watched her as she ate, wondering at her utter lack of sentimentality, her inability to understand how a mother might want to keep an old photograph of her only daughter. When I was fourteen, it was common among my friends to be ashamed of our parents. But I had never felt embarrassed by mother. It was, I always felt, the other way around.

I used to think it was because I didn't look right. Always by my side, at the age of fourteen, was the ghost of the daughter my mother should have had. Tall, not prone to fat, with hair that grew away from her forehead rather than clung, limp as wet seaweed, to the sides of her face. Someone who never had to be told that florals didn't go with checks . . .

But would it really have been any different if I'd been someone else?

She paused, wiped her mouth with her napkin, took a sip

of champagne, gave me a brief, abstract smile, quite unaware she'd said anything of particular significance. And I wondered – quite suddenly and piercingly – how often it happens that a daughter takes on the burden of what her mother lacks. How long she carries it before she sees that it doesn't belong to her.

'Aren't you hungry?'

I shook my head. 'It looks really good though. I'm sorry.'

'I didn't think I'd eat it all but look at me. Everything goes to the waistline when you get to a certain age . . .'

'You look great, Mum,' I said. 'It's the first thing I thought, when I walked in.'

The waiter cleared our plates. It was almost time to go. She wanted to know whether I was driving back to Oxford that evening and I told her I was staying at a friend's house for the weekend.

'Anyone I know?'

'Sarah,' I said, then, seeing her blank look, 'you know Sarah. I was at college with her.'

'Oh yes . . .'

'Her flat's in Islington. She's not there at the moment. She's in France. I sometimes stay there when she's away. She gave me the keys years ago.'

'Well, if the place is *empty* . . .'

'It's okay, Mum. Honestly.'

'You can always stay with me, you know,' she said, a touch hesitantly. 'I was just thinking only the other day that it's been a long time since you came.' She leaned forward and patted my hand, briefly, rather tentative.

'It's kind of you,' I said awkwardly. 'Perhaps next time.'

She paid the bill and we stood and gathered up our coats. On the way out, she paused by the large mirror in the lobby to adjust her hair and straighten her collar. While her hands were busy, I leaned towards her and kissed her cheek. 'Thanks for dinner.' She half turned towards me.

'But you didn't eat anything.'

'I'm fine.'

'About your job,' she said. 'If you get, well, stuck or anything, if it's a question of money . . . you'll ask me, won't you?'

I didn't say anything. Just kissed her again, once, very quickly, and left her there, arranging the folds of her scarf to hide the deep lines in her neck, frowning slightly in concentration at the task.

II

I woke late the next morning and lay motionless for a while in the stillness of the empty apartment, watching the light making unfamiliar patterns across the ceiling and wondering how I should fill the day ahead. I was glad that I was alone; that there would be no witnesses to my vacillation; no one to dilute – with their talk, their questions, their very presence – my sense of private undertaking. With a companion I would have found myself explaining the situation, there would be discussion, and the essence of the thing would be revealed, fixing my course. As it was, I had no idea whether I would keep the meeting, made so casually, so long ago and now only a few hours away, or whether I would finally decide against it; commonsense giving an idiot's voice to the murmuring of my hope. I didn't even know, when the moment came, how I would make the decision at all. And while all this remained unclear, it seemed that anything might still be possible.

I drank my coffee standing by the sink, then washed the cup out carefully, dried it and put it back in the cupboard. I wasn't hungry and besides, there was nothing to eat in the place, my friend having cleared the fridge before leaving for her trip. I walked around her flat for a while, noting the additions, the items she had moved from one place to another, then gathered up my coat and bag and went outside. It was in my mind to catch a bus into town. Some breakfast in a café, a little shopping, perhaps a gallery visit or a film in the afternoon. Packaged up in this way, the hours ahead seemed manageable, almost pleasant.

But I did hardly any of these things. I was twenty yards or so away from the stop on Upper Street when the bus overtook me, discharged a single passenger and then moved on. I knew I could have easily caught it. A short dash forward was all it would have taken. But I found my feet slowing. I told myself it was too far away, that I would catch the one following and that the best way to pass the waiting time would be to continue down the street to the next stop.

It wasn't until I had passed two more stops that I acknowledged that I had no intention of getting the bus at all. Instead it felt enough to be simply walking, with no particular goal or direction other than to follow the route of the bus for as long as it was clear to me.

It was a good day for walking; mild, windless and overcast; the light doing nothing to distract the eye, but giving the city a flat, businesslike aspect, one building much the same as another. I walked a touch self-consciously at first, surprised at myself, wondering whether I was being absurd, then settled into a steady rhythm, my mind drifting.

I abandoned the bus route after half an hour or so and soon found myself in unfamiliar streets. I didn't know London well and had no map but these facts seemed of little importance. The desire to lose myself, to turn away from all known landmarks, grew upon me as I walked. I stopped to eat in a café somewhere in the City, then carried on, a mile, two miles. I

walked with my head down, noting nothing more of my surroundings than the patterns on the pavement, whether a
particular street was residential or given over to office buildings.

I didn't look at my watch, knowing that hours were passing,
my legs still untired, my mind calm. I thought that this was
how a person might walk across continents; the vast land
measured by their own stride, the ocean nothing but a distant
theory . . .

My right heel began to rub painfully sometime in the early
afternoon and I stopped at a chemist's for plasters. I sat down
on the edge of the pavement to remove my sock and patch
the blister, feeling as little embarrassment as a hiker pausing
on a remote hillside, then carried on across some nameless
bridge, momentarily astonished by the sudden expanse of
river, the traffic a thundering blur beside me.

I thought of Julia, Nancy and I and the last time we were
all together, which, if the dead can ever be said to be present,
was the day of Nancy's funeral when we sat there in the
church with her coffin beside us. They came easily to me, the
details of that day; memory running steady beside my pace,
given freedom by that most ordinary of things: the placing of
one foot after another.

There was barely room to move in the church. I remember
being surprised by this, at the sheer number of people who
had come. They packed the seats and stood two or three deep
at the back, with latecomers obliged to remain half in, half
out of the open doorway. I didn't know who most of these
people were or where they had come from. I sat with my
father on one side and Julia on the other and watched the
church fill up. Cousins had come. I had not known she had
so many. A grandmother, three uncles, a dark-haired woman
who stood at Mrs Packenham's side and held her hand. Friends

of the family, four or five girls wearing the uniform of Nancy's school, snuffling and wiping their eyes even before the service got under way.

'That's her English teacher,' Julia whispered, as well-informed as always. 'And her doctor. I think a couple of nurses from the hospital came too.'

'How do you know?'

'My mum told me. Seems like half her class turned up,' she added, giving the huddle of girls a scornful glance. 'Bet they're the same ones who always ignored her, the cows. Look at them. Little drama queens . . .'

But I couldn't reply, too frightened I think, by the sight of all these people. The whole weight of adult authority was there, the whole grave-faced, shuffling weight of adult helplessness. My hands trembled slightly in my lap. Julia leaned towards me and touched my fingers very lightly. 'Miss Pemble took her shoes off,' she said.

I looked towards the opposite pew where Miss Pemble sat. She seemed older suddenly, as if she had aged ten years in the space of a few days; a thin, yellow-faced woman in a shabby brown dress, sitting alone. Julia was right. The lace-ups had been replaced by a pair of black Mary-Janes; the kind that only old women wore; with a small heel and misshapen toes where the leather had been deformed by long years of wear. I wondered what she had thought about when she put them on that morning. Her funeral shoes.

My own shoes were new, as was my outfit, purchased from Eaden Lilleys only two days before. It was my mother's idea to take me shopping, there being nothing in my wardrobe quite right for the occasion. If the venture struck her as incongruous, she made no mention of it. Perhaps she thought it would provide some distraction for me. Or for her.

I let myself be taken without argument. Since the death,

I had become entirely passive. On the rare occasions that I spoke, it seemed to me that someone else moved my lips to form the words and someone else's legs carried me into town with my mother, and stood uncomplainingly in the changing room while she slipped various garments through the door for me to try. We bought a suit in a dark, tweedy material. It was tailored at the waist with a brown velvet collar and tight sleeves that puffed slightly at the shoulders. I thought it was horrible, but said nothing, it being someone else entirely who held this opinion, who stood there looking at her demure reflection in the changing-room mirror with silent loathing.

Almost the whole of Oakville Street seemed to be at the funeral, even the Spanish landlady who stood towards the back of the room with folded arms, a proud, almost defiant expression on her face. A couple of her lodgers were there too, having wandered in by mistake perhaps, or being simply in the mood for an outing, the church only a short totter from their customary berth.

And there was Ivy, making something of an entrance on arrival by leaning heavily on the arm of a helper and groaning repeatedly and very audibly while a seat could be found for her. I glanced quickly at her as she passed, at her doughy face, her resentful bulk. She was keeping a fierce hold on the sleeve of her companion and there was something about that grip of hers that made it impossible to tell whether she genuinely needed help, or wished – for as long as she possibly could – to prevent all chance of the other's escape. Perhaps, I thought, not even Ivy herself knew. If she had ever made a distinction between the two, it was long forgotten.

I caught her eye and looked quickly away. She would never die, I thought. No matter how old she got. She would live for ever, planted there on her sofa, her wide lap empty, her curtains drawn against all the cold summers and long, bone-damp winters to come.

During the entire time in the church, I could hear her, two rows behind me, sighing heavily and grunting as she shifted position. As if she was the injured party, I thought, the chief mourner. The one in need of solace and sympathy instead of Mrs Packenham up there in the front row, staring at the vicar giving the service with desperate fixity as if warding off some imminent cataclysm by the power of gaze alone.

'She'll be doped up to the eyeballs,' my mother had said, that morning. 'God knows how else she'd be able to get through the thing. I can't imagine what it's like to lose a child.'

I wasn't sure what a person actually looked like who was doped to the eyeballs but Mrs Packenham didn't seem at all the way I imagined it. She was not staggering or lurching, or even weeping, but remained quite silent and utterly still, while all around her people coughed and shifted and cast their eyes around. I thought perhaps that like me, she too had someone else who had taken over the running of her body for her. And the real Mrs Packenham, the one who had fretted so over a single cigarette and who had always been bewildered by finding nothing but coppers in her cancer research envelopes, had simply been put to bed somewhere very quiet and far away. All her jangling bracelets taken off and the sheet – folded over in a perfectly straight line – drawn up and carefully laid across her neck . . .

The vicar giving the service didn't know the family well, since Nancy and her mother had only attended the church on a few occasions, and it was clear from his speech that he was basing his comments on the small amount of information that Mrs Packenham had been able to give him before the funeral. He was a fairly young man, with an air of concentrated gravity, as if the requirements of his job that day were not things that came naturally to him, but could only be assembled by great thought and effort. He had been up until late last night, I thought. He had been working on what he was going to say.

'Nancy was a loving daughter,' he said. 'A gentle girl who loved poetry.'

I glanced sideways at Julia, wondering if she was thinking the same thing as I. Not poetry. It was a *poet* she had loved.

'Beauty mattered a great deal to Nancy,' the vicar continued. 'The beauty of words and the beauty of the natural world. Taking walks in the country was one of her favourite things to do . . .'

I didn't know what he was talking about. Nancy had never taken any walks that I knew of, had never expressed to me, at least, any particular affection for nature unless you counted her strange attachment to the Hating Tree. For a second or two, I felt a prickling of embarrassment on the vicar's behalf. He was doing his best, but he had got it wrong. And then I realized that he was not referring to the girl that I knew, but an earlier Nancy, the one that Mrs Packenham remembered.

We had not been asked to speak at her funeral, Julia and I. She did not belong to us any longer. She had been returned, in death, to another place. To some familiar footpath along the side of open fields where she ran full tilt against the wind, her mother walking far behind, watching the small, headlong figure of her child, keeping her in sight.

I started to cry quietly. My father must have thought it was the service that had moved me; that had finally broken my numb silence. He took my hand, not looking at me, keeping his gaze fixed ahead. My tears ran unwiped down my face and the church fractured around me but I knew that it would be back in place again when my weeping stopped. For the first time in my life, I cried in the way that adults do, who know that their grief changes nothing.

'What sense can we make of this tragedy, the cruel loss of this young life?' the vicar asked, coming at last to the meat of his presentation. He paused, narrowing his eyes, as if expecting that the answer to his own question might, despite everything, still miraculously occur to him.

'Whether you have religious faith or not,' he continued finally, his shoulders sagging slightly, 'the answer is not one that is easily found. We may, in fact, never find it . . .'

I wept on, aware in the midst of my tears that something had separated in me for ever, that hard as I cried, there would always be a part of me that did not weep, that remained at a distance, watching. I cried for Nancy and for myself, for the mysterious splitting of my own soul that made it possible, even as my body shook and the velvet collar of my suit grew mottled with tears, to register – quite coolly and effortlessly – the multitude of small sounds that now filled the church; the slight gasp my father made as he fought for composure, Julia's escalating sniffs, the ripple of sighs and half-broken coughs all around, the vicar's words rolling onwards.

'. . . We may never find it. But that should not discourage us from the task that has been given to us today. The task of searching, in Nancy's life and in her death, for meaning of our own. No life, however short, is wasted, no death so terrible that it can destroy what we have known and loved . . .'

Beside me, Julia gave a small moan, slumping forward and covering her face with both hands. The sobbing from the back of the church was more audible now, a mewling, stuttering sound, as first one mourner and then another gave way. Miss Pemble's back stiffened, one knuckled hand grasping the seat in front of her. Ivy groaned again, louder than before. Far up at the front, Mrs Packenham swayed once, gently as a feather turning on a breath, and then was still.

The vicar spoke on, but I was no longer listening. I sat

perfectly calm, dry-eyed at last, my eyes fixed on the coffin resting on a low wooden plinth at the front of the church.

Nancy would not be buried. Her mother would have her cremated, returning home with the small hoard of ashes safe in her keeping. I would never know where she chose to scatter them, not having the courage to ask her. At the time I thought she blamed me for Nancy's death, and after the funeral took to avoiding her as much as possible. I don't think I was the only one who felt this way. It became hard to see her as anything other than a living embodiment of misfortune, a reminder to everyone of their own failure, and so it was a relief when she moved away shortly afterwards.

I must have walked for fifteen miles, perhaps twenty, through a city that I had not seen. My stride had lost its buoyancy sometime after crossing the river again, and I moved woodenly, my feet sore, my legs aching. I tramped up the long curve of Regent Street, the pavements thick with people, the lights beginning to come on in the shop windows although it was barely four o'clock.

It was probably just as well that I hadn't been asked to speak at Nancy's funeral. I wouldn't have known what to say and the prospect of standing up in front of everyone in the church would have filled me with terror. But now I thought I knew what I would say. Not as a fourteen-year-old, but with the hindsight of all the years that had passed since then. A common enough fantasy; the impulse to frequent one's own past; infinitely wiser, braver and better informed than a thousand previous selves. But I allowed myself the indulgence, solemnly rehearsing the funeral speech I had not and could not have made.

I would tell it like a story, I thought. I would say, there were once three girls and their names were Sophie, Julia and Nancy.

And they lived in the borderland between one territory and another. They were all travelling – faster than they knew it – towards the high country up ahead, but all of them carried something of the place they had left behind. Three gifts of childhood not yet put aside. Sophie had a child's emotions, Julia, a child's body. But Nancy had the dreams of a child, the greatest gift of all . . .

My interior monologue was interrupted by a group of four or five men coming towards me, taking up the whole pavement. I had to step into the street to avoid them. They passed me by without seeming to notice my presence, talking amongst themselves, too confident in their number or wrapped up in their conversation to pay attention to their surroundings.

No, my story was not right at all, I thought abruptly. It was too meandering and annoyingly whimsical. I'd have lost the entire congregation before I got halfway through. I could imagine the baffled looks, the awkward shifting of bottoms on chairs. But how else, then, to explain what it was that I felt?

Perhaps it could be expressed by simply saying that Julia, Nancy and I – such different people, friends of circumstance, not choice – had, for a brief time, seemed to complete each other. And that when I lost Nancy, it felt as though I had lost a part of my very own self. Something of mine, left behind there in that coffin, scattered with her ashes in a place unknown to me . . .

I stopped at the entrance to Liberty's, hesitated for only a second, then went inside. I chose a white shirt with beautiful, unnecessarily long cuffs and a pair of black, light wool trousers. Expensive clothes that I couldn't afford. The sort of clothes my mother would have bought for me. I stood in the changing room listening to her voice telling me how the trousers made my legs look longer, her eyes squinting a fraction as they always did when examining something which met her approval. 'You see how that shirt makes your skin glow?' she asked me. 'Do you see how it reflects light on your face? You get what you pay for. I've always said that.'

'Yes, you have,' I said out loud, turning this way and that in order to look at myself from all angles. 'And in this case, I think you may be right.'

I took a cab back to Islington, too weary to face the crush of the underground or to wait for a bus. It was quite dark now, night already. I would hang up my new clothes when I got back to the flat, I thought, then take a bath and wash my hair. I would get dressed at the last possible moment to avoid creasing the pristine lines of my shirt and then go out again, walking with purpose, this time. With a destination.

All day I had wondered about the meeting, but now I knew that the decision was already made. It had been made for a long time, before my marathon walk, the getting on the bus to come to London, the half-hearted attempt to contact Julia. I had agreed to it sixteen years ago, lying in my bed, listening to the voices of my friends in the dark.

I leaned my head against the window of the cab, watching through half-closed eyes as the line of lights streamed past, the whole city that step by plodding step had taken a day's labour to unroll, now ravelling itself back again in a matter of moments.

I had believed at fourteen that I would keep the meeting. Faith was an easy matter then. But I still believed it. Believed in my presence there, the importance of that single moment. I would not see Julia, I felt almost certain of that. But I was glad that one of us at least would be in the appointed place at the appointed time. Nancy, I thought, would never have forgiven me if I had not come.

III

I calculated that I would need an hour to get to Trafalgar Square. But time had grown miser's hands; doling out the minutes in ones and twos as the train rattled from station to station. I was at Leicester Square before I knew it, emerging onto the street with at least twenty-five minutes to spare.

I set off, walking as slowly as I could. I didn't want to be early, to be standing there, waiting, while the remainder of the minutes passed. I would rather arrive slightly late. In lateness, I thought, would lie some measure of comfort; the small, far-fetched, but nevertheless real possibility that Julia and I had simply missed each other.

She would not be there, of course, either early or late. And that was another reason I took my time: to delay, for as long as possible, the confirmation of that fact. One can be convinced of something before one understands it as a truth and between one kind of knowing and another, there exists a slender gap; too narrow to be called hope, but wide enough for a person to breathe awhile and gather their thoughts.

The streets were crowded, people milling about the theatres or standing in expectant groups, bright-faced, chattering, their evening not yet done. I moved among them, side-stepping, apologetic, feeling truly alone for the first time in that long, solitary day. Further down, towards the dark entrance of the National Portrait Gallery, the crowds thinned out a little, and I glanced again at my watch. I was going to be far too early. No matter how slowly I walked.

I hadn't been to Trafalgar Square in a long time and it was smaller than I remembered. The lions, the slender rise of Nelson's Column, dwarfed by the noise and movement of traffic all around, still fairly heavy despite the lateness of the hour. There were more people gathered there than I thought there would be, although I didn't exactly know what I was expecting. It had been different when I was fourteen; when I had visualized this scene. The lions were vast then, the air breathless with the significance of the moment. And the three of us dramatic figures, alone in a deserted city.

I waited to cross the road, watching the cars, keeping my eyes averted from the people in the square. I didn't want to look. I didn't want to be standing there, looking for her, my eyes passing from one figure to another, foolish in my new clothes.

A space opened in the traffic and I darted forward mechanically, head down. So many people there. Ordinary people doing ordinary things. Another night like all the others, nothing remarkable or different about it . . .

She was standing with her back to me, in a long shearling coat and black, high-heeled boots. Her hair was changed; layered and blonder than I remembered. But I knew it was her. I stood stock still, my heart pounding.

'Julia?'

She turned, her face thinner, far more beautiful; differences that only strengthened the utter familiarity of those features. Her eyes widened.

'I don't *believe* it!' she cried, dashing forward.

I thought that we would kiss, in the normal way of friends, but even that suddenly seemed too formal, too passing a gesture. She flung her arms around me and I found myself standing there, with my cheek pressed so hard against hers that it made the bones of my face ache. She smelled of shampoo and cigarettes and of herself.

'I don't believe it,' she said again. 'Why on earth are you crying? Oh God, I'm crying too.'

She pulled away to wipe her eyes. 'I thought you wouldn't come,' I said.

'I called you! I didn't think you'd got the message and then I got that message from you at work . . .'

'When did you call?' I could not take my eyes off her. Up close, she had the same slightly scruffy appearance that I remembered. Her hair, thrust haphazardly behind her ears, her lightly tanned face free of make-up, the beginning of fine lines around her eyes. She did not have the kind of skin that aged particularly well, I thought. But with her, it would not matter a great deal. The carelessness of her appearance was half of her beauty.

'I called ages ago. Some woman answered. Seemed a bit dopey.'

'Oh that would have been Michaela,' I said.

'God, Sophie,' she said, seizing me again by the shoulders. 'You got so *pretty*.'

'Did I?'

'My mum always said you would turn out pretty. She was right.'

'How is your mother?' I said, slightly amazed that we could be talking in this ordinary way given the circumstances. We were both of us grinning so broadly it was hard to get the words out.

'I thought that I might not recognize you. I don't know how I could have thought that,' she said, shaking her head, staring at me in delight. 'Sorry, sorry, what were you saying?'

'Your mother . . .'

'In Papua New Guinea of all places. Helping to build a school. She joined VSO after my dad died. She said it would give her something to do. You know my mum, always wanting to look after everyone.'

'Oh Julia, your dad . . . I didn't know . . .'

'Yeah. Five years ago,' she said. 'Totally awful. Let's not talk about it. What about you? What have you been doing?'

'Nothing really. Well, not *nothing* . . . I love your stuff by the way. Your writing. I always knew you'd go off and do amazing things. Do you remember the séance we had?'

'Séance?'

'Don't you remember? You made the glass move. You made it say that you'd be famous.'

She gave a hoot of laughter. 'Sounds like something I'd do. I was such an evil little cow.'

'I can't believe you don't remember that,' I said.

She smiled, reached into her handbag. 'Do you want a cigarette?'

'I don't smoke.'

'Are you sure?' She shook the box gently in my direction.

'Well, okay . . .' And just like that, I knew that nothing had changed between us.

We stood with our backs to one of the lions and shared a light. The cigarette made my head spin slightly. 'So,' she said, inhaling pleasurably, 'Let's catch up. We've got so much to catch up on. Tell me stuff.'

'Well . . . like what?'

'You know, events. Are you married yet?'

'God no. Never anywhere near. You?'

'Married and divorced,' she said briskly. 'What a cock-up that was. He was in New York half the time. I should have known better marrying another reporter. It only lasted a couple of years.'

'Any children?' I asked, a little timidly.

She grimaced. 'No. That's another cock-up. I can't have kids. Just can't do it. You remember how everyone got their periods before me? You know, one by one and there I was, still waiting for the blessed event to occur?' She paused. 'I even had a special drawer with packets of tampons and towels at the ready. Well, it never happened. Not properly at least. Which makes conceiving a bit of a problem as you can imagine.'

'That's awful,' I said. I hadn't expected this; to feel sorry for her. Whatever I had imagined feeling on meeting Julia again, it was certainly not pity.

'Oh well,' she said, flicking the butt of her cigarette away and grinding the heel of her boot over the ember, 'as any number of well-meaning morons have told me, there's always adoption.'

'Suppose so.'

She gave me a look that I remembered well. The kind of look that told you, without any need for words, that though the world was full of idiots, you were not one of them; that you were, in fact, perhaps the only person alive who could understand just what it was she was talking about.

She was smiling again. 'I still can't get over it,' she said, 'you being here. It's so good to see you, Sophie.'

'You too. I really, really thought you'd have forgotten.'

'*You* didn't,' she pointed out.

'I know, but . . .'

'I wrote it down, the date. It took me ages to think of a place I could write it where it wouldn't get lost or thrown away. A notebook was no good and I didn't keep a diary or anything like that. I thought of writing it somewhere in the house, on a wall or something, but my mum was always painting everything over and anyway, what if we moved? In the end, I put it in the one place I was sure I wouldn't forget it.'

'Where was that?'

'On the inside lid of my suitcase. God, I was so desperate

to leave home. I kept that suitcase for ages, right through college and when I started work. I chucked it out in the end, but by that time, the date was kind of engraved in my mind.'

'I didn't need to write it down,' I confessed. 'It just stuck in my head. You know what I'm like . . .' I pulled my coat tighter around me, feeling cold for the first time. I should have worn a jumper, I thought. But I hadn't wanted to waste my new shirt by covering it up. 'Maybe we should, well, go and get a drink or something,' I suggested.

'No,' she said, in a tone that brooked no argument. 'Not yet. Have another cigarette.'

'The first one made me feel a bit sick actually.'

I watched her light up. 'Well, here we are,' she said.

'Yes.'

We looked at each other solemnly. 'I had to be in London anyway,' she said. 'For a boring awards ceremony. Not that I won anything. Those things are complete mind fucks.'

'I thought, well, I suppose I assumed you lived here.'

'I'm in and out,' she said, 'it's complicated.'

'I had to come in too, to meet my mother. Well, no, it was just an excuse really.'

'Your mother!' she said. 'She was something else. I was always quite scared of her, you know.'

I stared at her with some surprise. 'I didn't think you were scared of anything.'

She looked at me with an odd expression on her face, as though weighing something up. 'You were always like that,' she said at last.

'Like what?'

'Remember that horrible shopkeeper? What was his name?'

'Mr Watson.'

She thrust her cigarette towards me excitedly. 'Yes! Watson! Christ he was creepy. Total paedophile if ever I saw one. Not that I imagine he could do very much more than look, fat bastard.'

'I used to think he was actually stuck behind that till . . .'

'Yes, well, anyway . . . do you realize that we never actually went there to steal things by ourselves? Nancy and me, I mean. It was never just the two of us. We only ever did it when you were there.'

'I didn't know that. Why?'

'It wouldn't have been the same if you hadn't been out there, staring in at us, looking like you were about to pee yourself.' She paused. 'Dead giveaway, that face of yours.'

'So I've been told . . .'

'God, we were stupid, weren't we?'

'Yeah,' I said, more heavily than I wanted to. 'Very. But I still don't see what me watching has to do with anything.'

'You were our audience,' Julia said simply. 'For that and other things. I think you . . . somehow believed in us, in what we wanted to believe about ourselves at any rate. Whatever craziness it was.

'I miss that,' she said.

'I never saw it that way. Is that what you really thought?'

She shrugged. 'I don't know. But I don't think I'd have been friends with Nancy at all if it wasn't for you. You kind of held us all together.'

I thought of Nancy in Ely, her hands among the candles. 'But I didn't hold us together,' I said, 'I didn't, did I?'

She looked at me steadily for a moment. 'You shouldn't think like that. It's pointless.'

'I can't help it. I can't help thinking I should have . . . how different it would have been if I . . .'

'You were lucky,' Julia said, cutting me off. 'You weren't there in the shed that morning. You didn't have to see it. I remember your dad shoving me behind him. He gripped my arm so hard. But I kept looking. I've seen some bad things. In my job you do. You go looking for bad things in my job. But Nancy was different.'

'How?'

'When I first saw her, the way she was lying, her face, I thought . . . she was looking at me. No that's not right, not looking at me, looking *for* me.' Tears shone in her eyes. 'I can't explain it any better than that.'

'Oh Julia . . .'

'The thing is,' she went on, 'the thing that really gets to me, is how it just *happened*. Do you know what I mean? It was all over so quickly and it didn't make any sense. I never really knew why or how.'

'She left us in the dark,' I said.

'Yes.'

We were quiet for a moment. The noise of the traffic seemed suddenly louder, almost oppressive 'We should go somewhere,' I suggested again. 'We should get a drink if there's anywhere still open. There must be a place around here.'

She shook her head. 'No. We can't do that.' She glanced quickly at her watch. 'It's still only ten to.'

'But Julia . . .'

'Are you cold? Let's walk then. We'll walk around the square a bit.'

'All right,' I said, unwillingly. She seized my arm, suddenly very animated, her sadness put aside.

'So do you think she would have come?' I asked as we circled around, up towards the National Gallery. 'Do you think she'd have been here?'

'Who, Nancy? She'd have been the first to arrive.'

'Yes, she would have,' I said, smiling. 'And we'd have never heard the last of it if we hadn't shown up. I wonder what she'd look like now. What she'd have been doing all this time.'

'I never think about that,' Julia said. 'I can't imagine it.'

'I can't really imagine it either. But I'm certain she'd have been an extraordinary person. She'd have *done* something, you know?'

'Do you think so?' She looked at me, a little sadly, I thought. 'I think she might have become a poet,' I said. 'A war poet of course. She'd have gone travelling with you, both of you hunting for wars to write about.' Julia laughed. 'You sound exactly like her,' she said. 'That's just the sort of thing she'd have said.'

We were silent for a while, both of us perhaps feeling Nancy there; her presence as strong as if she walked beside us.

'I wonder what happened to Christopher,' I said.

She made a face. 'I expect they put him away somewhere. I don't know.'

'Poor Christopher. I don't think he was a bad person at all. He seemed quite sweet.'

'Ironic, isn't it? Sometimes I'm truly glad I can't have kids.'

'Do you remember Miss Pemble?' I asked her. 'Those shoes of hers. And the book. I told you about the book didn't I? I must have done. She left it at our house once and we sneaked a look inside. I think she was mad. Partly mad at any rate. A very quiet, restrained sort of lunacy but definitely certifiable . . .'

But Julia had stopped listening. She kept looking back in the direction we had come in a tense, rather expectant way, unlinking her arm from mine so that she could glance at her watch every few moments.

'What's the matter?'

'Nothing, nothing.'

'What is it?'

'Nothing,' she repeated, taking my arm again and steering me forward. 'What I want to know is, why we didn't do this years ago,' she chattered. 'Meet up, I mean. Too easy to say we were both so busy, although time does tend to carry you along a bit doesn't it?'

I stopped in my tracks. 'Julia,' I said, 'what are you up to?'

'Oh God, I suppose I have to tell you don't I? I'm crap at keeping secrets, completely crap.' She was half babbling now, her face alive with excitement. 'So. So, I have a surprise for you. Something to . . . show you.'

'What?'

'At least I *thought* I did,' she said, looking at her watch for the tenth time. 'I think we should head back to where we were before.'

'What sort of surprise?'

'You know, I used to send Nancy's mother a card every year,' Julia said, apparently changing the subject. 'On Nancy's birthday.'

'Did you?' I looked at her with astonishment.

'For a long time I never heard anything back, then she started sending Christmas cards. And I happened to be in Norwich once – that's where she moved to – and I dropped in to see her. She's not like she used to be, you know.'

'In what way?' I asked, marvelling a little at how wrong I had been about Julia. I had assumed she'd cut all ties with the past, ruthlessly leaving all behind. But instead, it had been I who'd fled, too timid – or too ashamed perhaps – to keep in touch. She had always been the generous one, I thought.

'She got her act together,' Julia said. 'You remember how neurotic she was?'

'I suppose so. She did seem to worry a lot.'

'She's not like that any more. She got help and I think she realized she couldn't afford to fall apart. She'd been given a second chance, you see.'

We'd arrived back at the spot where we'd first met, in the

shadow of one of the lions. Julia's head was up, her eyes eagerly tracking the swift movement of the traffic.

'A second chance?' I repeated stupidly.

'She'll be here any minute. At least, she should be. She's staying with friends of the family. They said they'd put her in a taxi. I made all the arrangements. Mrs Packenham allowed her to come, as long as I promised to get her back safely. I told you Mrs Packenham had changed didn't I? She'd never have let Nancy out of her sight. But Lily is sixteen now. Totally independent of course, far more than we ever were. Probably hates the idea of me clucking over her . . .'

'Lily?'

'*Nancy's girl*,' Julia said, as though explaining something to a half-wit. 'We couldn't have had the meeting without her could we? It wouldn't have been right. She's my surprise.'

Out of the rush of traffic, a vehicle slowed and drew to a stop. The door opened. Beside me, Julia waved her arm high above her head. 'Over here!' she called.

A girl gets out, stands for a second or two, looking around her. The taxi waits as it has been instructed to do. In a minute she will see us, but for now we watch her. She does not look like Nancy. She is tall, robust, wearing the kind of clothes I would never have dared at her age. A short skirt, cropped sweater, tall black boots with preposterously high, chunky heels that would look ridiculous on anybody who was not so young, so full of confidence. Perhaps up close, I will see something of Nancy; the line of her nose, her eyes, but for now I simply stand there, thinking how much I love Julia, how she will mock me later. 'You should have seen your face,' she will say, in the way she always used to. 'You looked like you'd just seen the Holy Ghost.'

'*Li-ly!*' Julia calls. 'Over here.'

She sees us then, two women staring at her. She is out very

late at night, in London, all alone. She is having an adventure and so she does not smile, but steps forward with great seriousness, as her mother would have done, to meet these strangers, Nancy's friends.

IV

The woman at the information desk in the National Portrait Gallery has bell-shaped dangling earrings that tinkle minutely as she shakes her head. 'No,' she says. 'Not at the moment, no.' She pauses, giving me an apologetic smile. I can tell she is the sort of person who hates disappointing people.

'We do take him out from time to time,' she adds. 'Special exhibitions, things like that.'

'Oh,' I say, 'I thought . . .'

'You can find him on the computer,' she says brightly.

'Yes,' I say, 'I'll do that.'

I stand for a second or two in the pale, light-filled entrance hall, not knowing what direction to take. Everything is so clean, so well ordered, the portraits hung at perfect right angles, the lives of their subjects all straightened up and put in place . . .

Perhaps the First World War room, I think. Seeing the place where the photograph might once have been displayed is surely better than nothing. And there is the small hope that the information lady could be wrong, despite her air of authority, her desire to please.

I find my way easily enough and see at once that my hope is unfounded. The First World War room is small, rather shadowy and completely deserted. Somewhere above my head, the heating system gives off a muffled rattling sound; a suggestion of neglect matching the scarcity of the portraits on display. A couple of flying aces, a rather crude stone carving of Lawrence of Arabia and little else to draw the eye apart from a very large oil painting taking up one whole wall. *Some General Officers of the Great War* runs the title at the bottom.

I stand for several minutes, studying this picture. Twenty-two men, forty-four tan boots, lined up together between two pillars. A long, khaki horizon, broken only by the intermittent red flash of collar and medal and the subtle gleam of ceremonial sword. A dreary picture, I think it, for all the commanding looks on the faces of the men, their spurs and sticks and leather. Probably only kept on display because it happens to be painted by John Singer Sargant.

He does not belong beside these men, I think, turning to leave. It is not the place for him at all. It would have been a kind of grief to see him there, among these empty uniforms, the war – his war – nothing after all, but drab pomposity.

I go at last to the gift shop and find him among the postcards. They have the selection arranged in alphabetical order and I wonder briefly whether the same system was in place when Nancy stood here, years ago, scanning the shelves. I go to the counter and buy the thing, watching as the shop assistant carefully slides it into a small paper bag and then make my way downstairs to the café and find a seat in an empty corner with a cup of tea.

It is exactly the same picture as I remember and it gives me a strange feeling to have it in my hands. I turn it over and read that the photograph was taken by John Gunston in 1916. Owen must have been newly commissioned then, his experiences in the trenches – and the best of his war poetry – still to come. I turn it over again and sit for a long while looking at his face, my heart steady, my mind quite still.

I take out my phone and dial Peter's number, the new one that he gave me only last week. 'I'm here, in London,' I tell him. 'I came in Friday night.'

'That's great,' he says, his voice lifting, 'I wasn't sure whether you'd come or not.'

'To be honest, I wasn't either. Not until the last minute.'

'I'm not working today,' he says. 'I took the day off. Just on the off-chance. Where are you? Can you . . . do you have to go back straightaway?'

I pause, thinking suddenly of the afternoon Peter visited me in the shop and the walk we took. How I broke the string of my necklace and for a single, breathless second, filled the air with shining glass. They fell everywhere, the beads; bouncing and tumbling across the pavement and into the road, making me dart in all directions to retrieve them. And Peter, half kneeling on the ground, a little awkward, ungainly almost in his eagerness to be of use, collecting up the tiny blue treasures and slipping them in dusty twos and threes into the pocket of my coat.

An ordinary enough courtesy, perhaps. One might have expected it from anyone. But it catches in my mind, this act of kindness. A windy day; a shower of broken blue; the tiny chink of glass on glass meeting in the folded dark. Small things, easily forgotten, but how important they suddenly seem to me. How full of secret, wordless value.

'I don't have to go back today,' I say at last. 'I don't have any plans.'

We make arrangements and as we talk, I finish my tea and gather up my possessions, placing the postcard back into its wrapping and stowing it in the zippered compartment of my handbag. I can hear the sound of my own feet, clacking busily across the tiled stretch of gallery lobby, then I am through the door and out onto the street, moving swiftly towards the crowded entrance of the underground. It is nearly lunchtime. I will have to hurry.